RETURN OF THE GRAIL KING

The Power Places Series

Theresa Crater

Crystal Star
PUBLISHING

Crystal Star Publishing
1303 Alexandria St.
Lafayette, CO 80026
https://crystalstarpublishing.wordpress.com

Return of the Grail King
by Theresa Crater

Digital ISBN: 978-0-9971413-5-1

Print ISBN: 978-0-9971413-6-8

Cover art by Earthly Charms

To Ashley, Aubria & Aldrin Jr.

Prologue

Sand drifted down from the cave ceiling and settled on Hashem Sayeed's blue cotton shirt. He straightened as much as he could and brushed off his shoulders. Ali and Moustafa paused in their digging, hunched under the low dirt ceiling. They listened.

Silence.

Hashem gave a nod, picked up his spade, and went back to cleaning the earth from around a large stone. Ali and Moustafa filled sacks with dirt they'd cleared. They'd been digging this tunnel for a few months, working their way at a steady downward angle, and finally found rock. Behind rock, there was usually a tomb. In a tomb, artifacts. Ancient statues. His family could hawk the small figurines of the gods and *ushabtis* to the tourists, such as they were. The Giza Plateau had been practically empty since the revolution. Nothing like the old days when you could barely shoulder your way through the crowds. But things were picking up again.

Hashem stabbed his spade into the red earth, venting his frustration and hunger. He hoped for a large sculpture, perhaps two or three. Rings with gems, ancient necklaces. Maybe even gold. Something for the black market to tide them over for a year or more. Until the rest of the world realized Egypt was safe and came back. He'd sell this house, buy something in Abu Sir, put his feet up, and watch his grandchildren play in the pool he'd build. Just like those big hotels down the street from his house. He smiled and shook his head at this. The crooks in the black market never paid a fair price, but what choice did he have? At least they would eat.

His spade pushed through the dirt into emptiness. A rush of musty, stale air pushed through the opening.

He rocked back on his heels and shouted, "*Alhamdulillah.*"

Ali threw down his shovel. "What?"

"A tomb, son. *Inshalla.*"

The three crowded close, pulling the earth away with their hands, pounding at the hard places with the spade. Once they'd cleared a large enough spy hole, Hashem shined his flashlight through. He pushed his face up, moved the beam of the light around. Something flashed in one corner. He angled the light toward it. Gold glinted in the darkness.

"*Alhamdulillah,*" he shouted again.

Moustafa pushed his face to the hole, pointed the flashlight around, then looked back at his brother. "We've found gold."

"What is it?" Fatimah's voice came down to them from the hole in the back of the kitchen where they'd dug.

Hashem crawled toward her and stuck his head and shoulders out. "A tomb."

She threw her arms up. "*Alhamdulillah.*"

Hashem reached up, and she leaned down to throw her arms around his neck. This time she didn't make a fuss about how dirty he was. She poured him a cup of water and he drank it thirstily, then crouched and crawled back down the passage.

Ali had already doubled the size of the opening. Hashem kicked the small pile of debris to the other side of the tunnel. They'd clean up later. He picked up the shovel and dug as close to Ali's knees as he dared. Moustafa disappeared into the house and came back with a hammer and another spade.

After another fifteen minutes of digging, the hole widened enough to allow a man to pass sideways. Ali and Moustafa stepped back. "You first," Moustafa said. "It was your find."

Hashem clasped his hand to his heart. "There will be enough for us all, my brother."

"*Inshalla,*" they both answered at once, but this time more from habit, because they had seen the gold and the statues and the gleam of a painted wood coffin in the corner.

2

Hashem stepped in. Fatimah couldn't wait any longer and came down to watch. She passed in a lantern. The light bounced off a large gold statue, hands folded in front. The head gave off a bluish tint. Finely chiseled feathers covered the body and the graceful lines of a many-tiered menit encircled its neck. The hands held a staff topped by a djed pillar and an ankh.

"Ptah," Hashem breathed. Even he recognized this god.

As if in response, the jet eyes of the figure seemed to shift in the light.

Hashem pulled back with a start. The others had crept in as he stood mesmerized by the statue. To his right, Ali reached out and gingerly picked up a bowl from a carved niche in the wall. He turned it upside down and held it to the light of the lantern on the ground next to his father's feet. Translucent yellow, thin and flawless. Finest alabaster.

Moustafa leaned over the coffin in the corner and rubbed the wood with the edge of his beige shirt. He could just make out features. It looked like a man's painted face, probably somebody important since this whole tomb seemed to hold only one mummy.

A loud rumble came from below their feet. Then the growl of rock filled the chamber. Hashem grabbed Fatima and rushed for the opening, Ali and Moustafa close behind. A cloud of dust rushed toward them, clogging their noses. Grit burned their eyes.

Hashem pushed his wife up the passageway, but the floor tilted. Fatima screamed and fell. Hashem took a breath of air and grit, trying to shout, but the ceiling fell in before he could let out a cry.

Above ground, the wall of the house crumbled up to the third story and slid into the pit. A huge plume of dust rose along with the screams of children. Then silence, followed by the barks of the neighborhood dog pack.

Lights switched on in the surrounding houses. Neighbors swarmed into the streets, pulling their clothes on as they ran. But they were too late. Where Hashem's house had stood, the mouth of a cave showed black against the greying horizon. The people gaped in silence for a moment, not believing their eyes.

The lone voice of the muezzin from a mosque several blocks away lifted into the coming morning as if in blessing.

Chapter 1

Michael Levy quietly closed the book he'd been showing to Anne and tucked the alpaca throw around her now sleeping form. She'd been doing that a lot this late in her pregnancy—just dropping off in the middle of a conversation. He gently pushed the soft wool under her rotund belly, tight as a tick who'd feasted undiscovered. He frowned at the unbidden thought. This was his child he was thinking about after all. Boy or girl—they'd elected not to know.

He picked up the 1458 edition of *The Book of the Sacred Magic of Abra-Melin the Mage* and replaced it inside the small glass case they kept it in. The Le Clair library, filled with rare books and ancient manuscripts, not to mention all the important texts of esoteric literature, could content Michael for the rest of his life. Except he wanted to add some books on Egypt and archaeology. Michael had left his position at the Metropolitan Museum when he and Anne married. The Le Clair fortune made him not just secure, but able to do the kind of collecting he'd always dreamed about. He stayed involved in his field, though, consulting with his colleagues at the Met and Smithsonian, the Natural History Museum, and occasionally the British Museum. Another dream come true.

He returned to his seat by the fire and reached for coffee, but found nothing. How many cups had he already had this morning? Should he ring for some? He still couldn't get used to having servants, but Grandmother Elizabeth told him she wouldn't get rid of excellent workers whose family had been with hers for several generations just to satisfy his plebeian sensibilities. "Besides, the economy is still in recovery," she'd added. That he'd even considered calling a servant for coffee told him how much he'd already assimilated.

His cell phone vibrated across the table. Grateful it was on mute, he grabbed it up before it woke Anne and walked out into the hall, closing the door quietly behind him. The name on the screen surprised him.

Azizi Tau. The guide and security expert Michael always added to his entourage in Egypt. Second only to Tahir Nur Ahram, the indigenous wisdom keeper also trained in Western archaeology and Egyptology.

Michael took a few more steps away from the library door and answered. "Hello, my friend. What a surprise!"

"I'm glad I caught you," Azizi said. "Have you seen the news?"

"No. What's happened?" Michael walked back down the hall to a family room that had a television.

"A house collapsed this morning on the edge of the Giza Plateau. The family was digging underneath the foundation for artifacts—"

"Like everybody," Michael quipped.

Azizi gave a short laugh. "Yes, except this time it got a bunch of people killed. Only the family on the top floor survived, a niece and her children. The husband was in the tunnel though."

Michael switched on CNN, but they were covering US politics. BBC World Service News showed a crowd of soldiers circling a blocked part of the road that ran next to the Sphinx enclosure. A large group of people milled around in front.

"That's terrible." He waited. Azizi had not called to tell him this news.

"The military has cordoned off the area. The thing is, the collapse opened a huge underground cavern. We've found tombs on the periphery, but further in are ceremonial chambers. Lots of artifacts."

"Exciting." Michael grimaced at his enthusiasm. "Except for the tragedy."

"Of course." Azizi's tone was dismissive. Egyptians took births and deaths much more in their stride. Sometimes Michael appreciated their more philosophical view.

"We need you, Michael. Even with the stability of the new government, the Antiquities Department is still recovering from the Revolution. The President didn't want to just reappoint all the old crew."

"Amazing he cares about the appearance of corruption."

Azizi didn't answer immediately. Michael chided himself for speaking so openly. People in Egypt had to watch their backs again. Be careful what they said about the new regime. "The President is doing an excellent job," he said for any listening ears.

"Yes, he is," Azizi parroted back.

"I'd love to come, but we're expecting a baby."

"Mabrouk. A son? Is he your first?"

"We don't know if it's a boy or girl. The baby hasn't been born yet, but Anne is due very soon."

This silence was different. Clearly Azizi thought that was plenty of time, plus what did birth have to do with fathers?

"I could probably come for a couple of days. That's all," Michael found himself saying to bridge this cultural gap. The find intrigued him, but he wondered how Anne would take this.

"Excellent. I will book a room for you in the Mena House."

"Thank you, Azizi."

"When can we expect you?"

"Day after tomorrow, I suppose. I'll text to confirm."

"Of course you should go." Anne waved her hand at him as if to dismiss him already. "I'm fine. Honestly, you and Grandmother treat me like I'm some fragile Ming vase. Women have been having babies for thousands of years now, in case you didn't know."

Michael mimicked shock. "Is that so?"

She repeated this every time he asked about the trip during the day and while he packed the next morning.

"I promise not to take long." He headed toward the closet for a couple more shirts to add to his suitcase, but Anne caught his arm when he walked by the bed and pulled him to her. She planted a sloppy kiss on his cheek. He turned his head and found her lips, touching delicately at first, but she deepened the kiss, locking her arms around his neck. She leaned back, taking him with her.

Michael caught himself before he fell, steading himself with a hand on either side of her face. He stared down into those sapphire eyes, his torso just brushing her pregnant belly, then settled behind her and laid his hand on her stomach. The child stirred, then gave a kick. Michael pulled his hand away, but Anne took it and held it against the ripple beneath the skin.

"It doesn't hurt when he does that?"

"No, only when she gets mad if I'm sleeping on my back. Then she kicks until I wake up and move."

He pushed his face into her waves of blond hair at her neck. "She must have a temper."

"He's stubborn, like you." She turned in his arms. Her kiss was genial.

"I'd better get going," he said, but didn't move.

"Don't worry. We'll be fine. We'll wait for you to come back."

"It's just that—"

"You should go."

"It's a first for me. Not wanting to go to Egypt."

She laughed and pushed against his chest.

Michael kissed her forehead and headed into the bathroom to check for last-minute toiletries. He usually kept a travel kit packed, but had been home for the winter holidays and hadn't planned on traveling until well after the baby was born. He threw in an extra tube of toothpaste and slipped a packet of homeopathic tablets to help with jet lag into his front pocket.

Back in their bedroom, Anne held up the lid of his suitcase. He tossed in the toiletries bag and she zipped the case shut. "I left you a surprise."

They walked hand in hand down to the car.

The Le Clair family private jet pulled in next to a larger Gulfstream with the Oman flag painted on the side. Uniformed soldiers stood on either side of the tail of that plane, their guns holstered on one side, swords gleaming in scabbards on the other. Michael nodded at them as he disembarked, but neither moved a muscle. The sun burned down and the temperature had been reported at 95 Fahrenheit, hot for late January.

Azizi had sent one of his helpers to expedite the visa process. A bored guard finally stamped his passport after waiting in line for half an hour, and they headed out to the terminal. Michael grabbed a cup of coffee before they jumped into the waiting Nissan. Azizi's helper seemed young, so Michael didn't ask him any questions about the situation. He tuned out the young man, who pointed out the tourist sites along the way as if this was Michael's first trip. He indulged the kid, thinking it was good practice, and watched the Presidential Palace give way to the Mosque of Muhammad Ali and the long stretch of the cemetery. Soon the pyramids rose in the distance. The driver turned off the Ring Road and fought the traffic next to the canals. A herd of horses and one huge water buffalo stood in the middle of the canal, their owner washing them off. Further down plastic bottles and trash clogged the surface. They kept driving and the water cleared again. Village life buzzed around him, but his eyes were getting heavy. On the plane, he'd reviewed secret files about the Giza Plateau from several mystical organizations. The possibilities of what had been uncovered intrigued him.

When they entered the village of Nazlet-el-Samman, Michael pressed his face up against the window. A wooden fence blocked the site, but the dozen men in military uniform carrying SIG 552s marked this as the spot of the collapse. They'd gotten that fence up fast.

The black sedan pulled into the driveway of the Mena House and a bellhop dressed in a black-fringed vest and sporting a matching fez stepped up to open his door. Michael tipped the guy—he'd gotten generous since the marriage—and stepped through the metal detector which buzzed. The guard casually waved him in, never budging from his seat.

Azizi threw up a hand to catch Michael's attention, and he walked over to the bar just off the lobby. "I've already checked you in," Azizi said. "Come have something to drink. Relax."

Michael rubbed at his gritty eyes. "I thought this was an emergency," he said.

"We've got permission from the Antiquities Department to go in after dark. They want to limit visibility as much as they can."

Michael ordered tea, hoping it would wake him up. Outside the window, the pyramids soared into the blue sky, golden and indomitable. "What do we know so far?"

Azizi's smile was conspiratorial. He leaned forward, speaking in a quiet voice. "You won't believe it. Looks like a big ceremonial court with Osiris standing in the middle. It's surrounded by smaller temples. We've been able to get into the Anubis sanctuary. May be a Sekhmet shrine next to it, but they were still shifting rock when I left."

"Hmm, think the others will be Anput and P'tah?"

Azizi squirmed in his seat like a kid at Christmas. "I think there's more than four. The smaller temples might circle the large Osiris statue in the middle. We've hit the mother lode." Oxford educated, Azizi's English sounded like the upper crust of England, but his vocabulary was sprinkled with American slang. "There are stairs up and down. Might be a shrine for each major group of Neters." Neters was the ancient word for Egyptian gods and goddesses.

"What do you need me for?"

Azizi glanced around the bar. "This might be the major ceremonial site the traditions have always talked about."

"Maybe, but the question remains."

"There's more. You'll see."

"I should go over to the house. Say hello to the family."

"Tahir will meet us at the site tonight. Get some rest. We may be at it all night."

Michael glanced wryly at his tea, but the caffeine had barely scratched the surface of his fatigue. He wondered if he was coming down with something.

After agreeing to meet Azizi at eight o'clock, Michael followed the labyrinth of hallways to his room in the main palace building. He loved staying in the old section of the hotel, with its sudden steps up or down, checkered carpeting, and honey-colored paneling. When he arrived in his room, he found a gilded headboard on the bed in the shape of a round mandala. Too bad Anne wasn't with him this trip.

He showered and unpacked, finding Anne's surprise tucked between his shirts. It was a picture of the last sonogram, taken from an angle that left the child's gender unidentifiable. She'd written "Come back soon, Daddy," on the picture. He tucked it into the corner of the gold frame of the mirror and checked his watch. He had two hours before going to the site. He set an alarm and lay down on the bed.

Sleep came immediately, and a dream. Towering Neters whispered to him, looming dark forms, their faces hidden. Try as he might, he couldn't make out the words. The alarm sounded and he woke, still tired. He grabbed a quick snack, then headed outside.

Azizi lounged on the front wall and stood when Michael came out. "Let's take the short way."

They walked up the hill in front of the hotel. Azizi showed his ID and pass to the guard and they made their way up to the parking lot in front of the Great Pyramid. Across the now empty paving stones, a cluster of aspirants dressed all in white waited near the door of the giant structure to be let in for their private session. Azizi and Michael slipped through the shadows over to the causeway and walked down toward the Sphinx, her cone shaped head just visible in the growing dark.

"Looks like Cayce might have been right," Azizi said casually.

"What? But—"

"I know, I know." Azizi held up a hand. "You said you'd opened the Hall of Records already, that it was a spiritual place and not physical. But there is a hallway in the uncovered temple that goes over to the Sphinx toward a chamber." He paused for dramatic effect. "Right beneath the right paw."

"How can you tell?"

"It matches the ground-penetrating radar done a few years back. That crack the Antiquities Director made fun of?"

"The 45 x 45-foot perfect square? The crack was in his head."

Azizi laughed. "The hallway goes straight toward it."

People just couldn't let go of the Hall of Records, Michael thought. But maybe there was something stored in that square room. Still, he'd known deep down they'd opened Cayce's famed hall last time. And it had not been artifacts or lost technology from Atlantis. It had been an exalted state of consciousness—powerful enough to bring a huge energy surge into the earth's grid. Many things had changed for the positive afterwards, but the dark forces had redoubled their efforts.

"How about the staff of Osiris?" Michael asked.

"The real one that's supposed to open all the secret chambers in Egypt?"

"The very one."

"I think the Sayeed family already did that for us."

"The Ring of Isis?"

Azizi shook his head.

"Or the Seeing Stone from the great oracle of Ammon in the Oasis."

"But that's way south."

"It's never been found. Perhaps it was moved. Hidden away here in the North."

Azizi patted him on the shoulder. "Who knows what we'll find, my brother? Who knows?"

They walked in silence, the sand soft beneath their feet. A group of men waited close to the new fence near the ragged hole in the ground. Rubble from the house sat on the side. The front stoops of adjacent houses had been boarded up. Michael could only guess how these people got in and out of their residences now. The street up to the new fence was empty. Maybe the army had evacuated the whole neighborhood.

Michael spotted a tall figure in a flowing woolen galabeya, a white turban on his head. "Tahir!" He sprinted forward and grabbed him in a rough hug.

"Michael, I am so glad you came. Who knows what we will discover." His eyes gleamed.

A man with a muscular build and sporting a traditional beard stepped out of a knot of soldiers. "Azizi, is your group ready?"

"Yes. Eiham, this is Dr. Michael Levy, curator of the Egyptian collection at the Metropolitan Museum in New York."

Former, Michael thought, but decided not to correct him. "Pleased to meet you, Eiham." They shook hands.

"You know Tahir Nur Ahram, of course." Azizi nodded toward Tahir.

"Everyone knows Tahir," Eiham said. "Shall we go down?" Without waiting for an answer, Eiham walked behind a pile of rocks twice the height of a camel's head and picked his way down the steep drop. The cave ceiling closed over their heads. Electric torches lit the way forward.

"They've been busy," Michael pitched his voice for Tahir only.

"Very," he answered. "Many trucks."

Michael knew this meant the top black market dealers had already had their pick. They'd leave some things for the museums and universities to study, but given the difficult economy, Michael imagined the site would be more picked over than usual. What they'd left stopped the group in their tracks.

In front of them stretched a level area, blue and white marble tiles showing here and there between piles of sand and rock. In the middle rose an enormous statue of Osiris, his crowned head stretching maybe twenty feet, almost to the top of the cavern, his hands folded in front, the crook and flail resting on either shoulder. Dust still covered the head and shoulders, but the gold gleamed beneath it. The eyes seemed to shift as Eiham played his flashlight over the statue.

"Amazing, yes?"

"Beautiful," Michael breathed.

"The house stood there." He pointed the flashlight up, illuminating a gutted structure, stairs rising up to a precariously perched bedroom, the door to an armoire open showing what looked like children's clothes. "We think they discovered this tomb."

Eiham moved his light down on what now looked like a cave pockmarked with niches. One wall was painted with typical feast scenes. A wooden sarcophagus stood unopened and several gold statuettes littered the ground. That these had been left told Michael how rich the find was.

They turned back to the towering statue of Osiris. The piece dominated the cave, standing like a good shepherd ready to guide his sheep—or goats in the case of Egypt. Michael walked around the statue, marveling at the careful etching in the folds of his garment, the inlaid turquoise and coral in the crook and flail held in his crossed arms. "It's a miracle this statue survived. It looks untouched," he said.

"Over here is the Anubis chapel." Eiham walked to the west, behind

Osiris, but Michael was drawn to the south where the workers had just cleared another entrance.

He walked across the even tiles, avoiding a pile of rubble near the wall, and stood in front of the chapel entrance. Inside, the great lioness regarded him quietly, her lotus staff blossoming just at her heart. This Sekhmet had a gold disk on her head.

Eiham gave out a low whistle. "Would you look at that?"

Michael stiffened at Eiham's intrusion. He'd rather be alone with Tahir down here. Even Azizi's presence was a bit of a distraction. Eiham had no metaphysical training. Azizi had studied some, but he was a natural. He'd probably been a member of a mystery school in a past life. Now, he was down-to-earth, concerned with making a living for his growing family, as Michael would be if he hadn't married into money.

Michael snapped a picture of the newly revealed Sekhmet, apologizing to her for the impertinence, but he feared the disk that topped her head would disappear. At least he'd have evidence. One look at Azizi was all it took.

"Eiham," Azizi called from near the ramp. Thankfully, the man walked toward him. After a brief discussion, Azizi called out. "An hour?" his voice echoed off the walls, setting the large space reverberating.

"That would be excellent," Michael said in a softer voice. The sound carried as if he held a microphone.

"*Shokran*," Tahir said.

"Yes, thank you," Michael said.

Michael stood in front of Sekhmet and steadied his breathing. He stepped over the threshold of the chapel and dropped to his knees before her, silently asking her permission to search the area and for her protection. She stood quietly for a long moment, regarding him. Michael felt the same urge he always did before this great mother. He stood and leaned his head against her staff, his forehead resting between her breasts. She was the same height as the Karnak statue.

Be prepared, my son. A great test awaits you.

Michael wondered what it might be. Resisting the wealth that lay all around him? Documenting the find before the black marketers stripped it clean? Perhaps he'd discover something entirely new, unknown to Egyptologists before now.

Go West.

He bowed his head to her and walked toward the Anubis shrine, hardly hearing Tahir tell him he would try to get through the crack and enter the chamber to the East.

Anubis stood in the shadows, his dark skin barely reflecting the light of Michael's flashlight. He held a gold ankh in his left hand. His *was* staff gleamed dark mahogany. The jackal head peered down at him, quartz crystal shining back from the iris. This ancient technique made the eyes come alive, giving the viewer the feeling of being watched.

Michael stood in front of the statue, silencing his mind, waiting. He intoned a sacred sound, letting it fill his body and the chamber.

Nothing stirred.

He intoned the sound again, willing himself to patience. Michael listened as the tones filled the room, ringing like a bell at first, then softening as the vibration stretched out, thinned, and disappeared, leaving silence.

Something took a long, shuddering breath. Then the breathing steadied. Became regular and deep.

Michael opened his eyes. The statue's chest rose and fell.

The Great Opener of the Ways shifted in the dark.

Reached out his left hand and pointed the shaft of the golden ankh at Michael.

Michael steadied himself internally, then grasped it.

The Neter stepped down from his pedestal and led Michael back into the yawning dark cavern behind the chapel.

Chapter 2

Anne leaned over the white kitchen counter to smell the freshly ground coffee beans.

"Want me to make you a cup?" her grandfather Gerald asked, emptying the grounds into a paper cone.

"Can't." Anne patted her protruding belly. "I can only smell them."

"I've always thought they smell better than they taste, anyway." He poured steaming water over the beans.

Anne took a deep whiff. "I wish. I'm so sleepy these days, I can hardly keep my eyes open."

Estelle, the cook, looked up from the sink where she was peeling potatoes. "You should rest as much as you can. Once the little master is born, you'll be wishing for some uninterrupted sleep."

"You think it's a boy?" Anne ignored the 'master' part. Estelle was incorrigible when it came to social status. She took her pride from the family's position.

"I've always been right." Estelle pointed her peeler at Anne.

She hoped Estelle was making her famous potato leek soup. Not only was she sleepy, she couldn't seem to eat enough. Potato leek soup with crusted country bread and butter. Her mouth watered.

"I knew you were a girl and that Thomas, God rest his soul, was a boy."

"I wish he were here," Anne said. "He would have loved being an uncle." She still thought about Thomas every day. Death was something the Le Clairs were all too familiar with. She'd lost her uncle and aunt to assassinations.

15

Gerald squeezed her hand and she straightened her shoulders. "Grandma thinks it's a girl," she said.

Estelle snorted. "She might be the famous psychic, but I know babies."

Anne smiled, a little surprised that Estelle had taken to speaking so openly about family secrets. The public thought of the Le Clair family only as a political dynasty. Not many knew they were founding members of an ancient mystery school. And then there was the bloodline controversy. Garth, her late Aunt Cynthia's lover in Glastonbury, had scoffed at that. Said the evidence was scanty. She didn't much care one way or the other, but Grandmother Elizabeth was adamant that it was true. She said Garth was a plebeian, her favorite word of late, whose ignorance could be excused. The aristocratic families of Europe knew the truth.

Estelle pulled leeks out of the refrigerator.

"Yum! My favorite."

"Now you two skedaddle so I can finish this up."

Anne grabbed a glass of water and they left Estelle to her own brand of magic. Gerald carried his coffee to his study to finish the day's business. Anne pulled herself up the stairs and walked to their section of the house. Now that she'd married and was expecting, she'd exchanged her room for an apartment inside the rambling mansion.

Each family had their own contained space, with bedrooms, bathrooms, sitting rooms, and an office. The family shared some rooms—library, dining room, and den. The public face of the house—the reception hall, formal living room, and ballroom—got dusted regularly, but was rarely used except for events.

The family ritual room, which Anne had only discovered when she'd become a Keeper of the Crystal after Aunt Cynthia's death, opened off the ballroom, the entrance well camouflaged. Grandmother Elizabeth called it the temple. The job of cleaning it fell to the newest initiate, in this case Anne. She'd passed it off to Michael, but figured she'd have to give it a go over sometime this week. A few other ritual spots and a labyrinth dotted the grounds. They all passed as gardens to the casual visitor who might stumble across them.

Anne settled down in front of the fireplace and checked her text messages. Michael should have arrived already.

Checked in. Going to the site when the sun sets. Love you both.

She typed an answer: *Hope you discover wonders. Then hurry home. Love you, too.*

She turned on the TV and surfed through the channels. Her concentration had suffered, so she'd given up on serious reading until the baby arrived. She wasn't in the mood for the news. Maybe she'd binge-watch one of the shows her friends liked, a spy show or the latest Sherlock. She found the series and started with the first season.

She chuckled over the dry, British humor, but found her eyes closing. She jerked awake at a loud bang from the TV. The shoot-up scene. Rubbing at the creak in her neck, she gave in and took a nap. The big bed felt empty without Michael. She called the two Egyptian Maus, Viviane and Merlin. They'd been a gift from Thomas after her divorce a few years back. She called again and Viviane appeared. Then Merlin popped out of her closet. Anne held up the covers and they snuggled down, their purrs sending her off to sleep again.

After some time, from far away, Anne heard someone calling her name. She turned over and pulled a pillow close.

Anne. The voice came again, faint but distinct.

She strained to hear.

Come to me.

Anne looked around and was surprised to see a long hallway. A dim light escaped from under a door at the far end. She briefly wondered why it wasn't still daylight, but the thought faded away with another call of her name. Anne followed the light down the hallway, pushed open a door, then walked downstairs, her bare feet chilled on the marble floor. Why was the house so dim? It had been late morning when she'd gone back to bed.

Anne Morgan.

"Yes?" The sound of her own voice woke her up enough to open her eyes, but not enough to find it strange that she was walking through the formal living room into the ballroom. She paused in the middle of the hardwood floor and tried to shake herself fully awake, but the seductive voice called to her again, soothing her back into her dream-like state. She walked to the secret panel in the left wall of the ballroom and pushed the lever. The wall swung open.

Anne entered the family's temple, not thinking anything of the lit candles marking the quarters. She moved toward the center of the room to lay her hands on the family's ancient crystal ball. A family story claimed the crystal came from Atlantis and had stood in the main temple of the Crystal Guild. She reached out her hand to steady herself with the ball's firm presence, but instead she found a statue standing in its place. She jerked back, almost waking once more, but the voice soothed her back.

Welcome, Anne Morgan Le Clair.

She opened her eyes—or had she? Either way, somehow she saw a Celtic warrior standing before her, glaring. A rugged beard covered his lower face. His hand hovered over a sword sheathed at his side. An elaborate Celtic knot decorated his belt buckle. He was wrapped in a rough wool forest green cloak.

"Who are you?" Anne whispered.

The statue stirred. A deep, malevolent intelligence lit the eyes.

You have come. Kneel.

"What is your name?"

You don't recognize me?

A name swam into Anne's mind. "Mordred?" she asked. But how could this be? What was Arthur's murderer doing standing in her family's temple? What did he want?

Kneel before your true king.

Anne strained against the commanding voice, but some part of her wanted to obey, to kneel before this man and swear him fealty.

"No," she said and tried to take a step back, but her limbs were heavy, her feet sunk in a pool of energy that felt like quicksand. She struggled against its grip.

Kneel, Guinevere. The time has come to answer for your deeds.

Yes, Anne thought. *That was my name.*

Mordred drew his sword. It gleamed in the dark. A name seemed to flicker on the blade. *Excalibur.*

No, it couldn't be. That sword was safe in Arthur's hands. Buried in the hollow hill in the tomb Vivienne had made for him. He would bring it back with him to save England—maybe the whole earth.

Mordred touched her shoulder with the glowing sword and the force pushed her to her knees.

"Please, no," she whispered.

Something dark and thick as tar spread from the blade down her spine and into her womb. The squirming child went stone still. Anne struggled to push the energy out, but it turned and rose up her torso, into her throat, closing her mouth, her eyes. The flame of her awareness snuffed out and she sank into darkness.

Elizabeth Le Clair, grand matriarch of the family and High Priestess of the Lodge of Isis, sat at her oak desk, the golden sheen of the wood mellowed from two centuries of use, answering correspondence. She had to decide if they should go to the president's grand gala. Would their presence be read as an endorsement of the administration? She did need to fly to Washington for the Smithsonian Board meeting. How close together were they? She flipped the pages in her appointment book. No computer for her. She still enjoyed her Visconti Medina Rose Gold fountain pen. An extravagance, but considering how much time she spent at her desk, she'd indulged herself.

Without warning, a deep cold stabbed her. She let out a sharp gasp and pressed her wrinkled hand against her abdomen. Despair—dark, suffocating despair—took her heart. She bit off the cry of anguish rising in her throat. Had there been an accident? Had someone in the family died? A close friend? She'd felt a similar darkness when Thomas' plane had gone down over the Indian ocean, but this was worse. More powerful.

She probed out with her mind, questing for the source, and came up against a dark wall sealed with the bitter scent of hate, like burnt rubber. Elizabeth jumped from her chair, still bent over from the phantom pain, and walked toward the sensation, stretching her senses to follow its trail. She sent out a psychic alarm to Gerald, who was somewhere around. Arnold. Was he here? But this was no physical threat. Not that she knew.

She moved into the hallway and raised her palm out, feeling for the right direction. It seemed close. Perhaps even in the house although how such a thing could be possible was beyond her. The Oaks was expertly shielded. She reinforced the wards herself every new moon. Sometimes more often depending on what was happening in world power circles.

Elizabeth moved down the hall of the west wing of the house and took a shortcut through a small courtyard, skirting herb beds, into the kitchen. The aromas of leek soup and baking bread wafted toward her.

"Lunch in half an hour, madam," Estelle said, a wooden spoon poised before her mouth.

"Have you seen Gerald?"

"He came to make coffee a couple of hours ago. I think he headed to his study." Estelle's voice grew shaky as she sensed something was wrong.

"And Anne?"

"She went up for a nap."

"I don't think so," Elizabeth said and hurried through the door to the dining rooms.

"Is anything wrong, ma'am?" Estelle called after her.

Elizabeth didn't spare the time to answer. The darkness thickened as she headed toward the front foyer and seemed to push back at her as she made her way across the living room. When she tried to open the door to the ballroom, it stuck. It took several hard shoves before it suddenly gave way. She almost fell through it.

She paused to catch her breath, then refocused. Dark tendrils of fog rippled in the air, almost obscuring the open panel in the left wall. Someone had gotten into the temple. The fog reached for her, wrapped around her ankles. She ran toward the opening, almost tripping on the astral murk. An invisible membrane blocked the opening, thick and malicious, murmuring some menacing chant just below normal hearing.

The dark was so thick that Elizabeth couldn't see the room. She drew herself up, sank deep into her consciousness, and from her heart brought out a surge of light and wrapped it around a word of power she spoke. The fog disappeared instantly.

Instead of the family's Atlantean crystal, a black granite statue stood in the middle of the room at the center of the pentagram. Stretched on the floor at its feet was her granddaughter, Anne.

Elizabeth ran to her. Checked for a pulse. Strong and steady.

"Thank God."

She looked up again at the statue, but found the crystal ball on its metal stand, the same magical symbols running around the edge. Elizabeth closed her eyes and tuned into her inner sight. Hovering over the ball stood a dark shadow, a cloak around his shoulders, a gleaming sword in his hands.

She recognized him at once. Mordred. How had this traitor invaded her sacred temple?

Elizabeth opened her eyes again and checked Anne. Her coloring seemed normal. Her breath came easily. Elizabeth gently shook Anne's shoulder and called her name.

No response.

She stroked her cheek. "Anne, darling. Wake up." She shook her harder, but Anne didn't stir. She put her hand along Anne's head and probed deeper. She found fear, confusion. A strange desire to obey. Resistance.

Elizabeth straightened out Anne's arms, grabbed a pillow from the side of the room and placed it under her head. Then she ran for help.

"Gerald," she screamed as soon as she reached the living room. "Arnold. Estelle. I need your help." She ran to the foot of the staircase and shouted for Gerald again.

He appeared at the top of the stairs, his blue shirt rumpled, his reading glasses on top of his head. "What's the matter?"

"It's Anne. She's unconscious. Something's invaded the house."

"What?"

Elizabeth shook her head, impatient, and shouted, "I need your help."

Estelle blundered in, her large bosom heaving from the uproar. "What is it?"

"Find Arnold. Something's wrong with Anne."

"Oh, my God. And the baby?" Estelle clutched the dish towel she carried closer.

"The baby is fine. Find Susan. She knows where everything is."

"You gave her the day off."

Elizabeth shook her head in exasperation. Just when she needed her secretary. "Call her. This is an emergency. Tell her to get Winston Stuart out here ASAP."

"Shouldn't we call an ambulance?"

Elizabeth turned on her and Estelle blanched. "Right away, ma'am."

Gerald and Elizabeth moved with a speed surprising for people in their eighties. From the door to the ritual room, tendrils of fog swirled, reaching out long arms as if seeking for something. Elizabeth pointed at it and blasted it with a stream of energy. It dissipated again.

Gerald stopped. "What was that?"

Elizabeth grabbed his arm and pulled him into the temple. He ran to Anne as soon as he saw her.

"Her pulse is steady. She's breathing fine," Elizabeth said.

"What happened?"

Elizabeth told him about the sudden pain and finding Anne.

Gerald eyeballed the center of the room. "I see the crystal ball. What do you see?"

Elizabeth squinted. "I see a double image. The ball is here in the physical, but Mordred is superimposed over it. Like a dark shadow."

"Mordred? As in King Arthur's nephew?"

"Or son," Elizabeth said.

Arnold ran into the room, gun drawn.

Elizabeth gasped out a laugh. A wave of relief washed over her, even though the threat wasn't physical, even though she was more suited to handle this threat than he was. "Arnold, thank God you're here."

Arnold pivoted in a circle, his gun aimed in front of him.

"There's nobody here," Elizabeth said, "Not on the physical plane."

Arnold holstered his weapon and knelt beside Anne. He checked her pulse, using his watch to count. Rolled her eyelids back. Shook his head. "She seems to be asleep."

Elizabeth trusted Arnold's battle-trained first aid knowledge. "The baby?" she asked.

He shook his head. "There's no way to tell without a stethoscope." He reached for her rotund belly, but paused, looking to Elizabeth for permission.

"Please," she said.

Arnold prodded around the child, put his ear to her stomach and listened. He sat up and shrugged. "It's hard to be sure, but they both seem all right. Should we take her to the hospital?"

Elizabeth made a sudden decision. "Yes."

Arnold gathered Anne in his arms and headed for the door. Halfway across the temple, her body stiffened. Her fingers and toes splayed, and she convulsed.

Arnold swore, set her down, and tilted her head so she didn't swallow her tongue.

Half a second later, the convulsion stopped, but her breath was ragged.

He picked her up again and took two steps before she convulsed again.

"Carry her back here where she fell," Elizabeth said.

Arnold settled Anne back in her original spot. Her breath immediately smoothed out and her color returned to normal.

"Seems like we can't move her yet," Gerald said.

"Winston is coming," Elizabeth said. Winston Stuart was not only a physician. He was a member of their lodge, a skilled adept, able to deal with a psychic as well as a medical threat.

"What should I do, ma'am?" Arnold shifted his weight from one foot to the other, restless with no target.

"Double security."

"Yes, ma'am." He started for the door.

"Then check the black lodges, their corporations, anyone involved with them even peripherally," she called after him. "See if there's any unusual activity."

"Right away."

Chapter 3

Small puffs of dust rose from Michael's footsteps as he followed the Great Opener across the even paving stones into the darkness. Anubis kept up a steady but gentle pull through the ankh in Michael's grasp. A sharp cold wind blew on his face, smelling of the sea. A light drizzle fell. Michael reached out to steady himself and found a rough-hewn stone wall.

"Stand still."

"What?" Michael looked around and found a tall figure standing just to his left. He wore a dark woolen cloak. A white robe peeked out from under it matched by a long beard as white as cotton. The figure's hair hung long, grizzled gray.

"I said hold still, Uther."

"Who?"

"Focus! Do you want to have this night with Igraine or not?"

The man pulled Michael so he stood straight in front of him. Sharp blue eyes pierced his fog. "Merlin?"

"Who else, you numb—" Merlin started, then leaned forward, studying his face more closely. "What is this? You are both here?" He smiled, then whispered to himself. "So it will work."

He chanted, a low, crooning incantation, eerie in tune. To Michael's ear, there was something vaguely medieval about it. Then the sound got louder and buzzed in his head. Michael's body grew lighter, as if he would float. His breath slowed and deepened.

Michael watched, fascinated by the flourishes of Merlin's hands, the touches of his wand. The mage pulled a dagger with a bejeweled handle from its sheath, grasped Michael's hand, and drew a pentagram in his palm.

With the last flash of the blade, Michael winced and drew back, but Merlin held his hand steady. Blood beaded up from the last stroke that had closed the symbol, deeper than the rest, cutting flesh just enough to draw blood. The mage wet the blade of his dagger, then brought it, crimson and glistening, to Michael's forehead. Michael struggled to pull back.

Merlin made a scolding sound as if Michael were a child resisting having his ears washed. "Hold still."

The dagger touched his third eye. Dizziness took Michael. Merlin's face blurred and he heard a swooshing sound.

"Uther." It was more a command than a question.

"Is it done?"

Merlin pulled out a small mirror from his voluminous pockets.

Uther sometimes wondered if he kept his whole chest of magical tools in them. It reminded him of someone else, but he couldn't place him.

"Look," Merlin commanded.

Uther bent close to the mirror and squinted in the dim light. The face of King Gorlois looked back at him. That other watcher fell back into the recesses of his mind. Uther gave a grunt of satisfaction, a grunt full of lust and anticipation.

"You remember the castle layout?"

"Yes." He shook his head impatiently and stepped out from the wall shielding them. "How long?"

"You must be away before dawn."

Uther strode up to the gate of the castle. The two guards, young and inexperienced, not men to send to the war that was raging, scrambled to their feet. "My Lord. We thought—"

"I have business here and it is none of yours," Uther growled out.

"Yes, my Lord." The guard on the left of the gate fumbled with the bolt, then pulled it up. They both bowed their heads as Uther passed through.

He walked across the outer court to the entrance to the castle. Two more guards snapped to attention, eyes wide with surprise. With only a nod of acknowledgment, Uther hurried across the great hall, his boots a dull thud against the stone floor. As he passed, the tapestry displaying the family crest stirred in an imperceptible breeze as if to object to the intrusion. He slowed at the back of the hall, then turned into the hallway leading to the family chambers. Letting instinct lead, he passed two ancient oak doors, then paused before a third. Gathering himself up, he pushed the door open.

A fire burned low in the hearth, but one log still sported a flame that lit the room with a soft glow. Two settles stood before the fire on a bearskin rug, a low table between them. A large oak bed filled the opposite wall. The bed curtains were drawn on each side, but open at the end to allow heat from the fire. Uther moved to the foot of the bed.

Igraine lay there, a tumble of ivory limbs. She slept on her side, her golden hair sprawled on the pillow beside her. He drank in the sight of her, not wanting to disturb the moment. One shell pink foot protruded from the covers. A hand curled beside her face. Her skin was cream, her lips a blush rose. Her breath slow.

Quiet as a thief, he pulled off his cloak and draped it over the back of one of the settles. Unbuckled his belt and let it slide to the floor. He paused and listened. Her breath still came even and deep. Moving quietly, he unfastened the broach on his left shoulder and placed it on the table, then pulled off his tunic.

Igraine stirred.

Uther felt a sudden stab of fear, wondering if the disguise would work. What about his voice? Had Merlin thought of that?

She sat up. "Gorlois, is that you?"

Uther moved closer to the bed, his heart racing.

"My Lord." Igraine sat up straighter, grasping the cover close about her. "But I thought—"

"The war goes well, my love. We had a break in the battle. Leigh has command and I missed you."

She sputtered a laugh. "Surely not. . ." Her beautiful face lit by the soft glow of the fire was a study in confusion.

"And business. I have business that needs attending to."

"Should I call for a manservant?"

"No need." Uther toed off his boots and left them where they fell, then shed his tunic and leggings. He lost his balance in his hurry and fell part way across the bed.

Igraine jumped from the bed, her nightgown falling over shapely alabaster legs that Uther just glimpsed. "Let me help you."

Uther allowed her to pull off his leggings, reached out and touched her golden hair as she bent before him. "My love," he whispered.

She stood up and Uther rose also, taking her in his arms, pushing her hair off her face. "You are so beautiful."

"Gorlois?" She started to say more, but he covered her mouth with his. She pulled back slightly, but then her mouth yielded to him. Uther groaned and struggled to slow down. They had all night. But his passion welled up and he pulled her tighter to him, tugging at her soft wool nightgown.

"A moment," she whispered, and stepping back, pulled the blue shift over her head.

Uther caught his breath. The fire lit her curves, painting a golden tinge on the soft ivory of her skin, deepening her pastel nipples to rose. He bent his head and took one in his mouth, sucking gently at first, then deposited kisses between her breasts and up her neck.

A soft sigh broke from her parted lips and she nestled closer to him.

Uther's control broke. He must have her. Now. He pushed her back on the bed, moving his knees between her legs, spreading them. He gloried in the sight. Then taking himself in hand, he nudged against her, holding his urgency like a roused stallion, waiting for her to soften, to open. She soon did, and he lunged forward, sinking himself in the glorious warm wet.

Anne floated in a sea of dark. She stretched out in her sleep, reaching for the covers, but finding none, stirred. Her eyes fluttered. The warm dark turned to milky gray, like muffled fog near the English coast. She opened her eyes and the gray began to lighten, as if the sun were burning off the morning mist. Someone was speaking, just sound at first. She sat up and found herself in front of a mirror, a shadow behind the eyes of someone, a watcher.

"I'm tired of him," the woman said. "He treats me as an afterthought. No consideration. And I want to have a baby."

Anne looked down at the body she inhabited. She wore a simple sheath dress, a strap on either side coming over the shoulders, just covering her breasts. She shone like sunlit amber. Maybe her skin was oiled. Anne ran a finger down her arm, but it came up clean.

The mirror she was holding was gold in the shape of a woman's body, the mirror itself almost in the shape of an ankh. Egypt. She seemed to be in Egypt.

She looked into the mirror and her reflection came into focus. Kohl, yes, she'd been making up her eyes. She picked up the pencil and drew another line.

"Is this how Isis does her eyes?"

"Yes, mistress," the servant behind her murmured. The woman picked up a peacock blue shawl and draped it over Anne—no Nephthys, her name was Nephthys. The servant draped the shawl over Nephthys' shapely bare arms. Nephthys stood, pulled it off, and threw it down into a tangle of scarves— scarlet, cobalt blue, and grass-green silk, rich and luxurious.

She pointed to a servant who knelt in the corner. "Did you get what I asked for?"

"Yes, my Lady." The servant moved on silent feet over to a chest and opened the top. The inside of the lid gave a glimpse of Nut, gold stars in a dark blue sky above her burnished, bending body. The girl pulled out a long piece of lapis velvet. At least it looked like velvet to Anne.

The servant flicked it and the fabric unfurled to become a cloak.

Anne gave herself a shake. What was she doing in Egypt, anyway? Hadn't she been talking to . . . who had it been?

Another woman strode into the room, her spine straight, head held high. She wore the white gauzy robes of a priestess, a *weskhet* collar of carnelian, turquoise, and lapis dwarfing her small neck. "Nephthys—" she stopped just inside the door "—why have you bothered with lining your eyes? We are planning on disguising you."

"We're twins. It hardly seems necessary."

The priestess gave her a quelling look and waved her hands at the servant girl to hurry. The girl draped the cloak over Nephthys' shoulders.

"Ah." Nephthys ran a hand down the soft fabric, then sniffed the collar. "Yes, Isis always wears myrrh." She started to step toward the priestess, but noticed the servant bending at her feet. "Well done. You may go now."

The girl scurried away.

"Follow me," the priestess commanded and turned on her heel, not waiting to see if Nephthys obeyed. They left the family quarters and entered a long limestone hallway tiled with travertine. A murmur of voices came from a hallway to the left. They paused until the sound faded, then turned right and continued down another hall until they reached the end. Two tall cedar doors marked the entrance to the family shrine. The priestess pushed one open, lit a taper, and ushered Nephthys to the center altar, a square of blue-veined marble about waist high.

She lit a votive lamp. Golden statues glimmered in the shadows. The priestess held charcoal over the lamp until it gleamed a dull red in the dark, then dropped it into a stone dish. She sprinkled powder over it and a heady sweetness rose into the air, making Nephthys dizzy.

The priestess began a low murmuring chant, like a stream running beneath paving stones, almost subliminal. Calling on her temple training, Nephthys allowed her breath to slow and deepen. She listened, drifting on the sound.

The chant grew louder and with a sharp exhalation, the priestess touched her face. More sounds, another touch, this time over her eyes, then her heart. The priestess took a scepter and spread the energy down her arms, down the front of her body, her legs to her feet.

Silence.

The priestess took up the lamp and surveyed her work. "You are ready."

Leaving the priestess in the family shrine, Nephthys walked on silent feet toward her sister's apartments in the compound, moving quietly, hugging the shadows. A servant passed. His eyes flickered to her face, then with a frown, he asked, "My Lady Isis, I thought you had gone to sleep."

"I needed to look at the stars again, Qen. I'm going back to bed now."

He turned to follow her.

"I don't need any more help tonight. Please go to your own rest."

"As you wish, my Lady." The man bowed slightly and continued on his way.

Nephthys continued down the outside corridor, then entered another limestone hallway lit by evenly placed torches. She passed wooden doors, putting her head close to listen at the second door. The redolent smell of cedar filled her nostrils. She closed her eyes and listened. She heard faint, even breathing. Her sister slept. At the end of the hallway, Nephthys pushed open the tall door to Osiris's chamber and crept inside.

He lay sprawled on his back, his golden skin lit by moonlight from the open windows. His stomach rose and fell with his long breaths, the toned muscles distinct even in deep sleep. Shadow and light played in his shock of dark hair. His arm lay outstretched, his tapered fingers open as if grasping for something.

Nephthys drank in the sight of him for a moment, letting his muscled torso, the slightly opened mouth over the firm chin, the long, toned arms arouse her. Then she stepped out of her carefully chosen cloak, stripped off her shift, and walked on bare feet to the side of the bed. She knelt on the edge, lowering herself so that her round breast came to rest in his outstretched hand.

He stirred in his sleep. Nephthys stroked his side, the skin soft. A low moan escaped his open mouth. Nephthys trailed her breast up his bare arm, her nipple hardening in anticipation. She pulled the cover off his prone body. His manhood stirred. Her own moist center grew as wet as the lands after the inundation.

Nephthys straddled him and his eyes snapped opened. Now was the test.

"Isis." He placed his hands on either side of her waist. "But I thought—"

Nephthys leaned down and claimed his mouth, shifted her weight to open to him, and he slid home.

This is so easy. Perhaps I over prepared, she thought.

He gasped out his pleasure. "My love," he whispered.

Then there were no more words.

Nina Lockhart studied the scruffy man from across the restaurant, then pretending to adjust her pearl and diamond earring, pressed the listening device more firmly into her left ear.

"You've followed our instructions to the letter?" her agent asked.

The man—he called himself Zebulon—leaned back, his head at an arrogant tilt. He wore a wrinkled shirt that had once been white and brown trousers in equally reprehensible condition. "Well, if I'd done that it wouldn't have worked, but we're ready to lock up the—" Zebulon paused and looked around him, then waved his hand in lieu of naming anything specific "—as you instructed. Just say the word."

"And you guarantee our desired result?"

"Of course." The hacker wiggled in his seat, unable to contain his eagerness. He picked up his glass and took a quick sip of wine, spilling a bit in his haste. "There is the matter of my payment."

"The agreed upon amount will be deposited into your account on completion of the task. The last installment."

He glanced rapidly around, ferret-like. "One million more."

Nina's lip curled in distaste.

"If all goes as you say," her agent replied, his velvety voice containing the hint of a threat.

"Oh, it will."

The agent nodded. "We expect action by close of business today."

"No problem."

The agent pushed back his chair and rose with the grace of a dancer, or the highly trained martial artist that he was. The waitress rushed over and he handed her money, a large bill judging by her reaction.

Nina stayed, watching her hacker in the mirror above the bar, twirling the olive in the bottom of her martini glass. After a rather conspiratorial conversation with the waitress, the hacker ordered and sat back, a look of satisfaction on his face. He picked up his phone and poked at it. Nina wondered at him using it in a public setting, but assumed he knew his business.

She nudged her own phone to life and clicked on the pineapple icon

Gregor had installed to piggyback on Zebulon's devices. Gregor had assured her it infiltrated other systems on a public network and would not be detected. She watched for a few minutes, but the hacker didn't text or email anyone. Just scrolled through some technical computer journals.

Suddenly, Zebulon sat up straighter, his gaze darting around the restaurant. Nina lowered her eyes to her drink. Zebulon bent to his phone, furiously typing. He put it down and seemed to turn it off. Nina nudged her phone again, and when it sprang to life, she saw the pineapple icon had disappeared.

She snorted, ironically satisfied that her spying had been detected. She'd hired the very best.

Nina asked for the check, paid, and left the restaurant. She needed to prepare for the next step.

Chapter 4

Elizabeth rested on the floor beside Anne. Arnold had placed Anne on cushions, then spread more pillows beside her and created a make-shift back support for Elizabeth, who held her granddaughter's head in her lap. Gerald sat on the floor beside her. Both their eyes were closed, Elizabeth's hands resting on either side of Anne's face. Elizabeth had sunk deep, swimming amongst the thick currents running in the temple, probing the murky tides that ran between her granddaughter and the astral figure of Mordred that stood silent, hovering like a battle crow over the sacred crystal that had always stood in their family temple. Elizabeth firmly believed in the crystal's provenance—from their temple, to the European temples of her ancestors, the Temple of Isis in the ancient land of Egypt, all the way back to the main temple of Atlantis. Gerald was a steady pillar to her left, his firm strength upholding and protecting her.

Before she could penetrate the fog any further, the sound of footsteps pulled her from meditation. As quietly as he could so as not to disturb her, Winston Stuart set down his black doctor's bag and pulled out a stethoscope.

"Winston. Thank God." She told him what had happened so far, slowly at first as she surfaced from her meditation.

Winston listened to Anne's heart and lungs, then pulled out a blood pressure cuff. Pulled back her eyelids, took her pulse. "She seems stable. Her blood pressure is slightly elevated, but that might just be what's normal for her at this stage of the pregnancy."

"What is going on?"

"Let's check the baby." Winston placed his stethoscope on Anne's abdomen, moving it a few times, his eyes closed in concentration. "Good heart beat."

He prodded her rotund belly, checking the position of the baby. "The child seems to have dropped lower in her pelvis. Just what you'd expect this close to birth."

"Yes, I've had children." Elizabeth chuckled.

"It's hard to know more without taking her to the hospital."

"Is it safe to move her?"

"Physically, yes, but these seizures must have a psychic origin. What have you been able to ascertain about this—" he pointed at the crystal in the center of the temple "—situation so far?"

Arnold pushed two large cushions across the floor for Winston and he settled awkwardly beside Elizabeth.

"Somehow, the spirit of Mordred has taken control of the crystal."

"Mordred?"

"Or an entity taking on his appearance."

"How can this be? Our wards are strong. The temple is highly protected."

"This is the question." Elizabeth stroked Anne's forearm. "I haven't been able to break through yet. The resistance is powerful."

"Does Michael know?"

Elizabeth shook her head. "I've been here. Susan is trying to contact him. He was called to Egypt. She hasn't reported back."

"Shall we try to move her again?" he asked.

"Do you think it's wise?"

"Let me put some monitors on her and then we'll see what happens."

Elizabeth stood up on stiff legs, hanging on to Gerald until the blood flow returned. Then she moved back a few steps to make room for Winston to work. She leaned against the wall and set herself to watch the psychic currents as they tried to move her granddaughter.

Winston reattached the blood pressure cuff to Anne's arm and positioned his hand over the pulse in her wrist, then nodded. Arnold knelt on the other side of Anne, slid one arm under her knees and the other behind her shoulders, then lifted her. Even heavy with child, she seemed easy for him to manage.

Winston checked her pulse, then motioned for Arnold to continue.

Arnold took a couple of steps toward the door.

"Hold here," Winston said. He closed his eyes, counting her heartbeats, then inflated the blood pressure cuff and watched the meter. "Good. Another few steps."

Arnold moved toward the door again, then paused. Winston checked her vitals. "Same again."

Arnold readjusted Anne's weight in his arms. Her head lolled to the side and Winston gently pushed it back against Arnold's large shoulder. Another few steps. Winston repeated his examination, then nodded for Arnold to continue.

After two steps, Anne's body suddenly stiffened. Arnold halted. Anne twitched, then convulsed, her fingers going rigid, sticking out at angles. Her face twisted, her body jerking back and forth.

"Go back," Winston ordered.

Arnold jumped back a few steps and Anne relaxed once again in his arms. He stood waiting for instructions.

Winston looked to Elizabeth. "What is causing this?"

She pointed to the crystal. Above it, the malevolent figure of Mordred hung like murky smoke, clear for all to see. The figure flickered like a dark candle flame. He pointed at Anne, who twitched in response.

She stays here, he said.

"I thought I saw his mouth move," Winston said. "What did he say?"

Elizabeth repeated Mordred's message for everyone to hear.

"This is outrageous," Gerald shouted.

Winston faced the flickering figure. "What do you want?"

Mordred's only answer was a bone-chilling laugh, loud enough for them all to hear.

Arnold balled up his fists and took a menacing step toward the apparition.

"Stop," Elizabeth commanded sharply. "I wish you could wring his neck, Arnold, but unfortunately, he's dead already."

35

Arnold let out a frustrated growl.

Elizabeth squared her shoulders and marshalled her energy. The lives of her granddaughter and great grandchild were at risk. With Thomas gone, the family's future generations. This situation would take all the occult skill she'd learned in her long life studying, meditating, and leading rituals.

She sent a probe of energy toward Mordred, calling upon the large crystal she'd worked with for decades to respond to her, to throw off this interloper. The heaviness in the room seemed to lighten for a moment. The crystal, now as dark as a deep smoky quartz, cleared bit by bit.

The fog in the room swirled again and Mordred's face appeared in her mind's eye. Arnold gave a shout. From the gasp the other men surrounding her let out, she supposed the apparition was visible to all of them now.

He shall not return, Mordred sent, his voice almost a growl in her mind.

"Who?" Elizabeth asked aloud for the benefit of the others. "Who shall not return?"

You know, Mordred whispered.

The fog drew back, then rose in a wave. The building force was so powerful, Elizabeth opened her eyes to look. The wall of energy continued to rise, blocking out the others in the room around her. It rose to the chandelier, the hanging crystal tinkling, then reached the ceiling of the temple, almost fifteen feet.

"Elizabeth." Gerald's shout reached her through the black wave, roiling like the waters of a storm.

The grand matriarch raised both hands, rooted herself deep into the earth that had sheltered her and her family before her, opened her crown, and brought down a river of light, then directed it all at the heart of Mordred's menacing upsurge. But the dark wave broke over her, scattering her energy, throwing her against the wall behind her. She landed with a thud.

The wave receded, pulling back into the fog that hovered around the crystal, leaving Elizabeth gasping for breath. Winston was there in an instant, feeling her head for bumps, checking her pulse. "Does anything hurt?" he asked.

She shook her head no.

"Look at me," he said. "Follow my finger."

She did as he asked.

He sat back on his heels, apparently satisfied.

Once she could speak evenly, she said, "Gerald, call the Lodge. We'll work tonight." She felt around Anne's neck. "But first, go find the crystal key. She isn't wearing it. It's probably on the bedside table. Maybe in the bathroom on the countertop."

"I'll bring it right away." He stood and walked toward the door, but then waited, turning back to hear the rest of her orders.

"Winston, how can we make her more comfortable? She must stay here for now. Until we can break this link."

"So it would seem." Winston stood. "Her vitals have all returned to normal, but she can't lie on the floor. I'll get a hospital bed brought in. Monitors. We'll need a nurse."

Elizabeth nodded. "Do you know someone with esoteric training?"

"Mary Shak might know someone. She's involved in several esoteric organizations."

"Good. I'll stay here and work on this . . ." Elizabeth waved her hand at the brooding figure.

"I think it's best to leave it be for now."

"I can't leave my granddaughter." Elizabeth closed her eyes against the tears that welled up.

"Of course not. Sit with her. Perhaps meditate. You might connect to Anne," Winston suggested.

"I'll stay, too." Arnold stepped forward. "You both need protection."

"I appreciate that, Arnold, I really do, but there is no physical danger. I need you to run a security check on the house, our properties and finances. All the businesses. See if there is some corresponding threat in the world. That might give us a clue to who is behind this."

"It's already done," he said, turning on his heel, his head held high, shoulders pulled back, his face grim.

The others followed him out.

Elizabeth settled down as best she could on the pillows Arnold had brought her, closed her eyes, and went in search of her granddaughter. She matched Anne's breath, questing out to follow the thread of her consciousness. After a few minutes, the dark behind her eyes lightened slightly and she saw a low bed hung with gauze curtains. A fresco lit by a stray moonbeam depicted women with lyres and sistrums.

Egypt? What did Mordred have to do with this ancient scene?

Quiet sounds of love-making drifted to her ears.

"Isis," the male figure called out as his back arched up in the final throes of passion.

But was it Isis? Elizabeth studied the woman's face, lit by an almost full moon. No, this woman was more domestic, projecting the feel of home and hearth. Yet there was something of the night about her. Some hidden purpose.

Tucked into the Egyptian woman's energy field she saw the outline of Anne.

After delivering Anne's crystal to Elizabeth in the temple, Gerald went to his study and started making calls. After half an hour, he put down the receiver of the desk phone and ticked off another name on his list. Gerald ran his finger down the list of names in front of him. Most of the lodge would come tonight around seven o'clock. The Hardy's had just left town, but would come back and make it by tomorrow if they were still needed.

His first call had been to Dr. Abernathy, the man whose family had sworn to protect the bloodline for centuries. Abernathy said he'd arrive within the hour. Gerald pushed back his chair, preparing to return to the temple and check on Elizabeth's progress, but the phone rang again.

He hesitated, but picked it up. "Yes?"

"Oh, thank God I got through to you."

He recognized the voice of the family financial manager. "Sydney, I'm rather busy at the moment—"

"I'm sorry, sir, but this is an emergency."

"I already have one of those at the moment. Can this wait until tomorrow?"

"I'm afraid not, Mr. Le Clair" Sydney said. "I'm so sorry. I don't know how this happened, but it seems—"

"Spit it out, Sydney?"

"Sir, your money is gone."

Gerald put the phone on speaker and brought up the DOW on the computer. "The markets are doing well." He started to search bonds and commodities.

"Yes sir, but your trust has been drained."

Gritting his teeth, he asked, "What do you mean by drained?"

"I mean," came Sydney's clipped words, "gone, as in empty."

Gerald grabbed his head and pressed on his temples. He took a few breaths before he asked, "When did this happen?"

Someone knocked on his office door and without looking up, Gerald shouted for them to come in.

"Sometime this morning. The banks started calling, asking why we were moving our money. We got on it immediately, but whoever did this was fast. They emptied all the trust funds under our noses. The money just evaporated."

"This is impossible. We have the most up-to-date security."

"I thought so, too, Mr. Le Clair."

"Do you know who did it?"

"Of course. The signal bounced through Bulgaria, Zimbabwe, Hong Kong, Chile, Cambodia, and finally the UK. We could only trace it back to a specific IP address with an unusual domain name."

"And?"

"Well, sir, we don't know what to make of it."

"What was it, Sydney?"

"The name was HeShallNotReturn.'"

Gerald tried to speak, but only made a choking sound. His vision narrowed.

"Sir? Are you all right?" Sydney's voice sounded thin and distant.

"Arnold," came a shout.

An arm reached in front of him and picked up the receiver. "Mr. Le Clair will have to call you back," Dr. Abernathy said and disconnected the call. He shouted for Arnold again.

Running footsteps grew louder and the big bodyguard burst into the room. Gerald fought for breath. Someone lifted him, carried him to a couch. Fingers felt for his pulse. Someone opened his shirt. A head pressed against his chest.

"Do you feel any pain?" Arnold asked.

Gerald's vision began to return. "Can't breathe."

A brown bag appeared in front of him.

"Sit up." Arnold supported his shoulder and pulled him to a sitting position. "Now lean forward and put this over your nose and mouth."

Gerald tried to object.

"You're having a panic attack. You need to breathe into this bag." Arnold's tone brooked no argument.

A panic attack? He'd never had a panic attack in his life. But he stuck the brown bag over his nose and mouth as directed.

Arnold crouched in front of him. The tightness in Gerald's chest began to ease. Arnold's expression slowly relaxed. Finally, Arnold nodded. "You can stop now."

Abernathy sat forward in a chair near the couch. "What's happening?"

Gerald caught them both up. His words tumbled out and soon he got short of breath. Arnold threatened him with the paper bag again. Dr. Abernathy went over to the sideboard and poured a finger of Teeling Single Malt Whiskey. Gerald drank it in a gulp. Warmth spread from his stomach to his chest. He took his first deep breath, sat back, and finished the story.

"To sum it up, Anne is in some sort of coma, Michael is in Egypt and can't be reached, and now the trust is drained?" Abernathy ticked off the problems on his fingers as he spoke.

Abernathy's steady voice warmed Gerald. Together they could figure this out.

"Who could possibly have done this?" Abernathy addressed himself to Arnold.

"We don't know anything yet. But the message is the same as what Mordred said," Gerald said.

"How in the hell could a medieval knight know anything about hacking?" Abernathy asked.

"He couldn't, so this means someone in this world, in this time, is behind this. We can deal with that," Arnold said.

"How?"

"We need to hire our own hacker," Arnold said.

"Surely someone from the corporation's cybersecurity team could come over," Gerald said.

Arnold frowned. "We need to hire the best, sir."

"Don't we have the best?"

Arnold shrugged.

"Who's the best, then?" Gerald asked. "An old friend from military intelligence? Maybe a CIA contact?"

Arnold's face turned beet red.

"What?"

"Sir, the best hacker I know goes by the handle Night Wing."

Two blank faces met Arnold's statement. "I know how it sounds, but these guys like to remain anonymous. They go by code names."

Abernathy frowned. "Surely a man of your abilities knows the hacker's real name."

"I do."

"So, what is it?" Gerald was losing patience.

"Preston Royce Westwood III."

"What's the name of his company?"

"He doesn't actually own a company or have a job, per se."

"Good. Then he'll be available."

"That's not exactly what I mean, sir." Arnold wouldn't meet Gerald's eyes.

"Spit it out, man."

"He's not old enough to have a job. He's still in high school."

This stopped Gerald dead in his tracks. "Excuse me?"

"Yes, sir, but he freelances."

"This high school student is the best you can come up with?" Abernathy asked, incredulous.

"My granddaughter's life hangs in the balance, someone has stolen our family fortune, which I might remind you is hundreds of years old, and you want to hire a high school student?" Gerald's chest tightened again.

Arnold held up the brown paper bag. "He's the best anybody can come up with, sir."

"Where does he live?"

Arnold shrugged. "It doesn't really matter in this day and age."

Gerald sat for a moment, certain the world had moved beyond his grasp. He gave himself a shake. "Get in touch with him, then. I'd prefer he come here. I think I'll call Dana Goddard in. She's head of cyber security at Maris."

"I know who she is," Arnold said, "although I think Preston prefers to work alone."

"Just get Preston here."

"It's already done."

Arnold's new phrase was beginning to grate on Gerald's nerves.

Chapter 5

"The rains will come, brother. Be patient." Osiris stood up and walked toward Set, placing a calming hand on his shoulder, but Set shook him off.

"So you say, but where are they?" He turned to his true audience, the leaders of the forty-two nomes of Egypt, gathered for their annual meeting. "Aren't you the life-giver, the one who brings the green to the land after the inundation?"

"We have done the ceremonies. The priests assure me the rains will come." Osiris looked around at the gathered rulers, spreading his hands.

"Is Isis not the hand of Ma'at for Khemit? As her consort, do you not bring cosmic order to the land?" Set spoke to the gathering, not his brother.

"Of course—"

"So where is your heir?" Set gestured to Isis.

Anne started, realizing he was pointing at her. Wait, how had she gotten here? She sat on a high throne. The arm rests were the spread wings of a goddess, inlaid in ivory, carnelian, and lapis. The front legs ended in the golden heads of lions. Her feet rested on a golden stool covered in vivid scenes depicting a feast. Anne shifted uneasily, then another consciousness brushed her to the back of their shared mind.

You are here to observe, Isis told her.

"You cannot even bring fertility to the woman of the High House, the one who chose you to rule."

"Patience, brother," Isis said. "Are you always in such a rush?"

The rustle of laughter spread through the room.

"This might explain the restlessness of your consort, who remains childless herself." Isis smiled to the men surrounding the raised dais.

Set's face flushed a dusky red. His smile was more a grimace. "I believe Nephthys is with child."

Isis turned to her sister, seated to her right. "What happy news." Her smile was genuine.

"The Hathor priestess confirmed it just two days ago," Nephthys replied.

Isis stood to embrace her sister, but the dark glitter in Nephthys' eye disturbed her. There was something hidden here.

"If we are to judge who is to be king by who produces an heir first—" Set puffed out his chest and turned to the leaders of the nomes "—then perhaps the Neters have chosen me."

Osiris lounged at his ease, his smile indulgent of a younger brother, if younger by only a few minutes. He waved his hand to the women seated to his left. "Is it not our custom to allow the High House to decide who is to lead?"

Set bristled as he turned to study Isis and Nephthys.

Nephthys glanced down at her leather sandals, avoiding her husband's eyes.

Something is not right, Isis thought.

"We are satisfied with our choice, brother Set," Isis said, enunciating clearly so the entire court could hear. "Your service is important to us. Please continue in your current position."

Set's nod to her authority was barely perceptible, but it was there. Set took his seat to the right of Osiris and the leaders of the regions began to speak, bringing up the real business of the day. Isis allowed her attention to wander. Her sister watched Osiris with an uncomfortable intensity. Isis would have to find out what was happening.

Michael found himself standing in the dark. The wind buffeted him and he reached out for Igraine, for the solidity of the bed he'd just left, but found only empty air. He stumbled, disoriented from the sudden change, then caught his balance. Where was he? He squinted his eyes against the tempest, but couldn't spot the room he'd been sleeping so warmly in just a moment ago. He must be outside Gorlois' castle in the dark, but as his eyes adjusted to the night, he saw with a start not the fortress, but the ancient Tor rising before him. The Isle of Apples. How had he gotten all the way to Glastonbury?

Michael studied the slope of the hill, but Anne's house wasn't there. In fact, no houses at all stood beneath the ancient trees. Nor was there a tower rising from the top.

"She will see you now."

Michael snorted in surprise. He had thought himself alone. "Who?"

A priestess stood before him, her white robe covered in a dark blue woolen cloak. She studied him a moment, her face giving away her thought perhaps Uther was getting too old, but she caught herself and soothed her expression to neutrality again. "The Lady of Avalon, my lord."

"Ah, yes," Michael murmured.

"Please follow me." The priestess moved with quiet steps around an oak, her fingers trailing along the trunk in a casual caress. The ground rose gradually and soon they walked beside a sprawling clear stream, lush ferns giving way to wild irises. They reached a grove of yew trees and Michael's escort motioned for him to go forward without her.

After a few steps, he saw a dark-haired woman sitting next to the wellhead, her blue robes pooling around her. Her head lifted and she frowned, but gestured for him to join her.

"My Lord Uther," she said, making no move to get to her feet or acknowledge him as king.

"My Lady." Uther gave a curt nod.

She studied him a moment, taking his measure. Uther shifted uneasily. Her gaze saw a bit too much, as usual.

She finally broke the silence. "So Lord Gorlois is dead."

"Indeed he is. Killed in battle against my own forces."

"And you have married Igraine."

Uther concealed his surprise. "I have. News travels fast."

"Morgan has joined us."

"Her daughter? She has nothing to fear from me. She is welcome at court."

She looked up at him and squinted against a ray of sunlight that had made its way through the canopy overhead. "You will not send for her. The future of the kingdom lies in the balance."

"Over a girl?" Uther brushed leaves and yew needles off a nearby stone and sat down.

The Lady of Avalon's spine straightened, reminding him of a bristling cat. "You may have claimed the right to name the heir, Uther, but power still follows the way of the old lands."

Uther sneered. "And what way is that?"

"Power flows through the female line. The health of the land, the abundance and fertility of all, depend on a proper mating."

"Are you telling me I have violated this law?" His tone was challenging.

A slight smile softened her face. "It surprised me to find that you have not."

"How did you find this?"

Her face closed. "The ways of the Sisters of Avalon are hidden. Suffice it to say, the boy will be important."

"Boy? So it's a boy?" Uther could not contain his glee at the news.

"The future king," the Lady said.

"Thank you for this news, my Lady. Will his reign be long?"

Her eyes sparkled. "It will be of great import and well remembered."

"Excellent." Uther started to stand, but she stretched out a hand to stop him.

"We must hide the child away. His life will be in danger if he stays with you."

"What? Who would threaten him? I can protect my own son."

The Lady toyed with a crystal pendant that hung from a silver chain around her neck. It drew his eye. Something in the back of his mind seemed to recognize it, was pleased to see it.

She tucked it away. "We could not see who wishes to kill him, but it is vital he be protected. I have Seen it."

"If you say so," Uther said begrudgingly.

"No one shall know his true parentage."

Uther stood. "This is unacceptable. If he is to be my heir, he must be known. He must learn about the lands and the lords he will lead. They must see his character. He must prove himself."

"Sir Ector will school him in statecraft."

"Sir Ector? You mean me to send him north?"

"And Merlin will teach him magic."

"What? This is unheard of." Uther's hand went to his sword before he realized it.

The Lady stood up and stepped beside him, laying a placating hand on his shoulder. "We only wish to protect the child. He must be a master of this world and the other."

This intrigued him. He'd always watched Merlin's magic with wonder and a certain curiosity. His own son would know the mysteries. Ector was a good man. Loyal. Wise in the ways of court. Honorable.

The Lady interrupted his thoughts. "Send Igraine to us before her pregnancy shows. She will give birth here. Merlin will take the child to the Forest Sauvage."

"Am I not even to see him?"

"We will send word when the birth occurs. He may stay here with his mother for a few months." Her voice softened. "You are always welcome to visit, my king."

This assuaged his pride, a concession from the powerful Lady of Avalon. Her words eased the burning in his chest. But a son. He would have a son whose reign would be—what had the Lady said? Of great import. And history would remember him, which meant his own legacy would be honored for a long time. Uther knew his name would be remembered along with his son's. His heart soared like an eagle.

He cared little for mewing infants or young children. He would visit Sir Ector often. The child would know him as a friend of the family and the High King. What should he name him? He turned to ask the Lady for her advice, but decided against it. She had enough control of the child's life as it was.

"Tonight, I expect you at the Beltane fire. You and your men may stay in the lodge beneath the springs." The Lady was already turning away. He was dismissed.

This reminded him he was not the one in power here, but the mild discourtesy did not disturb him overmuch. He was to have a son. A son who would be well known.

Nina sipped her India Pale Ale and waited to see if the group of neophyte magicians around the table in the White Hart Pub would answer her question. After seeing to her hacker, she'd flown to London to find an artifact she now suspected had last been in Cagliostro's possession.

"I say he's dead." Angus set his Irish stout down decisively. "No one has seen Cagliostro in nine months, maybe more."

Callum wiped suds from his beard. The beer at the White Hart Pub in North London was almost as legendary as the magician they were discussing. "Last we heard he was in the Caribbean diving. Rumor had it he'd found a crystal from Atlantis."

Jessamy chuckled. "And you believe that? He used to spin stories to keep everyone in awe of him."

A surprised silence followed this statement. When Alexander Cagliostro had been among them, nobody dared question his ascendancy. Now his critics seemed emboldened.

Everybody in the magical world knew or at least had heard of Alexander Cagliostro. He'd been around a long time, and his silver hair showed it, but his face was smooth and wrinkle free. He kept himself fit. A scoundrel—or worse—his exploits were often the subject of gossip at many a gathering.

Everybody had an opinion on how deeply Cagliostro had dipped into black magic and even more theories about why he never seemed to face repercussions from his misdeeds. Perhaps his actions had finally come back three times three, Nina thought, although she'd stopped believing in such things. Light and dark—just two sides of the coin of the universe. That's what she'd finally realized.

"He was at Black Thorn in Wick last I heard," Maisie said in a quiet voice.

"Black Thorn?" Callum asked.

"His ancestral house. Wick is just northeast of Glastonbury, right behind the Tor." Maisie waved her hand over her shoulder vaguely. "But what Angus says is true. Nobody's seen him or heard from him in months."

A member of Valentin Knight's lodge in the States had connected Nina to Maisie. Apparently they were young members of a lodge Cagliostro had worked with. Why he still took students was a mystery to Nina, but they idealized him and would likely keep up with his whereabouts. Maisie was proving to be the most mature of this group of neophyte magicians.

"What does his family say?" Nina asked.

Callum snorted. "They won't talk to plebeians like us."

"Speak for yourself," Jessamy said.

Nina had done research on this group of friends before meeting them at the pub. Jessamy's family was of the peerage, although sitting here in torn jeans, a wrinkled blue tunic, and smudged mascara, she didn't look the part.

She spoke up. "I saw his cousin Nigel Ravenscroft at my father's New Year's party. We didn't talk about Cagliostro though."

"Cousin? How old is this guy?" Angus asked.

"Well, they're second cousins, I guess. I suppose I could ask Nigel, although it might be awkward since we only see each other at social functions." She took out her phone and scrolled through an app. "I don't see any events scheduled for the next couple of months."

"What ever happened to Paul Marchant?" Nina asked.

Blank faces stared back at her.

"You know, tall, gangly guy. Gives lectures on sacred geometry. Said the poles were supposed to shift."

"Why?" Callum finished his beer and looked back at the bar.

"I heard he was in Egypt with Cagliostro a while back," Nina said.

"Oh, yeah? I don't really follow his work," Callum said.

"Haven't seen him in about a year," Maisie added.

"Another round," Nina shouted to the barkeep.

"Coming right up."

Angus pushed his empty glass away and smiled, warming up to Nina now that she'd bought him another beer. "Didn't you hear? He died in Egypt after some mysterious ritual."

"Died?" Nina knew this was true, but she wanted to see how much this group knew. "Are you sure?"

"Went to a memorial service for him. Apparently his mother was senile. In some home. Marchant's friends arranged the funeral." At the incredulous looks, Angus added, "What? I have family in New York. I go there pretty often."

Callum leaned forward and said in a conspiratorial whisper, "I heard Cagliostro went into Paul's apartment and took all this research and magical tools."

Maisie frowned. "What would he want with those?"

"No, Cagliostro was involved in the same ritual that killed Marchant," Angus said. "I heard he walked up to his dead body and stole something right off it."

"That's disgusting." Jessamy made a face.

"What did he take?" Nina asked.

"I heard it was a crystal or something. Don't know what somebody as powerful as Cagliostro would want with a pendant from that guy. He was all intellect. No real power." Angus seemed well informed.

So Cagliostro had taken the Orion crystal key, Nina thought. But what had become of him?

"You're sure Cagliostro survived the event in Egypt?" she asked.

"I saw him in Glastonbury right before that big to-do about White Spring running dry. Months after the Egypt thing," Maisie said. "Seemed a bit off his head, if you ask me. My uncle said he confronted some guy right outside the Wellhouse."

"Has anyone seen him since?" Nina asked.

Angus shrugged, looked around the table. A few people shook their heads. "I guess not, but you know Alex. He'll show up. He always does."

Their beers arrived and Nina held hers up. "To the old rascal."

Maisie looked rather scandalized, but the rest laughed good-naturedly. "To Alex."

Nina sat back and let the conversation swell around her. After a decent interval, she slapped her glass on the table and pushed her chair back. "Nice chatting with you all. I'll see you at the next meeting."

"You've moved here?" Callum asked, his eyes sparkling.

Nina kept her face neutral. Let him dream. "I'll be around for a while. Got a temporary assignment from my firm in London. Thanks for helping me find a place to celebrate the holidays."

"See you around, then," Callum said. The others lifted their glasses to her in farewell.

Nina paid the bill at the bar, then waved and left the pub. The chill outside crept up from the sidewalk. She wrapped her scarf tighter around her neck, then pulled out the Tube map. She was closest to King's Cross Station. She could catch a train out toward Glastonbury from there.

Chapter 6

A wave of dizziness swept over Anne as the scene changed abruptly from the audience hall where she'd been sitting between Osiris and Nephthys. To steady herself, she pressed a hand against the warm sandstone wall she found herself standing next to. She sensed she was still inside Isis, who observed a two-year-old boy squatting in the dust drawing crude figures with a stick.

His parents argued just out of earshot, gesticulating wildly, mouths open in what must be shouts. The child always placed himself so he could not hear their arguments. Set's jealousy had grown worse since the boy's birth and their fights were now an almost daily event. Set quarreled as vehemently with Osiris, cultivating his own band of followers at court and among the leaders of the nomes.

"Anubis," Isis called softly.

The boy looked up and Isis caught her breath. He was the picture of Osiris, dark umber eyes, the look in them older than any child had a right to. Damp curls lined his high forehead above his nose, high and straight. The child's skin glowed bronze in the late afternoon sun.

Those eyes sparked joy when he spotted his aunt. He jumped up and ran to her, pudgy arms raised to be picked up. She obliged him, the sudden weight surprising her. "Oh, my. You're getting too heavy for me."

He giggled, then batted at her dangling earring.

Isis captured his hand. "Want to come stay with me and your uncle for a while?"

"Can I?"

"Yes, you can stay as long as you want."

He looked back at the still-arguing couple. "But Daddy will get mad."

When would they tell him, Isis wondered. It didn't really matter. Not in Egypt. The child was the *akh,* the shadow of his mother. Children belonged to the mother's family. Sometimes the father lived with the matriarchal clan. Other times not. But here in the royal household, they were all family.

"Don't you worry about that," Isis said. "We'll let Osiris handle him. Now, what toys do you need from your room?"

Anubis frowned. Isis realized to go to his room they would have to pass in view of Set and Nephthys. "We can come back later if you want something. What do you want for dinner?"

"Fish," the child shouted, then flinched and looked over his shoulder to see if his parents had heard him.

Nephthys had stalked away down the golden-toned hallway and Set was following her.

"I think we can find you some fish. Fresh caught from the Nile. And mangos."

"I love mangos." The little boy slid down to the floor and took her hand.

Isis's eyes teared up and Anne felt the heaviness in her heart. Too young. He was too young to live around such strife. He needed a cousin, someone his own age to play with, and yet she had not conceived.

Shaking off her sadness, Isis led the boy out of Nephthys' apartments across a courtyard toward her own rooms.

Michael walked down the slope of the Tor, his host Uther still contemplating all the news the Lady had given him. With his next step came the rustle of leaves against his boots. The wind swirled a few up and away. He squinted into the sudden dark and thought he saw movement. The sway of tree limbs. Pinpoints of light winked in and out above the crowns of the trees. He was in a thick wood at night. It had just been close to noon.

Then came the sound of hooves and heavy breathing. The pounding feet grew into a thundering, then the heavy snort of an animal desperate to escape.

A few seconds later he picked up another noise beyond—the galloping of horses and faint cries of men. Torches pricked the darkness, then lit the tree limbs. A great mass flew at Michael, hot breath and desperate squeals. He jumped out of the way just in time. The torches were bright enough to light up a huge boar. The eyes burned red as the animal ran past.

"He's just ahead," came a shout.

"We can corner him against the rocks."

Then the horses surged into view, a sorrel, then a bay followed by two blacks, their nostrils wide, eyes flashing in the torchlight. One young man, gleaming sword in his hand, saw Michael and his eyes lit with joy. "We've got him, your majesty. The court will eat well tonight."

And then they thundered past.

Michael stood in the darkness, grasping his own sword, his breath coming in gasps.

What's going on?

But before he could take another breath, he was sitting in a gilded chair at a round table in a stone room filled with laughter and the jests of comrades. Long tapestries hung behind each man—scarlets, azure and royal blue, forest greens, and dandelion yellow, depicting the family crest of each knight. Torches smoked, darkening the ceiling. Serving maidens carried pitchers of mead and platters of cooked meat and vegetables.

One man stood and lifted his cup. "To Arthur, for a good hunt. May Moccus bless our company."

Gareth, Michael remembered, Sir Gareth Beaumains. Michael sat back and lifted his own cup, brimming over with the honeyed drink. "To Arthur," he shouted.

The boy stood at the other end of the table, his face flushed, his blonde curls darkened with water from a recent bath, beaming with pride. He caught the Pendragon's eye and raised his pewter mug. And Uther Pendragon, whose eyes Michael watched from, surged to his feet, raising his flagon into the air. *To my son*, he thought. He dared not say it aloud. Not yet. Merlin and the Lady had forbidden it.

Nina rented a Mercedes in Salisbury, something to suit her cover as a rich girl looking for an old beau, and drove the rest of the way to Glastonbury. She picked a small bed and breakfast a few streets west of High Street, avoiding the spiritual landmarks next to the Tor, not wanting to attract attention or be recognized. The next morning, she added a few layers of paint to her face, dressed in an expensive blue dress with Italian leather boots and a cashmere coat, then drove out to Black Thorn.

The place was well named. Hawthorns outlined the property boundaries, an open invitation to the fae of the Tor. The main structure was brown stone, with a layer of darker brick dividing the ground floor from the upper stories. The upper windows were small, but numerous, and a gray slate roof topped the large house. She parked on the side of the circular drive and walked to the portico, gravel crunching beneath her boots. The knocker was a brass skull.

"Cute," she mumbled, then pounded on the door. The house was big and she wanted to be heard. After a minute, she pounded again.

Soon she heard footsteps and the door swung open to reveal a proper English butler, dressed in muted gray trousers and vest, topped with a black tailcoat. He'd finished off his ensemble with a red tie and white gloves. Nina wondered if he'd gotten dressed while she waited, but the delay hadn't been long enough for all this.

"Hargreaves, at last. I was beginning to fear no one was at home." She'd researched the family online and hoped they still had the same butler.

The man gave a slight bow. "How may I help you, madam?"

"I've simply been searching everywhere for Alex." Nina had decided mimicking her sister would strike the right tone, her voice high and lilting even higher at the end of each sentence. "I haven't heard from him in ages. I do miss the old chap." Maybe that was too much.

"Mr. Cagliostro is not at home at present." Hargreaves reached out his white gloved hand. "I will give him your card."

Nina forced herself to giggle. "Oh, Hargreaves, you're such a perfect relic. I mean that as a compliment, of course. Nobody carries cards anymore."

The butler looked up at her. Something swirled in his gray, green eyes that made her uneasy. "Whom may I say has called?"

"Isn't anyone else at home? I saw Nigel recently and he mentioned he might come out for a visit."

This was a bald-faced lie and it seemed Hargreaves knew it. His face closed. "The family is not receiving at present."

"I see." She gave a fake name and number. "Please tell him I'd simply love to see him. I'll be in London for a couple of months."

"As you wish, madam." Hargreaves gave another slight bow and closed the door.

Nina sat in her car, pretending to search for her keys in a capacious purse, studying the windows. She saw the curtains flip back on the second floor and a pale face look out for a moment. A female face. Not Cagliostro. She closed her eyes briefly and sent out a psychic probe, but came up against a firm wall. If his wards were still in place, maybe he was still alive.

She decided to check out White Spring.

Chapter 7

The ground dropped out from under Michael and darkness engulfed him, but before he could yell, he found the earth beneath his feet again. He stood in bright sunlight in front of a crowd of people, Merlin at this side. The old wizard's eyes twinkled, if such a word could be used to describe this formidable old man, venerable as an ancient oak, his white beard flowing over his blue robe set with astrological and magical symbols.

Why was Merlin so dressed up? Michael wondered, then looked down at himself and jumped when he found breasts beneath an equally fancy robe of dark blue. A familiar crystal hung around his neck, but this one was not his own. He could tell by the little song it sang, detectable only by certain finely tuned ears. This one belonged to Anne. He reached his hand up to grasp it and the contact brought him fully into focus.

A laugh escaped the lips of his hostess. "You'd think he'd never been a woman before," the Lady of Avalon commented to Merlin.

"He needs to see," the wizard said in a whisper, but before he could say more, a roar rose from the crowd.

A young man stood before a large, sunburned stone in the midst of a clearing. From its center rose a steel blade. Celtic knots wound their way around the black and gold cross-guard. A red jewel crowned each end of the pommel, sending out shafts of crimson.

They were choosing the High King, Michael realized. Uther's successor. He must have died. A stab of grief cut Michael, surprising him. He missed Uther in an odd way. He'd shared some of his most intimate and important moments and grown rather fond of the old letch.

The beam of light from the jewel in Excalibur's pommel seemed to point to a man who stood glowering in the background. But he seemed insubstantial somehow. Perhaps he was an astral visitor, like Michael.

In a flash, Michael saw the future laid out, the marriage, then the betrayal. The other child born from the ritual with Morgan, the snake in the grass at the final confrontation. Arthur carried back to Avalon accompanied by the chanting of the Sisters of the Isle. He shook his head against the visions.

The jeering of the crowd, good-natured but loud, snapped him away from that prescience. The Lady gently pushed Michael to the back of her consciousness where he could watch, but not make any movement.

"Excalibur is not for you, Sir Kay," said a young man with already burly shoulders and a patchy red beard moved in front of the stone, pushing the younger Kay aside. They both laughed.

The crowd cheered again. Sir Kay's friends patted him on the shoulder as he moved back into the crowd. Some jostled against him in a jovial way.

"Step up, Sir Gareth, and try your hand." The silvery voice of the lady surprised Michael.

The crowd quieted as Gareth took his stance, planting his feet a bit apart. He took two deep breaths. With the third, he grasped the handle of Excalibur and pulled, the tendons in his neck standing out with the strain. But the sword did not budge. Gareth gathered his strength and tried again, grunting with effort. He stepped back at last, wiped the sweat from his brow, and shook his head.

"Are there more contenders?" Merlin called out.

The young men searched each other's faces, shaking their heads, frowns and worried looks all around. A gust of wind blew the dried grass around the stone.

"All the sons of the provincial rulers have had a turn," Gawain said, his head hanging low.

Apparently Michael had arrived late in the contest.

"What shall we do, Merlin?" Gawain asked.

The Lady of Avalon was anything but dejected. Michael could feel glee bubbling up like the springs she oversaw. She'd been waiting for this moment, but he felt her tighten her cheeks to school her face. She must appear solemn.

The men spoke quietly among themselves, some shaking their heads, others standing, hands on hips. At last, an elderly man stepped forward into the middle of the field. He walked around with his back to the sword in the stone, looking each man in the eye. He turned to Merlin, his cloak billowing with the sudden movement. "There is one other who could make the attempt."

"Surely you cannot pull the sword out, father," Sir Kay said.

So this was Sir Ector, Michael thought.

"Not me, son, but my ward. Your squire for today."

Voices erupted in protest. "A squire? But we do not know his parentage," one man said.

"The people will only accept one born from royalty," someone in the back shouted out.

"Who is this boy?" another asked. Sir Ector's kingdom lay to the north and visitors were infrequent, although they knew Uther had visited a good deal toward the end of his life.

The Lady stepped forward. "It has not always been the tradition that the son of a king become High King. The Druids have always chosen," she said. "Let the boy try."

All eyes turned to Merlin, who made a show of weighing her words. Then he addressed the crowd. "What say you?"

"Where is this ward?" an elder asked.

A willow-slim youth, his head a mass of blond, his chin sharp, stepped forward and stood next to Sir Ector. The clouds parted again and the young man was lit by a shaft of sunlight.

The crowd murmured. A few recognized him.

"He slew the great boar just before the Pendragon died," one said in an undertone.

"Arthur, would you try to pull the sword?" Merlin asked, his voice soft, yet easily heard by all the crowd.

Arthur's glance darted to Sir Ector, then to the lady as if asking their permission. Sir Ector gestured toward Excalibur gently swaying still from the last attempt. Arthur stepped up to the bronzed stone and took his stance. He looked up at the Lady of Avalon again. She smiled, radiant as the light that had fallen through the clouds to light Arthur. He nodded and grasped the sword, planted a foot on the stone itself, and pulled. Excalibur glided free with a ring of steel.

It shocked the crowd into silence for a few seconds. Arthur's surprise was even more profound. He stood, eyes wide, jaw slack, staring at the sword he held in his hands.

He doesn't know who he is yet, Michael realized.

A huge roar erupted, every throat giving voice to welcome the new High King of England. Arthur stood with the royal sword still pointed in the air. He brought the sword down and laid it across his hands. The Lady stepped forward and held out a leather scabbard. He bowed low and took it from her, then turned in a full circle in front of the cheering crowd, holding the sword high for all to see. At last, he slid Excalibur home and buckled the sword around his waist.

Before the crowd could surge forward, Merlin stepped up next to Arthur and raised his hands for silence. Shushes filled the air. Some poked their neighbors to get their attention, pointing to the tall wizard who was a head above the youth. Merlin waved Sir Ector over to his side.

"Now is the time to tell you, Arthur, who you really are."

The boy's forehead wrinkled in confusion. He looked to the man he had always known as a father, the question written on his face. Perhaps Arthur had assumed he was a blow-by of this regional king.

Sir Ector shook his head slightly as if answering this unspoken question.

The crowd pushed forward, elbowing each other to hear.

Merlin held his head high. "Arthur, you are the son of the Queen Igraine and the High King of the Land, Uther Pendragon."

Arthur stumbled back a step.

Sir Ector grabbed his arm to steady him. Michael heard Ector say in an undertone, "It's true, but I have always loved you as a son."

Voices rose from the crowd, asking each other what Merlin had said, if it could be true.

Merlin held out his arms, gesturing for Arthur to step forward. He took the stunned youth by the shoulders and turned him around to face the throng. "I took Arthur away as a baby and hid him in the North to keep him safe. Educated at the side of Sir Kay, he was taught states craft by the honorable Sir Ector—" Merlin paused, waiting for perfect silence "—and magic by me."

Shouts of surprise rose from the crowd.

"Did he say magic?"

"The King a magician? But that's unheard of."

"In the older time, the King was always a magician as well as the ruler. In fact, this is the source of the family name."

"Another Pendragon."

And with this, the crowd surged forward, pulling Arthur up on their shoulders, chanting "Pendragon, Pendragon, Arthur Pendragon."

In the jubilation and chaos, Michael felt himself separating from the Lady of Avalon. The sight dimmed, but right before he rose above it all, he felt a sharp prick at the back of his neck. Had a bee stung him? He reached behind to feel, but all faded to black.

"Michael." Azizi's voice bounced off the walls of the cavern, echoing twice before falling back into silence. He listened carefully for any sound in the humid dark. He called again, but still Michael didn't answer.

Azizi walked back into the main temple space and looked around for Tahir. He spotted his tall form stooping down, his nose close to the wall behind the Sekhmet statue.

"Tahir," Azizi called.

Tahir whirled around, shining his flashlight in Azizi's eyes. He squinted against the light. "Sorry." Tahir pointed the bright LED beam down at the dusty travertine floor.

"Have you seen Michael? The guards only gave us an hour. We need to leave."

Tahir glanced back at the wall he'd been examining with regret. "When can we come again?"

"Perhaps tomorrow night, but only if we leave when we agreed." Azizi shrugged. "You know how they are."

"Where did Michael go?"

"Last I saw he was heading into the Anubis niche."

They walked across the temple, the sound of their footsteps reverberating off the walls. With so many workers moving around, the sand had cleared from the middle of the cavern. The dark jackal-headed god stood behind his father in his own small shrine, gold lining his ears and mouth, the eyes eerie. The lights the workers had rigged didn't reach into the gloom here. Tahir switched on his flashlight again, pointing the light in every corner of the niche. He stepped away from the shrine and shined his light into the dark beyond. About fifteen meters in, golden limestone walls rose in the back of the cavern.

"Michael," Tahir shouted, his voice gruff, long practiced at calling children in from play.

There was no answer.

The two walked toward the cave wall, shining the light along the floor. One set of footprints appeared leading away from the shrine.

"Ah, we'll find him," Azizi said.

But the faint impressions vanished halfway across the space. Azizi crouched down. Taking Tahir's flashlight, he examined the ground carefully, shining the light parallel to pick up any irregularities. The dust lay even, undisturbed. He pointed the light back toward the center of the temple, studying the ground carefully. There were no returning prints.

Tahir crouched beside him and took the light, aiming it into the black of the underground cavern. In the distance, a form lay on its side. Tahir shone the light over the ground between the figure and where they crouched. The abiding dust lay even and undisturbed.

"Michael," Tahir shouted.

The form did not stir. Azizi jumped up and ran to the figure, Tahir rising more slowly and following. Azizi reached him and pointed the flashlight into the figure's face. Michael's mouth was lax, his eyes closed, as if he were sleeping peacefully at home.

Tahir bent down, a low grunt escaping his lips as he kneeled on the hard floor. He took Michael's face between his two palms.

Azizi leaned back.

"The light, please."

Azizi aimed the flashlight back at Michael's face, now dwarfed between Tahir's two rough hands. He kept the light steady as Tahir hummed, gently massaging Michael's temples. After a few minutes, the hum turned into Michael's name. Tahir's low, deep voice called out several times until at last Michael's eyelids fluttered and his eyes opened. He squinted against the light, and Azizi directed the flashlight to a spot beside him.

"Tahir?" Michael sounded surprised. "What—Where am I?"

"You are in Egypt," Tahir's voice remained steady, not betraying any alarm.

"Egypt, but I was just in Camelot."

"What did he say?" Azizi whispered.

"You are in Egypt," Tahir repeated, loud and firm.

Michael sat up and clutched at his chest.

"Should I call a doctor?" Azizi asked.

Michael looked around wildly for a moment, then into Tahir's face. He panted for air. Soon his breath slowed and he stood up, dusting himself off. "I was just—"

"Wait until we are at my house," Tahir said.

Michael nodded, then again his hand went to his chest, grabbing at his shirt. He felt the back of his neck, then closed his eyes and shook his head.

"What is it?" Azizi asked.

"The crystal. I had it on when I came tonight. The crystal key—it's missing."

Chapter 8

Winston and Arnold had installed a hospital bed in the temple and a comfortable chair for Elizabeth. She sat next to Anne contemplating the situation. Still unconscious, Anne lay beneath white sheets and a thermal blanket, an IV drip in her arm. A bank of monitors stood in the corner, Anne's pulse registered by soft, steady beeps. A second monitor displayed the baby's vitals, its heart rate much higher. Elizabeth had asked it be muted except for the alarm because the rapid beeping had made her uneasy.

The new nurse, Emma Gallen, stood by the machines, her blond hair streaked with gray captured under a white nurse's cap. She made hourly notations on the clipboard in her hand. The woman had come highly recommended by Mary Shak, a member of the lodge whose family affiliation with the Le Clairs stretched back at least two hundred years. Probably more. Elizabeth and Winston had vetted her psychically, and Arnold had done a thorough background check. All rushed, yes, but that had been necessary given the circumstances. The woman had a solid metaphysical background and could probably understand Elizabeth's explanations and perhaps even take part as a support person in ritual. Arnold would probe further, and in the meantime, Elizabeth was keeping an eye on her.

And Anne.

Not to mention Mordred, who still hovered, a dark shadow, over the crystal in the middle of the temple.

Anne's condition had not changed. Her vitals were strong. The baby seemed fine. But the coma persisted, although Elizabeth wondered if that was the right word for what had happened. A powerful magician had entranced Anne. An unembodied magician at that, who, because of that, could access the energies of the upper realms much more easily.

Elizabeth paused at this thought. Could he? After all, he was intent on doing harm. Negative magic came at a cost. The more powerful, the steeper the price. Mordred wanted to stop the birth of the child Anne carried. The child who'd almost come to term, due in a week, if not sooner. These things could never be predicted accurately. Her own daughter Katherine had been late by almost two weeks.

Elizabeth smiled at this thought. It had become a character trait. Katherine was late in everything—finding her favorite subject in school, puberty, getting married. She'd never accepted the family legacy. Still scoffed at metaphysical teachings Elizabeth tried to share, something she'd given up on years ago. Learning this and the family heritage was Katherine's duty, the duty of all the matriarchs of the Le Clairs. To pass on the knowledge of not just their bloodline, but how to use the abilities that usually came with this inheritance for the guidance of humanity.

Elizabeth straightened in her chair. Katherine had shirked this duty since she refused to learn how to use her brilliant vision. She still shocked her mother with some of her insights, but they could not be relied on, coming as they did from an untrained and undisciplined mind.

It had seemed that Anne would follow in her mother's footsteps until Cynthia died and passed on the crystal key to her niece. Thankfully, Anne had risen to the occasion, much to Elizabeth's relief. She'd handed off most of Anne's early training to Roger Abernathy, a man who followed in the Templar tradition of protecting the bloodline. He was not a monk. The Templars had passed their duty on to householders, but the rigor remained. Elizabeth had hoped to polish off Anne's training with the female mysteries after the baby was born.

A soft cough got Elizabeth's attention. Emma stood at the foot of the bed, hands folded, the picture of an old-fashioned nurse in white dress, white stockings, and white comfortable shoes that apparently made no sound at all.

Elizabeth pulled herself from her reverie. "Yes?"

"Mrs. Levy and the baby's vitals are all normal, ma'am."

"Thank you." Elizabeth reached out and patted Anne's hand.

"You mentioned a lodge gathering at eight o'clock. It is now a quarter after seven." Emma kept her voice low as if she didn't want to wake her patient.

If only it were that simple, Elizabeth thought. Suppressing a sigh, she pushed herself up from the new cushioned chair Arnold had provided.

"May I help you prepare?" Emma asked.

"If you could keep watch, I'll go get ready."

"Of course."

"Let me know immediately if there is any change."

"Yes, ma'am."

Elizabeth stopped by Gerald's study and found him hard at work. He updated her on the hack.

She stared at him a full minute before responding. "So, we have no money now?" This idea was beyond her. They came from old money. Very old. She'd never thought a moment about what she would do without funds. It was incomprehensible.

"Arnold has hired our own hacker." Gerald explained the plan.

This shocked her more deeply. Finally, she roused herself. "Arnold, change the codes on the family vaults here. Unless those have been broken into as well."

"It's already done," he said.

Tangible goods. That she could wrap her head around. They had some gold bars stored away. The family had always kept gold or diamonds on hand, a tradition that stretched back hundreds of years. A sudden picture of Estelle trying to pay for a loaf of bread with gold bullion flashed in her mind and she almost laughed.

"Is the attack on Anne and this theft connected?" she asked.

"We'll check into that as soon as our computer experts arrive."

She shook her head, deciding to leave the business to Gerald.

In her rooms, she stripped off her clothes and stepped into the shower, turning the nozzle to a pulse of hot water. She let the spray beat on her tight shoulders, finally feeling the knots loosen. She dried off methodically, forcing herself to slow down. Applying her favorite lotion, she breathed in its scent of roses, letting it carry her to the garden where she tended the bushes herself in summer, picked and laid the petals out to dry, before blessing them for ritual use. Then she settled before her private altar in her sitting room and allowed all the turmoil and fear to rise. The dark clouds that had hovered on the edges of her awareness moved in and broke. Her throat burned and she wept for her granddaughter, for the child whose birth these malevolent forces were fighting to stop.

Her grief widened to include her grandson Thomas, lost in the Indian Ocean during his search for the crystal key in Tibet. She wept for Cynthia, her bright child who grew to be such a powerful woman both magically and in her life, who had fully embraced the family legacy and taken their knowledge to new heights. For her brother, George, cut down in his prime by an assassin's bullet, the man whose administration the American people still called Camelot, never realizing how close they came to the truth.

"Why not me?" she whispered.

Then the spiritual being who guided her, who oversaw their family, the real head of their Lodge, rose within her. Isis spread her blue cloak over Elizabeth's shoulders, comforting her, murmuring of her search for Osiris, sharing her grief at the loss of her lover. They wept together.

She allowed her feelings full reign, knowing it was the only way to clear them, knowing the storm would play itself out and leave her washed clean like a beach after a heavy storm, but with a treasure deposited somewhere on the sand.

Anne listened to the silence around her. Gradually, she noticed a sound, a faint, regular beeping in the distance, slow and steady, far above her head. The weight of something stirring inside her, a small form readjusting itself.

The baby, she thought. *That's right. We're having a baby.*

She kicked her legs as if to surface from deep water, trying to move toward the sound, but ran into a murky haze that thickened as she struggled to push through it. She strained to fight her way free, but a voice murmured indistinctly, just below the threshold of hearing, sending a numbness through her limbs. The weight within her went still. Too still. She wrapped her arms around her jutting belly protectively. Her throat burned with grief.

But the baby is still alive, she thought. *Why do I feel like I've lost my one, best love?*

The darkness lightened. She sensed air currents. In a few moments, she squinted against a tropical sun and found herself sitting in a gilded wooden chair, bent over, holding her stomach as if her guts would spill out, howling with grief.

A man stood in the middle of the room, his face streaked with tears, waiting. The woman in the chair gasped for breath. She gripped the table beside her for support. "Take me to his body."

Whose body? Anne wondered.

She studied the man before her. He wore a white linen kilt, pleated in front. His chest was bare, but around his neck hung three strands of obsidian, carnelian, and crystal supporting a lapis scarab at his breastbone.

Egypt again. Why do I keep traveling back here?

"I'm sorry, Lady Isis, I can't . . ." His jaw quivered. He wiped tears away with a square hand. "There is—"

"You can't?" Isis surged to her feet, anger replacing grief. "I command you to take me to his body."

"While you were away, Set made a beautiful box, and at the feast he held at Osiris' return, he offered it to the person who fit it most exactly. The coffin was beautiful, made of rare cedar from Lebanon, and inlaid with ebony from Punt, and ivory, gold and silver, and painted inside with the figures of Neters, birds and animals. Osiris desired it and when he tried it out—"

"He got inside it?" Isis asked, her eyes wide.

"He did, my lady. I wish I could say I tried to stop him, but Set's apology for his past behavior was convincing."

"Then what happened?"

"Once Osiris was inside, Set and his men slammed on the lid, nailed it shut, and carried it to the Nile. They . . ." the man shook his head. His voice sank to a whisper. "They threw the coffin into the water."

"Take me to the place."

The grief of the goddess pulled Elizabeth into harmony with Anne, and they watched this scene unfold. Did Anne sense her presence, she wondered. Perhaps not. Anne's link to Isis was almost seamless.

Once the scene ended, Elizabeth rose from her straight-backed chair, clear-headed now. She dressed for the coming ritual—shrugged into her robe, slipped her feet into velvet, soft-soled slippers, and donned one of the family heirlooms, an ancient, magical amethyst ring, on her forefinger. The gold dragons at the base seemed to slither into place, arming her.

Elizabeth made her way through the house to the temple, thinking about what she'd seen so far. Anne as Nephthys, then Isis. Why did Anne keep going back to Egypt when the scourge of Avalon stood in the temple, the one responsible for this psychic attack? What did these two stories have in common? Two men fighting for the throne, one a set of brothers, another father and son. Clandestine assignations and secrets about the parentage of children.

Downstairs, most of the lodge had gathered in the ballroom, their dark robes somber in the evening light. The quiet murmuring stopped when their head priestess arrived. The group arranged themselves in a semicircle, hands folded, eyes intent on Elizabeth.

She told the whole story since a few people had not heard it yet. She wanted to be thorough, to let the group think this through before attempting the banishing. Elizabeth added her latest experience.

"Gerald will not be joining us tonight. Our businesses and financial holdings have also been attacked and he is attending to that."

At a few raised eyebrows, she added, "I would advise you to see to your own affairs as soon as you can in case the attack spreads to the whole group." She paused, looking around at her colleagues, thirteen highly talented magicians, carefully chosen to form a balance of abilities. All of impeccable character. "Our identity is well hidden, but we don't know who is behind this. Clearly, they have ties to the metaphysical community. I'm just suggesting this out of an abundance of caution."

"Thank you, Elizabeth. I'm sure we'll all do our due diligence once we've attended to the more pressing business at hand." Winston straightened the purple cord around his waist. He explained Anne's medical condition, forgetting his audience couldn't quite follow his technical terms. After he finished, he looked around at the confused faces and smiled ruefully. "To sum up, her condition is stable for the moment. The baby is fine. But she could go into labor at any time. It seems the entity is here to stop the baby's birth."

Murmurs greeted this last statement.

"Thank you, Winston," Elizabeth said. "Now, given that Anne seems to be returning to Egypt in her astral traveling, presumably guided by the situation, how can we use this to our advantage? What does it tell us?"

The group stood quietly, some lost in thought, others with mouths pursed or foreheads wrinkled. Julia and Bill Hardy spoke in whispers. Finally, Cordelia Stuart raised a forefinger.

At Elizabeth's nod, she stepped forward. "We all know the stories that are at play here. The metaphysical tradition holds that both the Egyptian and Jewish traditions succeeded in bringing in the savior of their age, but in Camelot, Arthur left no child born from his marriage with Guinevere. Instead, he was killed and taken away. We still await his return."

"So, you're suggesting this child might be involved in the return of the King?"

Cordelia ducked her head slightly at hearing this stated so boldly. "Perhaps."

A tingle of energy set the hairs on Elizabeth's arms on edge, alerting her there might be something to Cordelia's idea.

Alycia Thompson spoke up. "I took the liberty of investigating Michael's lineage."

"Thank you," Elizabeth said. The family had already done this, but Alycia was an expert in genealogy and might have discovered something new.

"He does come from the Levite priesthood. Anne, as we know, is of the Magdalene bloodline, so the two parents are from ancient and powerful heritages. Two spiritual families combining again. The child could well be pivotal to the new era that is dawning."

"Where is Michael this evening?" David Wilt asked.

"He was called away to Egypt. We haven't been able to contact him yet."

Arnold spoke from the doorway where he would keep vigil during the ritual. If he had to leave, he'd assign another member of the security staff.

"Anne Morgan le Clair has been kidnapped." Elizabeth's voice rang out. "It is our duty to rescue her and the young prince."

This archaic phrase had the desired effect. The group circled around her, backs straight, eyes intent.

"Let us proceed into the temple. The west will enter first. You know your stations." She turned to David. "Guardian, let us know when the temple is ready."

Soon David called them in, and the group walked through the carved oak double doors, some pausing at the threshold to take in the sight of Anne lying in her hospital bed surrounded by monitors, but discipline prevailed and they made their way to their chairs. Some closed their eyes, further preparing themselves for their role in tonight's ceremony.

Those in the directions picked up the implements, a few ancient, each one representing the element, and called in their quarter in order. Elizabeth picked up her wand and flourished it. Bill Hardy in the South held a dagger with a long history. Cordelia stood opposite Elizabeth and picked up the sacred chalice, holding it with reverence. Julia balanced her husband in the North and called in the element of earth. David sealed the temple with a flourish of the ancient sword belonging to the lodge, and Elizabeth felt the air in the room tighten like the skin of a drum.

Elizabeth had taken David aside and instructed him to keep a close watch. He'd need to open the circle to allow the entity to escape once they'd driven it from the crystal. The nurse stepped back, and Winston stood beside Anne, his hands hovering above her. His job was to block any attempt to harm her or the baby. Elizabeth wished Michael were here to do it. Where was he, anyway? She also missed Gerald. Although his magical abilities were not strong, his special gift was his heart. His love buoyed her up, wrapping her in a cloak of warmth and optimism. She could use that about now.

Once the quarters were called, Elizabeth turned to the crystal ball in the center of the temple and began the rite. She raised her wand above her head. "I invoke the Defender, Archangel Michael. Sekhmet, the Protector. I invoke the guardian of this Lodge, Mother Isis and call upon Anubis, the Opener of the Ways. I call on the guardians of the soul of Anne Morgan le Clair Levy, the guardians of the spirits of the companions assembled here. Come to us now."

As she called each name, Elizabeth could feel the light intensifying on the inner planes. Lord Michael took up his station in the South, his sword gleaming. Anubis walked in and stood in the West, his dark robes almost cutting the air with the force of his presence. He wore his human face and a fierce expression. Sekhmet took her place on the other side of the western altar, her golden body shining, her expression serene.

Elizabeth began a chant to raise the energy of the temple further. The chant grew in intensity as the others joined in, spiraled up the scale, then right before it crescendoed, she pointed her wand at the center crystal and drew a banishing pentagram in the air. The others followed suit.

"Mordred, son of the Goddess and God, conceived of the high ritual at Beltane in the sacred Avalon, I expel you from this place. I call upon all the powers gathered to sever your ties to Anne Morgan Le Clair Levy. I command you to release her. I send you back to your place in the other world." She flourished her wand and then pushed the energy she had gathered with her words at the crystal.

A quiver went through the temple. Winston's face sharpened, and he moved one hand up as if to block something from reaching Anne. The Archangel Michael standing at the southern altar was suddenly engulfed in scarlet flames.

There was a pause, then a long, low laugh sounded like a gong, spreading a malevolent arrogance that set Elizabeth's teeth on edge.

Ah, my Lady, still the Lady.

Elizabeth wondered what he meant by this.

These powers will not interfere with my rightful claim. It is me, not him, who shall be reborn.

Elizabeth could see by the looks of shock and anger on the faces of the lodge members that everyone had heard these words in their minds, even the least talented. She looked to Anubis, who could banish this upstart with one wave of his hand if he chose, but he only smiled at her. Sekhmet's fury was legendary, although Elizabeth had only ever experienced her compassion and unconditional love, but she stood, holding her lotus staff, watching with a detached interest.

Elizabeth turned her attention back to Mordred. "What is your claim?" she asked.

A bright yellow glow began in the heart of the crystal and spread, rapidly engulfing the whole temple. The faces of her companions were lit with the light, Alycia's spectacles reflecting the luminosity like a cat's eyes caught by headlights. The energy did not feel malevolent, but Elizabeth lifted her hands to push back and suddenly found herself in a clearing surrounded by a grove of trees. Her knuckles had smoothed out, the age spots on the top of her hands had disappeared.

Her own voice rang out, clear and strong. "Arthur, Guinevere, join hands."

The young royal couple stood before her, Arthur decked out in his finest. His tunic sported the golden double dragons of the Pendragon coat of arms. The jewels set in his gold crown caught the sunlight.

The bride wore a gown of white, the layers billowing in the light breeze. Elizabeth abruptly remembered her family had converted to Christianity, which explained the color. Yet, here she was getting the blessing of the Druids and the Priestesses of Avalon. Had they already done a service in the cathedral just down the hill? Many of the Knights of the Round Table stood watching. She recognized Gawain and Bedivere.

At least we're in the right story, she thought.

Elizabeth shook her head against the enthrallment, but the Lady of Avalon—Viviane, her famous ancestor—steadied her. Elizabeth looked through the Lady's eyes around at the gathered crowd and saw her lodge companions had joined her, some overshadowing their past selves as members of this famous crowd just as she did, others standing as shades because they had not lived at this time. All watched intently.

The Lady's voice rang out again. "Stretch out your joined hands."

The couple did as instructed. Elizabeth noticed a ring shining from

Guinevere's hand. So, they had already been to the cathedral. The young bride looked up into the Lady of Avalon's face and Elizabeth gasped. Her granddaughter Anne looked back at her.

With a snap, Elizabeth returned to the present, to the temple. Murmurs rose from around the circle. Cordelia grabbed the rails of the hospital bed to steady herself.

"We were there," someone said.

"What an extraordinary experience."

"Let us maintain order," Elizabeth said.

The whispering in the lodge fell into silence.

Elizabeth addressed Mordred, who stood in his fighting clothes in the middle of the temple where she imagined many still saw the crystal. "How is this an answer to my question?"

I am the only born son of Arthur Pendragon, High King of Britain, and Morgan, the daughter of Igraine, High Queen, and King Gorlois. It is my right to rule.

"You, my dear boy, are a gift of the gods, a divine child born of the sacred Beltane rite. You are not the child of those humans who took part in the ritual."

It is my right to rule.

"You failed to understand your place during Arthur's time. Your human parents are of lesser stature than the deities who came into the people celebrating the ritual. You are higher than a king. This is the tradition."

Mordred shook his head, his jaw clenched, his face set in stubborn lines.

Elizabeth wanted to snatch him up like a recalcitrant child and throttle him, but she took a steadying breath and said, "It is the twenty-first century. The Pendragons do not rule England any longer. The monarchy no longer holds temporal power." Elizabeth fought the rising frustration. How could she explain the modern world to this medieval soldier?

The bloodline will always rule, he answered. *It is my time.*

Elizabeth gathered a ball of fire in her solar plexus, pulled it up through her arm, and sent it crashing across the temple at the surly warrior standing in place of her precious Atlantean crystal. Her companions joined in. Streams of fire flowed across the space, all meeting in the dark figure of Mordred. But he threw up his arms and to her great surprise, Anubis stepped in, surrounding Mordred with his cloak, deflecting their energy.

Not yet, he said.

Chapter 9

Michael ducked his head at Tahir's wife, Jamila, as she handed him a cup of tea. He sat cross-legged on a cushion on the second story of their tiered house just a block away from the Sphinx enclosure. Tahir nodded for his wife to set the tray in the middle of the rug and busied himself with the shisha pipe beside him. Michael rubbed the back of his neck. It still stung from the theft of his crystal—at least that's what he thought had happened. There had been only one set of footprints leading into where they had found him in the temple. None returning. How his crystal had been stolen might be a three-pipe problem, as Sherlock Holmes would phrase it. Tahir looked prepared for that as he broke up a briquette of charcoal and spread it evenly in the bowl of the pipe.

Tahir had sent Azizi home to his family. It was still the wee hours. Jamila went back to bed, the children and grandchildren still slept, so it was just the two of them. The night was silent—as silent as Egypt ever got. An occasional voice lifted from the street, the bark of a dog, the noise of distant traffic reached them through the open windows. Michael watched the now familiar ritual as Tahir stuffed the tobacco into the bowl and sprinkled a few grains of hashish on top. It was the only time Michael indulged in either substance—here in Egypt with Tahir. It seemed to take down the remaining barriers so they could speak mind to mind. Before smoking, Michael reached into his pocket for his cell phone, but remembered he'd accidentally left it in his room. He'd call home later. He hoped Azizi had taken pictures in the newly uncovered temple.

Tahir lit the mixture in his pipe and inhaled deeply. He blew smoke from his nostrils, reminding Michael once again of a dragon. Then Michael took a turn. They passed the hose of the pipe between them a few more times and fell into silence. The orange cat who had adopted the family jumped down from the balcony, stalked across the rug on silent feet, and curled up in Michael's lap. He stroked the old tom, who purred and kneaded his leg.

At last, Tahir spoke. "Tell me the whole story again."

And so he did.

Michael listened with a critical ear as he talked, surprised that sitting here in Egypt, he'd kept returning to Arthurian England. Tahir reloaded the shisha pipe, then lit it and they smoked again, then sat brooding on the story. Michael picked up his teacup, but found it empty.

After a few minutes, Tahir asked, "Do you have a strong connection to the story of King Arthur?"

Michael shook his head. "I've always felt more drawn to Egyptian stories, as you can imagine."

"But the two are connected."

"How so?"

"The followers of Akhenaton are not the only ones who have taken the true teachings out of Egypt. First, Bishop Theophilus and his mob burned the great repository of knowledge."

"The Library of Alexandria."

Tahir nodded. "The Greeks invaded and the seven Cleopatras ruled." He ticked the events off on his fingers. "Khemit fell to the Romans, and those who kept the knowledge went underground, but some fled north."

"Mary Magdalene."

"Yes, but others as well. Even before her. The wisdom keepers established themselves there as the Grail Kings, intermarrying much as the royal family here had done, continuing the mother line. Centers of learning sprang up in these courts. But the Roman Church grew in power and eventually brought their reign to an end. The kings who served the land and people gave way to the kings who served the church, and the knowledge was hidden once again."

"I guess I hadn't connected all this back to Ancient Khemit quite so clearly."

Tahir shot him a look of disapproval, but then he waved that away with his hand, like a teacher erasing a blackboard. "You have married into one of those caches of hidden knowledge. And also into an ancient bloodline of Egypt."

It surprised Michael. He'd never thought much about family lines. He knew the Le Clairs claimed a lineage back to Yeshua and Mary Magdalene. But Egypt? It made sense, based on what Tahir had just said.

Tahir pointed the end of the shisha pipe at him. "Plus, you bring your own powerful bloodline to the mix. The Levite priests—keepers of the Ark of the Covenant, the teachers of the priest king Solomon."

Michael squirmed, and the cat lifted his head and let out a meow, instructing him to hold still. Michael stroked the tom until they both settled back down. Part of him always felt uncomfortable with all this talk of bloodlines and royalty. It was the twenty-first century and monarchs had become figureheads. The Rosicrucians had escaped Europe to establish a New World Order in America, free of kings. At least, that was the popular story. But what if they were escaping the kings loyal to their old enemy, the Church of Rome? What if in establishing democracy, they also wanted to bring back the rulership of the old knowledge in a different form? After all, they had only allowed the aristocracy the vote in the beginning of the republic. Democracy had not been meant for the masses. Not then.

It had started earlier, maybe in Prague. The Thirty Years War at its heart had really been the Rosicrucians fighting the Holy Roman Emperors, trying to wrestle back control. Frederick V had taken his English bride to Prague to establish a different sort of New World Order, an enlightened society based on the metaphysical teachings of old. The Northern European kings had supported them, but James I doomed the rebellion when he reneged on his promise to come to their aid. What if there was something to a leader who was schooled in states craft and metaphysical knowledge—just as Merlin had declared Arthur to be? Frederick had been a mystic, and John Dee, who had spent time in Prague, had also advised Queen Elizabeth. But what did all this have to do with King Arthur?

Tahir interrupted his thoughts. "There is some reason you are reviewing the history of Anne's family."

Michael took a breath to protest, but Tahir's cell phone rang.

Tahir answered it in Arabic, then switched to English. He looked up at Michael, his bushy brows raised. "It's for you," he said, and held the phone out.

Michael put the phone on speaker. "Hello?"

"Michael, thank God we reached you," Dr. Abernathy's voice rang out. "Something's happened to Anne."

"What?" Michael stood up, dislodging the cat. "Is she all right? Is it the baby?"

Abernathy explained that they'd found Anne in the temple unconscious, that she could not be moved. That they had tried to banish the spirit holding her captive to no avail.

"Spirit? What spirit? Some spirit is stronger than Grandmother Elizabeth and the Lodge?"

A wry chuckle rose from the phone. "We can hardly believe it either."

"Do you know who it is?"

"Well, yes. It's Mordred."

Michael stood dumbstruck in the middle of Tahir's living room. "Mordred?"

"Yes. He keeps saying he should rule."

"Rule? Rule what?" Michael's hand flew to the back of his neck. "When did all this happen?"

"We're not sure. Elizabeth found her earlier today. We tried you immediately, but it seemed you'd already gone out."

Michael remembered switching off his phone so he could sleep. Had he checked it before leaving for the site? But he'd still had the crystal then. "I have a theory about how he got in, but the timing is off. I still had the crystal key when this seems to have happened."

"You lost your crystal?"

"I wouldn't say lost," Michael objected, feeling like a child being scolded by a parent. "It was stolen."

"Stolen?" Dr. Abernathy shouted. "We should have sent Arnold with you."

"Arnold couldn't have done anything." Michael told the story all over again, pacing the room. "I felt a sting at the back of my neck as I was leaving the ceremony for pulling Excalibur from the stone. I'd noticed a dark, brooding figure on the fringes of the crowd earlier. Perhaps it was Mordred. Maybe he took the crystal, although how he could have taken a physical object from the astral plane is beyond me."

"Mordred hadn't been born by that time," Abernathy objected.

"True, but maybe he was there on the astral, like I was. Maybe that gave him access to the crystal key somehow."

"We must think about it," Abernathy said. "While you were traveling in Arthurian England, Anne has been jumping through the Isis and Osiris story in Egypt."

"What do you mean?"

Abernathy shared Elizabeth's visions of Anne's experiences. "Her last trip was to Avalon, though. At the end of the ritual, everyone in the temple saw where she was on the astral. She joined Guinevere for her wedding to Arthur."

Michael and Tahir stared at each other. "What is going on?"

"That's the question."

"But the timing is off. I still had the crystal when Mordred broke into the temple and entranced Anne."

"Time is flexible on the inner planes. You know that. This is the strongest theory we have so far. You need to recover that crystal while we work to dislodge Mordred here."

"I still can't believe he bested Grandmother Elizabeth."

"Well, it wasn't really him who beat her."

"What does that mean?"

"We attacked Mordred with the consolidated force of the group—"

"That should have done it."

"But Anubis blocked us."

This stopped Michael in his tracks. "The Opener blocked the attack?"

"He did."

"Did he explain? What does Grandmother Elizabeth say about it?"

"We all heard him. He said, *Not yet.*"

There was a prolonged silence. Tahir scooted closer to the phone. "Dr. Abernathy, we will work on recovering the crystal, but Michael must remain here for a little while longer."

"No, I have to get back to Anne," Michael said.

Tahir reached out a restraining hand. "Her safety depends on solving this riddle and getting the crystal out of Mordred's hands—if he has it."

"Who else?" Michael said, arms raised.

"It's the best idea we have." Dr. Abernathy said. "Anne and the baby are fine for the moment. Winston is taking care of her in the temple and we've hired a nurse. Someone with metaphysical training in addition to her medical expertise."

"That's good," Michael said, then he heard muted voices in the room with Abernathy. Abernathy answered back, but Michael couldn't make out his words.

Abernathy's voice came clear again. "I have to go. There are other things going on."

"What?"

"Nothing you need to worry about."

"Tell me," Michael demanded.

Abernathy exhaled heavily. "Someone has hacked the family accounts."

"Hacked?"

"Yes, and the money stolen."

"What?"

"The Le Clairs are broke," he said, "for the moment."

Michael waved his hand, dismissing this. "The museum will take me back. I can support my family."

Abernathy let out a broken laugh—Michael did not understand the sums of money they were talking about—then seemed to catch himself. "Good man. Let me know how things turn out with Tahir's plan."

Michael heard Arnold shouting in the background, "Now, Abernathy."

"You go," Michael said. "I'll talk to you later. Take care of Anne," he said, but the connection had already been severed.

Michael turned to Tahir. "So, what's your idea?"

"We need to go to the Serapeum."

Michael was too surprised to respond.

"Get some rest. I'll make the arrangements for tonight."

Abernathy followed Arnold into the Gerald's home office to find a scrawny kid in a black hoodie and ripped jeans giving orders to a woman well into her thirties. He recognized her, but couldn't remember from where.

"No, no, no," the kid said, "these need to be all in a row and connected to the same processor." He picked up a handful of cables. "Do I have to do it all myself?"

"I was just going to do exactly what you said, Night Wing." She laid heavy sarcasm on the name.

Then Abernathy remembered. The woman scolding the kid was Dana Goddard, head of cyber security at Maris Corporation. She stood behind the computer tower, hands on her hips, dressed in jeans and a long-sleeved tunic. Not her usual three-piece navy blue skirt suit with modest heels. They must have called her in on the weekend. Was it the weekend? He'd lost track.

"And I can't keep calling you Night Wing. What's your first name?"

The boy scowled at her as if she'd asked for some unorthodox intimate encounter. "I'm not going to tell you that."

Arnold snorted. "Preston Westwood III, meet Dana Goddard."

"How did you—" A flush of red crept up the kid's neck. He was a typical rich kid. Left alone by his busy parents tending to their fortune or vacationing halfway around the world. Trying to pass himself off as a genius from the wrong side of town.

"Now, let's get back to putting these machines together," Arnold snapped.

The two worked in silence for a few minutes, then the kid grabbed the chair in front of the bank of monitors, linked his own laptop to the system, and flipped a switch. They sprang to life. His fingers flew over the keys and rather than the company logo, the screens filled with different charts, a couple of maps, a list of what looked like phone numbers, and then gobbledygook that Abernathy felt sure was computer code.

Dana pulled up another chair, and the two talked, pointing at different monitors. Soon the map on one monitor sprouted red lines that jumped from New York City to the Philippines, to Croatia, then to Siberia, Belarus, and finally to Somalia.

"Gotcha," Preston said with immense satisfaction.

"So, this attack originated in Somalia?" Abernathy couldn't imagine how a country in such chaos could support a high-tech attack like this.

"No," Preston rolled his eyes. "It means the cloud service provider is there. The attack could have originated from any computer with access to them." He turned back to the monitors and clicked. A list populated on another monitor.

"What's that?" Arnold asked.

Preston waved his hand at the three older men standing behind him, but addressed himself to Dana. "This will take forever if I have to explain everything to these troglo—"

"All right, there's no call for that." Dana turned to Gerald. "Sir, the attack originated from the cloud service provider in Somalia. We're hacking into those servers to generate this list of computers that have used them. Then we need to find who owns those computers. Once we accomplish this, we'll see if any of those companies has ties to Maris."

"We'll want to check for connections to the family and this list of organizations." Gerald gave her a hand-written list. Abernathy caught a glimpse of the first few.

International Council of Princes

Noble Order of St. Germain

Royal Dragon Order

Royal House of Forester

Templars of Saint Joseph

Temple of Columbia

As Dana scanned it, a look of confusion grew on her face. "I've never heard of these companies, sir."

"They're not companies. They're—" Gerald shook his head as if trying to throw off lifelong habits of silence "—secret societies, some hundreds of years old. Their members might have reason to attack us."

"If you say so, sir." Dana looked skeptical.

"How long will this take?" Gerald asked.

"Hard to say. We could find something immediately or it could take hours. I'll let you know as soon as we have a list for you to study."

"Excellent."

"Ah ha!" Preston shouted. "Take that, you bastards."

Gerald frowned. "What?"

Dana put her hand on Gerald's shoulder and said in an undertone. "Don't mind him, sir. It's like a computer game to him. But he's good. Together, we should be able to crack this."

"I'll be in my—" Gerald blinked and looked around.

Abernathy guessed he'd been about to say 'study', but that's where they stood now. The room had been taken over by the cyber security team. "Let's adjourn to the library," he suggested, but Gerald walked toward a monitor displaying a growing list of companies linked to the Somalian servers.

"Look at this, Abernathy. Institute for the Workings of God," he read out.

"Bank of Vatican City? Don't they have their own computers?" Abernathy asked.

Gerald looked at Dana. "Is there a way to find out the amount of these transactions?"

"Assuming they're banking records. These could be anything—memos, emails, personnel files, illegal dossiers on public figures, real estate holdings. You name it."

"Can we open the files?"

"I doubt we can gain access to them," Dana explained.

"Oh, please," Preston said. "I can crack anything."

Typical teenage hubris, Abernathy thought. But the kid had a reputation. They certainly had promised him a pretty penny if he succeeded. Not that he needed money.

The list continued to populate.

Central Intelligence Agency

EU Intelligence

Coche Industries

Zenel

"That's a Saudi Arabian company, isn't it?" Abernathy asked

Gerald just nodded.

Chinese Offshore Oil Corporation

Royal Holland Oil

Britannia Petroleum

"Seeing a trend here?" Gerald commented.

"Looks like the usual suspects, as the saying goes," Abernathy said.

United Germanic Bank

Suisse Credit Financial

Dana snorted. "Now their bankers."

Knight Corporation

"What?" Gerald jumped back from the monitors. "That can't be."

"Is that Valentin's company?" Abernathy asked.

"Who is that, sir?" Dana asked.

Gerald shook his head, the habit of secrecy too deep even faced with this situation.

Abernathy came to his rescue. "Mr. Knight is an esteemed head of one of those spiritual organizations Mr. Le Clair gave you a list of."

"Abernathy—" Gerald objected.

"This information is to be kept in strictest confidence," Abernathy said to Dana, who nodded. Preston didn't look up. He took a step toward the kid, whose eyes remained glued to the screens. "Is that understood?"

"Whatever, man. I don't care about your moldy old secrets."

Somehow, Abernathy doubted this was true. Hackers thrived on secrets. "When can you get into the files that were sent?" he asked.

"Man, I'm looking for your data. It could be stored here."

"Excellent. How long—" Gerald asked.

"Forever if you keep hanging over me."

Abernathy put a hand on Gerald's shoulder. "Shall we adjourn to the library?"

"Good idea. Arnold, would you ask Estelle for some tea and sandwiches?"

Preston's head popped up. "How about pizza?"

Abernathy tried not to laugh at Gerald's chagrined expression. "Get them whatever they need," he said to Arnold, who'd been standing in the doorway observing everything.

Chapter 10

As soon as he got back to the room, Michael made another call to The Oaks to check on Anne and spoke to Abernathy again.

"Anne and the baby's vital signs are stable, but she is still entranced. Grandmother Elizabeth will sleep next to her and Mary Shak will keep vigil tonight. She has medical training."

"I should be there," he said.

"Elizabeth agrees that you need to recover the crystal. If Mordred has somehow gotten control over it, he will have a great deal more power than he would otherwise."

Michael shook his head. "If you two think that's what I need to do, then I will. But I'll come home as soon as I can."

"Of course. What's the plan?"

"Tahir won't say. He said he's taking me to the Serapeum."

Abernathy chuckled as if he shared a secret. "Enjoy your trip."

Michael ended the call and took a quick shower. With a large white towel wrapped around his waist, he pulled the curtains in the room tight, blotting out the bright Egyptian sun pouring down outside, leaving the room in almost total darkness. Still, he could feel the solar pull and wondered if he'd sleep. He threw the towel onto the bathroom floor and got in bed. He was certain he would toss and turn with his worries for Anne and his son. He felt certain it was a boy now. He wasn't entirely sure why. He flipped onto his side and fluffed up the pillow, ready to try and still his thoughts. But sleep took him immediately. And then dreams.

Michael felt his loins stir at the thought of the duty he would perform tonight for the land and the powers that ruled moon, sun, and stars. He half listened as Merlin reviewed the responses he should make to the Lady in the well-known ritual.

Merlin pulled at his robe to get his attention.

"What?" Michael asked.

"Haven't you been listening, you big lout?"

"Sorry."

Merlin just snorted in reply. "Now lean down, Arthur."

Arthur? He was watching through Arthur's eyes. The young man turned his head and Michael glimpsed the Tor rising behind him before he slipped into the back of the king's mind to watch.

Merlin hoisted up the heavy crown for the Horned Lord, the antlers reaching out in nine points, three times three. Arthur braced himself and Merlin fit the crown on his head.

The sound of women chanting rose and fell from the crest of the Tor. Merlin grasped his staff, the twisted oak crowned with a crystal that seemed to light up of its own accord regardless of the rays of the moon or sun. It brightened when Merlin thumped it against the ground. The old wizard bent his head, listening to the chant. One of the planetary signs in his plush purple robe gleamed out and Arthur took a step back, but Merlin grabbed his hand.

"It's time." They stepped out of the small hut at the base of the Tor and started the climb up. Arthur balanced the stag crown with one hand and pulled up the ceremonial robe with the other, feeling less than manly at this moment when he was to embody the cosmic male principle. Irritated, he pushed this thought away, focusing on the growing power of the chant. Something flashed white at the corner of his vision, and Michael glanced over to catch the white flag of a deer's tail as it bounded away into a copse of ash trees.

They crested the hill and the Lady of Avalon came into view, standing in front of the sacred fire, arms spread in welcome. "All hail the Horned Lord," she cried out, and the priestesses echoed her, "All hail."

Arthur made the proper responses, already detaching from his daily self, and the priestesses parted into two columns. Arthur took a deep breath, steeling himself to walk through this gauntlet of feminine power, a birth canal, a death channel. Merlin strode beside him through the corridor they formed, their mysterious voices swirling around Arthur, taking his measure, encouraging him, somehow caressing his skin like the promising brush of a lover's lips. His shyness melted as the sexual energy rose from them, the scents of rose oil and myrrh, the whispered suggestions.

Merlin began his chant, his deep bass grounding and intensifying the ethereal song of the women of Avalon, for the folk of the surrounding town and country had joined on the edges of the circle. A chant rose in Arthur's chest and he added his own voice, sounds that budded and bloomed, becoming the call of the bull to his cow, the challenge of the buck to any others who would contest him.

Through the line of priestesses now he saw another coming toward him, a woman wrapped in red and bedecked with flowers, her face glowing with light, transformed by the power of the Goddess she had already called into herself. She carried a chalice. Michael, watching from the back of Arthur's mind, recognized it as the same vessel used in Grandmother Elizabeth's temple at The Oaks. So the legend seemed to be true.

Arthur pushed Michael back and sent out a call to the God and a shaft of light fell on him from the parting clouds. His sense of himself as an individual faded almost completely. He let the God take him.

The Goddess danced around the God, slowly leading him away from the others toward a bower constructed further away in the meadow. There, she pulled at his robe, allowed hers to open, revealing the curve of her hip, a pink nipple, taut with desire. His body responded, energy flooding his limbs, his phallus rising fully to serve Her. At last, but it had only been minutes, she pulled off her robe to reveal her naked form, laid the robe on the ground under the bent willow branches, and beckoned to the God. A surge of joy filled what little remained of Arthur and Michael, such a gift to be welcomed into Her service like this.

The distant chanting intensified yet again, and somewhere distant from his intense passion, the Lady and Merlin spoke of the sun and earth coming together to bring the tides of summer back, to bring fertility to the crops and lambs to the hills, to create new life in the people. To rectify earth and bring her into harmony with the realms of the divine. The people of the surrounding villages scattered to find their own mates.

The Goddess stroked the God's limbs, pushed his robe off his arms, and ran her hands down his chest, kissing the scars he had gained in service to the sacred land, which she was tonight. Finally, she lay back and he could hold back no longer. He stretched above her, the sky above the earth, the sun above the crops, and sank into her warmth, her depths, the vast mystery of her fertility. He lost himself to the thrusts and gasps and wetness of burgeoning new life.

During that long night, he realized the priestess embodying the Goddess tonight was Morgan, the daughter of Morgause. Morgause had come here for safety after her father had died and Uther had married her mother, just as he himself had been sent away north and hidden from enemy eyes. Morgan was the product of a ceremony like this one, one between King Uther and the Priestess Morgause. This made the woman he made love with, laughed with, ate with from the baskets brought out to them, his sister.

He pushed the thought away. It was the old way, before the Christians taught it was wrong. They did naught but their duty. There was nothing personal in it. She carried the maternal blood, and it was only fit that he should serve the Goddess as well as the royal line. The Sun Child would be worthy. He turned back to the business, the pleasure, at hand.

Nina pulled on her black leggings and slipped a black turtleneck over her head followed by a black wool sweater. She matched this with black athletic socks, black sneakers, and topped her outfit off with a black slicker against the inevitable English rain. Studying her face in the mirror, she decided the hood of the slicker shadowed her face enough against recognition. She waited until the clock struck half-past two am, opened the door to her room at Pilgrim's Bed and Breakfast, and listened. Hearing nothing, she snuck into the hall and made her way outside.

Luck was with her. The street gleamed black beneath the lights, wet with light rain. She paused next to a vine-covered wall. Satisfied nobody was out at the moment, she made for the alley between the church and the Daisy Center Retreat. Huddled under her slicker, she walked across High Street to Silver, then up to Chilkwell, and finally onto Well House Lane. All was silent at the Berachah Guest House and it looked like her luck would hold.

Nina made her way past the Victorian pump house, keeping her breathing even. The faery lights that decorated the building and wall had been turned off. No vagrants or late night celebrants stood inside the small courtyard outside White Spring. No one filled a bottle at the small stream of water that fell inside the nook just past the courtyard.

Rose Cottage, the Le Clair house, stood dark. She walked the length of the road to The Hermitage, which she'd heard a new Australian couple had recently bought since Garth had disappeared. It seemed many people in the magical community had recently turned up missing or dead. Its windows were dark.

Nina retraced her steps to the round wrought iron door to the interior of White Spring, took out her hook picks and torsion wrench, and went to work. In a few seconds, the padlock at the top of the gate clicked open. With one more glance around, she slipped inside, closing the door behind her. She reached through and hung the opened padlock back in the slots of the gate. If anyone walked by, they probably wouldn't notice it was open.

Nina stood in the dark listening to the sound of gushing water and allowed herself to acclimate to the sacred cave. In the nineteenth century, an outbreak of cholera had led the local water board to desecrate the series of faery dropping wells that had lined the bank and build a stone well house, trying to contain the water in a series of pipes. The high mineral content of the water blocked up the pipes over several decades and the place had been closed.

Magic always pushed through the attempts to contain it, Nina thought. She was grateful the locals had finally gotten control of the building and turned it into a temple. In nooks and crannies, altars to the Goddess and God stood, with beautiful paintings, lit by candles during the day.

The spring itself fell into a round stone basin much like its twin spring across the street, but this one single, not double. The water brimmed over onto the floor, out the door and often, she remembered, down the street. Moisture had already seeped into her sneakers. Nina switched on her flashlight, thinking belatedly that a candle would have been more appropriate given that the Brigit ruled over this well and her day was a fire ceremony. She moved off to the left where she knew from an earlier reconnaissance that the stone would be dry.

She leaned against the stone wall, sank to the ground, sat cross-legged, and switched off her light. She sank deep into meditation quickly, the atmosphere redolent with power, ritual upon ancient ritual layering more energy onto the primordial potency that already existed here, the vital force of water as life, of mother earth, the higher beings who used this place as an anchor, of the elemental undines, and the fae just out of sight.

Nina sensed them watching. They were like her, she imagined, beyond the moral constraints of human religion. Primal beings, bringing comfort or cruelty as appropriate. She felt the brush of Brigit's attention, but it moved off. In the dark, she waited, letting her awareness open, deepen. The black of the cave grayed and she made out the dim outlines of the well wall, the altar table near the back of the cave. Beneath the gush of water, she heard stirrings, whisperings. A splash that sounded to her ears like a frog jumping into the water. But it was no frog. Giggles.

"Where is the Orion crystal key?" she whispered.

A renewed silence came after these words, the wary quiet of wild creatures, but it was short lived. Another splash. The sound of tiny feet. Deep inside the Tor, a laugh. The strains of a harp.

A breeze touched her face. Ghostly fingers? The breeze grew stronger. The gray of the cave sharpened and took on a touch of color—golden stone. The light seemed stronger toward the back of the cave. Nina stood as quietly as she could and walked toward the glow. She reached what seemed like a solid wall, but light escaped from one edge, revealing one stone overlapping another with a gap between them. Steeling herself for what lay beyond, Nina slipped through the hidden entryway. She switched on her flashlight with apologies to the powers that presided here.

The way was ordinary enough at first. The path widened into a larger tunnel, the remnants of an ancient cave. A stream bed led deeper into the hill. She followed it to a fork and felt an urge to turn left. A few feet in, she found a large chamber. Nine Sentinel Stones stood around the perimeter glowing faintly. The ceiling of the cave glinted in response, mica picking up the light and bouncing it back. Nina pointed her flashlight up and saw a rounded ceiling dotted with crystals. Light reflected from the ceiling and walls, stars within the earth. Crystals and gem stones sparkled from every direction.

Mentally she asked her question again. *Where is the Orion crystal key?*

She sat in the middle of the cave, lotus-style, and waited, schooling herself to patience.

Nimué, a voice whispered.

Was this the famous crystal cave where Merlin had been held captive by his traitorous apprentice? A different cave sprang up in her mind's eye, smaller, lined with faceted quartz, dotted with amethyst geodes and smaller tabbies just beginning to elongate. Farther north.

She let the image fade and sat in silent expectation. The back of the wall seemed to waver, like stone seen through water. A gleam caught her eye, something on the floor of the cave near the back. She stood and crept toward it. Another glint in the sandy bottom. She knelt beside it and felt around.

Gritty sand. Tiny granules of harder stone. Her hand passed over something larger with a rigid edge. She brushed sand away and searched again, palm flat. A faceted edge seemed to bump up against her hand like a cat asking to be petted. She pointed her flashlight into the sand and there it was, a three-inch clear quartz point.

She'd found it. She lifted the crystal. It was still on its gold chain. Under the light of the flashlight, she made out the detail in the setting, the head of Set, the brother of Osiris, the principle of duality.

Something stirred behind her. Turning, she saw two figures standing in an open field under a canopy of stars.

What had happened to the back of the cave?

The female's head was crowned with wild red curls, her skin ivory white.

Her beauty made Nina's heart stop a moment. The scent of spring flowers reached her nose.

The male—something about him seemed familiar.

"Cagliostro?" she called out.

The male cocked his head as if trying to place the name. His eyes sharpened a moment, uncanny blue eyes that were lit tonight with an otherworldly glow. Then he threw back his head and laughed. The sound both thrilled and terrified her. One of the fae.

"Finders keepers," he said in a sing-song voice.

The childish phrase in the mouth of one of the faery royalty unnerved Nina. She turned and fled down the corridor to the mouth of the cave. She tore the lock loose, ran outside, closed the iron gates to the spring, and then snapped the padlock closed.

Had it been real? She opened her hand. The Orion crystal key lay in her palm, a reassuring weight.

Chapter 11

Michael waited while Tahir paid the driver. He'd managed to get some sleep during the day, which surprised him, although he'd had another dream about King Arthur. Now, he and Tahir walked toward the entrance of the Serapeum at Sakkara. Stars began to appear in the deep purple twilight.

"I spoke to Grandmother Elizabeth and Winston. Anne is fine as long as they don't move her. The baby's vital signs are normal. I should get back there," Michael said.

"You must recover the crystal if you are to make her safe."

"I still don't see how coming here will help," Michael said. He took another breath to continue his argument.

"Quiet. We go in silence now."

Michael stifled a protest. This command meant he was to prepare himself for ritual—to quiet his mind and gather his energies. He allowed his worries to flow through him, the images of Anne lying helpless, of the child stillborn, Anne in her coffin, of Mordred lording it over them. As they flowed, he imagined them as a river and moved away from the banks, matching this image to his steps. Slowly, his worries faded. He started taking slow, even breaths. Imagining the outcome he desired. A healthy family.

Tahir nodded, feeling the shift and approving.

They reached the sloping entrance to the Serapeum in the growing dusk. Michael bent his knees to keep his stride even. A man in a white galabeya glided out from the shadows and greeted Tahir, talking with him quietly as they approached the wooden door. He drew a key from his pocket and opened the door, stepped back and nodded. Tahir slipped the man some baksheesh. Michael would repay Tahir for his time at the end of their work, being sure he added enough to cover all these tips, but Tahir's pride demanded that he pay now.

Once inside the entrance, they turned left and made their way along wooden walkways until they reached a corridor about thirty feet long. Large chambers had been carved out on either side. Each held an enormous stone box. Most were diorite, the largest about ten feet by fifteen, weighing seventy to a hundred tons. The interiors of the boxes were smoothed to space-age precision and gleamed like glass under a flashlight. The engineer Joe Whyte had once measured one and found tolerances of two ten-thousands of an inch. Michael chuckled to himself. That meant the surface was so smooth that any deviation was smaller than a human hair split in half. But the Egyptologists still claimed the ancients had used stone balls and copper chisels to carve them out. And that the boxes were coffins for giant bulls.

Michael almost bumped into Tahir who had stopped in the middle of the corridor. Tahir raised a finger and stared into Michael's eyes. He began to chant in the ancient Khemitian language, his voice low and insistent, somehow dissonant but soothing. The effect was eerie. Michael felt himself detach even more from time and space.

He allowed himself to float with the sound. Gradually the silent, dusty corridor on either side of them lightened, as if torches had been lit or some crystalline light had been turned on. Then came sounds, voices talking quietly. Michael looked around to see who had joined them and saw shadows moving toward them in the hallway. As they drew closer, he noticed they were not dressed in Egyptian costumes, but in the garb of many times and places. He blinked, but the shadows only grew more solid.

Tahir grunted in approval.

"What the—"

"Shh," Tahir commanded, his finger to his lips. He motioned for Michael to follow him.

They walked past the huge chambers filled with stone boxes. Once the chambers had held only the gigantic diorite structures, but now in each one an attendant stood expectantly. Every person held a staff with a different sigil at the top. And the stone walls of the back of the chamber had dissolved and now revealed distinctive landscapes. One opened to a water world with sun-dappled seas and a pod of orange and cream fish with bulbous, faded blue eyes. Another revealed an expanse of green lawn. A city crowded the horizon, soaring spires of crystal rising into a lavender sky. In the next, jungle vines draped over taller trees. Exotic birds sang. Michael paused, and a jaguar leaned out and licked his face.

He wiped his cheek with his sleeve and looked up to see Tahir trying not to laugh. "What—Where did—" Michael sputtered.

"Shh," Tahir said and gestured for Michael to follow him.

Dumbstruck, Michael trailed behind Tahir without another word. He did not understand what he was seeing. He'd always thought of the Serapeum as some sort of elaborate energy generating device. Others thought it was a storage facility for seeds. He'd never thought the place was a burial ground for the sacred Serapus bulls that it was currently named for.

As they passed by, Michael hesitated to look into the next chambers. Tahir stopped and nodded at the attendant in the room. Michael stepped up behind him and found a Druid priest standing next to the huge, dark box that gave off a deep hum. The man wore a white flowing robe with a torc around his neck. His beard almost matched the white of his robe. His skin was smooth, but his eyes seemed to have watched centuries go by and they took Michael's measure in one quick glance.

"Just in time," the man said in a curious, lilting accent.

Michael was rooted to the spot. He was afraid to look at the back wall.

"Come along, now," the Druid said.

Michael looked wildly at Tahir. He peeled his tongue off the roof of his mouth. "What's going on?"

"You need to recover the Sirius Crystal Key and save your wife and child," Tahir said in a firm voice.

Michael opened his mouth, then closed it. He looked from Tahir to the Druid, who stood with his arm out to usher him inside the chamber. Tahir started down the short flight of steps that led into the chamber, reaching behind him to grasp Michael's hand and tug him along. Michael allowed himself to be pulled into the chamber.

The Druid nodded and pointed his staff at the box. He sang a series of tones and the twenty-ton lid shifted. The man turned to offer Michael a hand up.

"In there?" Michael asked, his voice almost a squeak.

"If you please," the Druid answered.

Michael's chest flooded with heat. His heart pounded. He backed away and ran up against Tahir.

"It's okay, Michael. It's perfectly safe."

"What is happening?" He spat each word out with great emphasis.

"It's best we don't talk much." Tahir turned him around and took his face between his hands. "I promise on my life that it will not harm you. You have two lives to save."

"And a prophecy to fulfill," the Druid whispered.

"What? But—" Michael started to object, but then two nine-foot beings with conical heads walked by dressed in iridescent loose pants and tunics, laughing, one slapping the other on the back.

He looked back at the priest. "Where am I going?"

"It is not so much a matter of where," the man said. "Now, if you please."

How had he learned English, Michael wondered? Or maybe it was being translated in his head.

Michael took the man's outstretched hand and used it to push himself up to the side of the box where he perched.

"In you go. Do not cross your arms or legs."

Michael did as he was instructed, all objection driven from his mind by the strangeness of it all. The Druid sang another series of tones and the lid of the chamber slid back into place, but instead of darkness, the box filled with light. Startled, Michael reached out his hand and felt the light flow between his fingers, a little thicker than water. Panicking, he sat up and pushed against the lid, but the Druid's voice sounded in his mind. "Lay down and relax. You are in no danger."

The substance soaked into the backs of his legs, soothing his muscles. The back of his body felt lighter. Currents of light swirled through the fluid. Michael eased himself back down. The liquid light filled his ears and he heard a hum, faint at first, growing stronger. The hum differentiated, becoming a celestial choir, complex layerings of what could only be angelic voices, he thought, soothing, reaching into every nook and cranny of his being, singing him awake to his higher existence. The frequency called to a memory, and he found his body lightening, matching the vibration.

He dissolved into light.

His mind blanked.

Time stopped.

A voice spoke softly in his ear.

"Sir Lancelot?"

He opened his eyes and found himself lying on a green slope dotted with small violet flowers. A black stallion nosed through the grass nearby.

A squire squatted over him, blotting out the sun.

"We should go, sir, if we mean to be in Camelot before nightfall."

Anne discovered she was leaning out of a mullioned window, looking across a field dotted with early bluebells and the splash of wine-stained buds on the heather. A faint track wound down from a dark fringe of wood in the distance, tan against the spring green. The sound of swordplay rose from the yard below her. Geese honked a protest as a gangly girl herded them away from the feet of the practicing men. The smell of horse manure, human sweat, and venison stew mixed in the air. Two soldiers stood guard at the gates of the yard dressed in a livery that plucked at Anne's memory. Three golden crowns.

Camelot. She must be in Camelot. Then who—

"It should only take the summer months, Gwen. I must see to the lands and see that the peace is secure."

And just like that Anne slid to the back of the mind of her hostess and remembered.

Yes, I was Guinevere. Arthur called me Gwen.

She turned away from the window to find Arthur's expression a mix of sadness, anxiety—probably for her—and almost concealed excitement. Complain as he might of the hardships of campaigning, sleeping on the hard ground, his head on the flank of his favorite hound when there was no time to pitch camp, riding in a drizzle that gradually worked its way through his thick wool cloak into his tunic and linen shirt, and finally down to his skin, she knew he still loved the crisp morning air, the feel of the horse's haunches gathered beneath him ready to charge, and yes, the cheering for the high king when he rode into a town where he'd be feasted before the political talk the next morning.

"It's just that I'd hoped to be carrying before you left this time," Guinevere said. "I've gone to the healers for a potion."

Arthur covered the distance between them in three large strides. He swung her up and carried her to their bed, managing to wrap them both in the bed curtains and just catching himself from stumbling. "We still have a few days before the preparations are complete, my love. I mean to stay for the sacred day."

A ting of guilt tightened Guinevere in the stomach. *My love. He always calls me that. I do not love him like that, although I like him well enough.* Arthur's eyes were as clear and open as one of his favorite hounds when it looked up at him. She shook her head against that image.

"What?" he asked, finally managing to free his feet from the gauzy material. "You aren't—"

Guinevere smiled at this. Still squeamish about naming a woman's cycles, even after he'd won the hard wars against the Saxons, then the Picts when they'd joined forces with the invaders.

"No, love. In fact, the timing is promising. But we are dressed and expected downstairs for dinner. I will take the potion and perhaps you will return to me with a nicely rounded belly."

He leaned down and kissed her tenderly, then pulled back. "As you say. To business, then." Arthur straightened his tunic and donned a slender circlet of gold, then banged out the door before she could straighten it.

Guinevere laid back on the pillows, thinking back to her girlhood dreams of a love match, the perfect cottage in the woods. Well, as the daughter of a lord, she would have had a slightly larger house, but still, a cozy home, children playing on the floor at her feet, a spindle in her hands. Her beloved coming in of an evening from the fields, worn-out, but not too tired to give his young ones a ride on his shoulders before a kiss from her, and then supper filled with laughter and stories of the day. But they had chosen her to cement the peace, to seal the court of the High King of Britain in the old ways, for she carried the old maternal blood. It was an honor she'd never dreamed of as a child, but a duty she'd accepted when her father had spoken to her. She did love Arthur in her way. Her mother had told her that love comes with time. She could still hear her voice.

"The love that grows with knowing lasts, dearest child. The quick spark of a spring lust too often fades in the autumn."

But a girl blooming into her womanhood does not wish to hear such advice. Guinevere pulled herself up. She must go to supper, sit at the king's side, laugh at the jokes of the various lords gathered there tonight. Then tomorrow she had the household to look after.

They expected her to bless the seed before the planting. The young men would try their hand at plowing tomorrow. Soon the festival to mark the onset of summer would be on them. The people would pick the Spring Maid. The household must host the countryside and she needed to see to their stores, talk to the cooks, see to cleaning out the vegetable and herb gardens. She worked almost as hard as the farm wife she'd dreamed of being.

With a sigh, she stood, but instead of going downstairs, she found herself drawn to the window again. Purple shadows crept across the meadow now and the cool of late afternoon settled on the shoulders of the doves cooing in the eaves. Far out to her right she could make out the small figure of a shepherd and his two dogs going out to call in the cattle for the night. Her eyes followed the slope of the land back toward the woods, and there two figures emerged, the first riding a majestic black stallion, the second a dun two hands smaller.

Even though the shadows of evening were gathering in the corners and whispering together, conspiring to take over the day, as the knight drew closer, the sun came out from behind a cloud and cast a bright ray directly across the field that fell on him. Light flared from his armor. His shield was a yellow that shone like a sun-flower, and as he drew closer, Guinevere could make out the device, a red-cross knight kneeling to a lady.

Bells jangled merrily as his warhorse pranced on burnished hooves before the man leaned down to sooth the beast, his coal-black curls falling from beneath his helmet. His bridle caught the last ray of sunlight and flickered like the gem-toned windows of the chapel. A great silver horn hung from his baldric. The knight sat straight again, the feather in his helmet catching a breeze and flashing out like a flame.

He stopped at the gate, talking out of ear-shot with the guards, who leapt to attention once they heard his name, a name Guinevere couldn't make out. They waved him inside. The great stallion snorted at the sound of swords clashing, and with a shout from the captain, the men stopped their practice and made way. The horse pranced a few more steps, then came to a halt halfway across the yard, and the knight looked up and spied Guinevere in the window.

Their eyes locked. Guinevere felt a jolt of recognition, although she was certain they had never met. She would have remembered such a man. Then a wild joy clamored in her chest like church bells after a celebration. Arthur strode out of the door below and the knight dismounted and bowed deeply. "I bring greetings from King Hoel of Llydaw. He bids me make a pact with you, Arthur Pendragon, High King of Britain." His voice carried the accent of the continent, suggesting grape terraces maturing in the summer sun and fine perfumes.

Arthur started back in surprise. Before he could ask, the man answered the question on everyone's mind.

"I am Lancelot du Lac."

After the men went inside, Guinevere called her maid into her chambers before going down herself. "Hester, can you please pin my braids again? Did I hear we have company tonight?" She didn't know why she feigned ignorance of who had come.

"Yes, m'lady. A knight from across the water come to parlay with our Great Bear." Many still called Arthur by the name he'd earned on the battlefield.

She studied herself in the mirror. Her apron had a small stain from earlier work in the gardens and she wore an everyday muslin gown. "Should I wear something more formal?"

"Perhaps the blue?" Hester's eyes danced at the prospect. The girl busied herself helping Guinevere into a gown of lapis blue with star-like flashes of tiny gems on the bodice.

"What about the amber beads? Would that be too much?"

"On, no." Hester opened the chest beside Guinevere's mirror and lifted out the necklace, wrapped in a length of velvet. The amber beads, the size of young hazelnuts, picked up the glow of the candle as the girl picked them up and settled them against Guinevere's fair décolletage.

Guinevere donned the matching earrings, stood and shook out her skirts. "How do I look?"

Hester nodded, circling her and smoothing out the skirts of the gown. She went back to the chest holding Guinevere's little treasures and picked up something. She unfolded a silk shawl embroidery picking up the lapis blue of her gown and gold of the amber. "It is a special occasion, isn't it?" the girl asked shyly.

"Perfect." Guinevere turned her back and allowed Hester to wrap the shawl around her. They both studied her reflection in the mirror. The blue darkened her cornflower eyes to the mysterious depth of a lake. The gold reflected the highlights of her hair.

"You look beautiful, m'lady."

Guinevere squeezed Hester's hand and made her way down to the feasting hall, trying to school her steps to the sedate pace becoming the matron she was.

When she arrived in the hall, she found Sir Lancelot seated to Arthur's right. The two had their heads bent together, one golden, the other dark as a raven's wing. Arthur noticed her when she stepped up onto the platform that held their table and got to his feet to pull out her chair.

"You have changed your dress," he whispered.

"I heard we had royal company," she explained. "I thought I looked too plain for such a guest."

"You plain? Never."

Once settled, the servant filled her glass with mead and Arthur held his up. "We are honored tonight with a visit from our cousin, Sir Lancelot du Lac."

Guinevere smiled. The great families always called a distant relation "cousin."

Arthur continued. "He comes at the behest of King Hoel to parlay with us and keep the great peace."

A hearty cheer went up from the men and the knights close to the royal table nodded their approval.

"To Lancelot," Sir Kay shouted out.

Geraint cried, "To King Hoel."

And they drank.

Chapter 12

"We need to figure out who stole our money," Gerald said to his hacker team. Or at least to Dana. Preston hadn't stopped coding. At least, that's what he thought he was doing.

"I may have a lead," Preston mumbled.

Gerald rolled Susan's desk chair up behind him and sat.

"Dude, like I'll call you."

"I'll stay here. I'm sure my presence will not deter someone with your skill."

"Whatever, man."

Gerald marveled at the speed at which Preston turned out lines of code. He sat back in the chair, going through his muscle groups, tensing and relaxing them. He badly needed to punch something, but he was getting a bit old for that. Maybe he'd ask Leo to spot him in the gym.

His mind wandered to Anne. He wanted to be with her, with Elizabeth, but she had told him she needed to have a private consultation with the Opener. That meant she would ask Anubis why he'd blocked their banishing spell. He knew better than to interrupt her. Or his hacker. They'd both report their results when as they had them, but his experience with Preston so far suggested that could be soon.

"Yes!" Preston yelled.

Gerald jumped to his feet. "What?"

"I think your money was stolen by a Mr. Valentin Knight, owner of Knight Corporation. Clever name," he smirked.

"I don't believe it," Gerald said.

"Dude, believe it or not, the IP address is located in this neighborhood in Potomac, Maryland." He squinted at the screen "That's where Knight lives, right? Nobody else on this list corresponds to this area."

Gerald nodded his head slowly. "I'd have to double check, but it sounds about right. Could someone have rerouted the signal from there?"

"No way. Look." Preston pointed to the monitor slightly to his right with a series of lines bouncing around the world. "Look at all the different routes the packets are taking through the proxies. Every single one is coming from this point. It's gotta be the source."

"And there's no way to fake that?"

"I'd bet the family money on it." Preston realized what he'd said and blanched. "Um, sorry dude."

Gerald shrugged it off. He still couldn't believe that Valentin had been involved in this theft. Valentin Knight headed the most elite mystical lodge in the country, the one that led the rest of them. He was the lead spiritual authority in Western Metaphysics. You could say Valentin was the Merlin of America.

"Maybe it was someone on his staff," Gerald suggested. "His personal secretary. Or somebody might have broken in."

Preston shrugged. "Whatever, man, but the hack originated from a computer at this address. I'm sure of it."

"And the money? Where did it get moved to?"

"It's probably been converted to crypto currency, like BitCoin or Etereum. But this Knight guy is an old dude, right? He probably stashed it in the Caymans. Where else do old crooks hide their money?"

Gerald could think of several other places, but a rush of relief made him too light-headed to list them. He sat heavily in his chair. "Can we get it back?"

Preston's smile reminded him of a pirate. The kid rubbed his hands together gleefully. "Dude, hold my beer."

Gerald decided it was time to check on Elizabeth.

After last night's failure, Elizabeth had forced herself to sleep in her own room, not next to Anne in some make-shift arrangement, to clear her psychic palate so to speak. This morning she went into the temple with renewed determination.

"How's our patient," she asked Emma.

"She's fine. You'd think this was a natural sleep. The baby's vitals are strong and normal."

"Mary stayed last night?" Elizabeth confirmed.

"She did. She reported the same. A quiet night."

"Has Winston come in yet?"

"He went to his office to clear his schedule until we can get this resolved. He's seeing a few critical cases, then reassigning them. Said he'd be here in the early afternoon."

Elizabeth nodded. "Good."

Emma went back to a chair near the east wall of the sanctuary, and Elizabeth walked toward the crystal in the middle of the temple, palms out, feeling for Mordred. A wave of hatred swept through her awareness. She smelled horse sweat, heard the jingle of a bridle, then all that faded and the man's face formed deep inside the stone. But she didn't engage him. Not after last night. Instead, she turned back to Anne and Arthur.

Arthur? She shook her head against the name that had spontaneously come into her mind.

Elizabeth leaned over the cold metal railing on the hospital bed. She ran her fingers gently over Anne's forehead, then settled her left hand there. "We're here, love. We'll figure this out."

Anne lay slightly on her right side so the baby would not be resting directly on her spine, pillows supporting her back and one between her knees. Her blond hair fell over her face. Elizabeth smoothed the strands back, stroking her cheek. Then she placed her right hand gently on the dome of Anne's belly, closed her eyes and hummed, creating a link between herself and the baby. She searched for a spark of awareness that was the child and was rewarded with a return wave of energy that warmed her palm. Now she'd established a link with them both.

"Good."

"What is it?" Emma half rose.

"I'm going to do a couple of specific workings. Just keep an eye on her and touch my shoulder if her condition worsens."

"Should I stay here?"

"You won't disturb me. Can you pull that chair in so I can sit and keep my hands where they are now?"

"Sure." Emma pushed down the side railing of the bed, then lifted the chair and moved it closer, not making a sound. She placed it directly under Elizabeth, then guided her to a sitting position.

"Thank you."

Emma retreated to her lookout post.

Elizabeth went through her routine of preparation, relaxing all her muscles, breathing, clearing her energy field. She forced herself to take her time, being thorough, almost methodical. Once she'd achieved a fairly deep trance, she went in search of Anne. The gray mists of the astral swirled around her, thickening at first. She wondered if Mordred was interfering, but only felt him as a watchful, brooding presence nearby.

She schooled herself to patience, difficult to achieve now. After a while, the mist lightened. She heard laughter, the scrape of knives on plates, a dog gnawing a bone.

"How is King Hoel, Sir Lancelot? And his Lady Iseult?"

So, she's made it to Camelot, Elizabeth thought. *That must be a good sign.*

Lancelot had already arrived. Here was a court hosting another love triangle. Why did this theme keep asserting itself?

Anne seemed to be fully integrated with Guinevere. Elizabeth settled in to listen.

Guinevere allowed the polite talk between Arthur, Lancelot, and several of the knights to wash over her like a stream—all about the court of King Hoel, Arthur's victory against the Saxons and their allies, the challenges of keeping the regional kings loyal. The idea of a united Britain was still new, and as the peace continued, fewer people saw a need for unity. They were slipping back to the old ways. That had been the major reason for her marriage to Arthur.

"That is another reason they've sent me. To cement the alliances. The fiefdoms to the east are still restless."

"Not to mention those to the north," Arthur added.

Alliances. Was that the only thing life had to offer? Guinevere toyed with the venison on her plate, picked up her mug and drank the honeyed mead, listening to the tenor of Lancelot's voice more than his words, catching the flash of his eyes when he looked past Arthur to her, watching his long fingers as he gestured or picked up his mug. A languid dreaminess crept through her, relaxing her limbs, warming her belly, making her heart stir awake like the buds on the apple tree in the meadow, promising the green growth of summer, the sweetness of an autumn harvest. She allowed herself to float, imagining the growing season spent with this new addition to court, showing him her favorite glen in the woods.

He had been here only a week, but already he'd won Arthur's friendship. The two rode together every day, sat in Arthur's council room going over maps, talking strategy for winning back the lords to the east whose people were a mix of Saxon and Normans as well as English. She saw the admiration for Lancelot in Arthur's eyes. They'd quickly become as brothers.

The knights had welcomed him. Gawain took it easy on him when practicing in the yard—that is until Lancelot landed Gawain on his backside. Bors the Younger hung around him, eyes shining with hero worship. Gaheris, third son of Arthur's sister and King Lot, plied him with questions when he could, asking about Llydaw and King Hoel.

Lancelot spared her a few hours, walking out to see the gardens, speaking to her beneath the bows of the orchard. A visitor from the western isles had made it to Llydaw and shared news of her family whom she heard from less and less.

"What do you think, m'lady?" Arthur's voice jolted her out of her reverie.

Guinevere sat up straighter. "Sorry. I wasn't following."

Arthur threw his arm across her shoulders, pulling her closer. She tried not to stiffen. "I was saying rather than riding out immediately, perhaps our cousin could rest here with a few of his men while I visit some of the closer lands who still hold me dear to their hearts. He has traveled far already. His horses could do with more rest. His retinue will swell the number of soldiers I leave to guard Camelot. Not that much is needed in peace times."

Heat flooded Guinevere's face, and she tried to sit back, away from the rushlight, hoping no one would notice, but Arthur held her close. "If you think that is best, my lord. We will do our best to amuse our cousin while you attend to your duties."

"It should only be two months. Not much longer. Then we can circle back and he can join us to march east," Arthur said. Then he released her and raised his mug. He called for another toast to Lancelot, but the knight grabbed his arm. "They have had enough of me, Arthur. To the queen."

"To Guinevere, the light of my life," Arthur shouted.

And the host answered him, "To Guinevere. To the Queen."

All but Agravain, who frowned, but held his cup up so Arthur would not notice. But Guinevere had seen and it chilled her heart like a sudden early spring rain.

So, it has begun, Elizabeth thought, pulling back from Anne. The call between two souls, two bodies, the eventual consummation. The giving of sovereignty, held by the woman carrying the blood bond with the land to another, making him king in spirit, but not in the law of this time, laying the road for the one son of Arthur's to claim his right to kingship. It was a story every school child knew.

Her eyes strayed to the western altar where the temple's chalice stood gleaming in a ray of morning sunlight from an eastern window high above. This cup had its own stellar history, like so many artifacts her family kept and collected over the years, but nothing like the grail itself. Arthur had sent Bors, Galahad, and Percival after that holy cup. Percival found his way to the castle where the grail was kept, but he failed to ask the right question. Elizabeth hoped she did not make the same mistake.

Elizabeth cleared her connections to Anne, pushing back from the bed a bit, then resettled into her trance. She needed to know why Anubis had stopped the banishing. Returning once again to the silver gray of the astral, Anne called out the name of the Opener.

Anubis, son of Osiris and Nephthys, Ab-Nub, Opener of Pathways between the worlds. Sacred Guide through the Ways. Come to me now.

She heard a chuckle. *So formal. Am I ever so far from you, beloved Priestess?*

So that was the mood he was in this morning. The ghost of a smile lifted her lips. She would come straight to the point.

Why?

We must let events come full circle.

Impatience swept through her limbs, but she controlled her response. *These two lives hang in the balance, Great One.*

More than that hangs in the balance.

What then?

The Opener shifted. His black jackal head blurred and when he was visible again, a tall, handsome man with jet black hair and sharp eagle eyes stood before her. *Finish the story of Isis and Osiris tonight. Enact the ritual. This is the next step.*

With a snap, he was gone.

Elizabeth took her time coming back to the world. She allowed herself to consider the message. When she found herself simply listening to the beep of Anne's heart monitor, she rose heavily from her granddaughter's side to find Gerald lingering near the doorway.

"How is she?"

"Physically the same. Both she and the baby are well."

"That's a relief. Do you think we could risk moving her yet?"

Elizabeth shook her head. "Not until we've resolved this situation. In her visions, she's moved from Egypt to Camelot."

"You told me that before."

"Lancelot has shown up."

Gerald walked to Anne's bed and stood looking down at her. Relaxed in sleep, she looked younger. He remembered reading bedtime stories to her when she'd visit with her mother. "Have you figured out why she's living through these stories?"

"Her connection to Guinevere is deeper than just watching. It feels like she's remembering a past life."

"Is that significant?"

"Perhaps there is something unresolved for her, something she needs to be finished before Mordred will relent."

They both heard a murmuring from the crystal in the middle, like distant thunder. They glanced at the large crystal ball uneasily. Elizabeth tightened her shawl around her.

"I spoke with the Opener. He wants us to perform the Isis ritual."

Gerald frowned. "Why?"

"He just said, 'We must let events come full circle'."

"What circle? What does he mean?"

"The only way to find out is to take the next step."

"What should I do?"

"Call the group together. Tell them what we'll be doing."

"I will." He kissed her cheek. "Get some rest. Estelle still has that potato leek soup."

"I should eat light if I'm to face the trials of Isis tonight."

"So eat a small bowl. You've hardly eaten since this started."

"Was it just yesterday?"

"Can you believe it?"

She squeezed his hand and he left her. It was only after he was gone that she realized she hadn't asked about the hack. Oh well, perhaps being penniless would help her become the pilgrim Isis had been as she searched for the pieces of Osiris.

Chapter 13

That evening, Nina stretched her hands out over the blue-veined marble altar in the middle of the temple of Knight's lodge. She stood in the west, sending energy and the whisper of a promise to the priest, none other than Valentin Knight himself. Regal in his white robe, he stood, eyes closed, palms open, almost swaying. Then his eyes opened with a snap and he smiled benevolently at his priestess, those blue eyes pure as a robin's egg. Guileless. He took up his wand and intoned the opening phrase of their ritual.

Nina leaned back into the abundant energy she had raised, allowing it to lick up her spine, over her head, and back down to her forehead. She rode the current, pulling the energy in until she was wrapped in a cocoon of light. The ritual flowed like a mighty river, directed by the High Adept himself. Or so they thought him. The responses came automatically after so many years.

Once he turned away from her, Nina reached into the pocket of her robe and grasped the Orion crystal key. She ran her finger down the smooth, faceted edges, calling into her mind the spell she'd breathed into the crystal on the full moon. Her goal was to finish what she'd started so many years ago. He had escaped her at some point—she couldn't remember how—but she would capture him again, tame his will, distract his mind, seal him back in the cave. Steal his knowledge and power.

Sometimes she wondered how she'd gained access to this group, how she'd fooled them all, but squashed the thought in case anyone around her picked up any jarring vibrations. Like a chameleon, she sank into those memories of the past when she truly had been the high-minded student of this man, letting that frequency flicker over the surface of her mind.

The ritual ran about an hour, and Valentin closed down the circle, the energies quieting gradually, small eddies and echoes spinning down until the latent vibrations settled into quiescence, but Nina kept her cone of light wrapped about her tightly so no one would detect it. The group filed out of the temple, went off to change into their street clothes, and gather in the common room for some refreshment and conversation. Nina waited until most of the group had left, then snuck into the women's room, still smaller than the men's even after a generation of more equal participation. She went to her corner toward the back and changed, folding her robe carefully, cradling her power objects inside a soft cloth. She pulled the Orion crystal over her head, then hid it beneath the front of her black dress that clung in all the right places, draped a soft wool shawl in fall tones over it, and braced herself for small talk. She despised all the niceties of polite conversation.

"Wait up," Faye called to her. The younger woman brushed out her gleaming chestnut pageboy—weren't those from the fifties? Nina half listened as her sister lodge member told her the story of how her teenage son had been in a fender bender as they walked to the common room together. Faye pushed open the venerable oak doors and a sea of voices washed over them.

Her companion headed straight to the buffet table and filled her plate with stuffed mushrooms, dates stuffed with blue cheese, and artichoke turnovers. "I just adore these," she informed Nina. The mushrooms did smell earthy and rich, so Nina took a few, added a variety of olives, and a couple of Russian wedding cookies for decoration, then made her circuit, greeting the important members of the lodge. She took a glass of sparkling cider from a tray. She needed to keep her head clear.

Spying Ralph, she made her way to his side and waited for the conversation to lull. "Has my secretary gotten in touch about the benefit?" she asked.

Ralph's gaze sharpened a touch as he searched his memory, making it back to earth a little more with this question of practical matters. His feet floated above the ground too much to be a serious magician, but it was important to stay on his good side. Seeing that he didn't know, she smiled. "I'll check tomorrow. I'm looking forward to the event."

His eyes shone at this. Ralph was a sucker for putting art education into the poorest schools. Really, they tagged their whole neighborhood. She thought they had plenty of practice.

After an hour, the platters held only a few stray cookies and bits of cheese. The group gathered their coats and headed out, with all the hugging, shoulder pounding, and hearty goodbyes that entailed. Nina sank back into a dark corner and wove a cloak of shadows around herself. Soon, the group had gone except for Valentin. He sank into a deep chair by the fire and sighed. Nina drew the spell she'd prepared for him into her mind, fortifying her intention. She took a step out from the corner next to the antique cherry sideboard, letting her cloak down gradually.

Valentin jerked in surprise, almost spilling his whiskey.

"It's just me," she whispered, adding a touch of husk to her voice.

"I thought everyone had gone." He struggled to stand, pushing against the armrest, the blue veins showing against his white hands.

Nina closed the distance between them and put a hand on his shoulder. "Stay. May I join you?"

Valentin gestured to the matching chair on the opposite side of the fireplace. "Can I get you a—"

"Drink?" she interrupted. "I can pour my own. You relax."

She went to the sideboard and picked up the bottle of Glen Alba whiskey. She took an appreciative whiff, but chose the Lagavulin scotch instead. That was one thing about Valentin. He had the best of everything—drinks, food, magicians. She put two ice cubes into her glass, added a dash of angostura bitters, then poured two fingers. She picked up the whiskey bottle and held it out to him. "More?"

"Oh, no. Only a sip or two after a night like this." His tone was warm. It had been a strong ceremony.

Nina kicked off her shoes and folded herself into the chair across from her former mentor, took a sip of her scotch, and let the silence mellow around them.

After a minute, she asked, "Are rituals taking more out of you these days?"

He snorted, then studied the flames for so long she thought he wouldn't answer. "I suppose so. But tonight I felt some kind of . . ."

"Disturbance in the force?" she suggested, then wondered if Valentin had ever seen *Star Wars*.

His chuckled reassured her. "I suppose you could say that. I thought we'd turned the corner on the new age, especially after last Christmas."

"What happened then?" she asked, but he didn't answer. He went back to watching the fire as if he could divine the solution in the color or shape of the flames. She'd drifted away until his voice called her back.

"You are so sensitive. Did you notice anything off tonight?"

She stroked the butter-soft leather of the chair, pretending to consider his question. "I'm sorry, Valentin, but everything seemed crystal clear to me." She rose and stood behind him, dropping her hands on his shoulders, kneading the tight muscles, but he stiffened beneath her touch.

Not yet, she thought.

Nina settled in front of him on the Persian carpet, not touching. She lifted her eyes, pushed a sorrowful look onto her face. "Perhaps it's something else. Are you well?"

He waved this suggestion away. She noticed he still wore his magical ring—a deep amethyst singing its high note, set in the middle of a compass and square. "I'm healthy. I just had my physical last month."

She smiled and rested her hand on his knee. "I'm glad to hear it. I hope there is nothing just developing that the tests couldn't find."

He frowned.

"But you would know."

She let her hand grow heavier on his knee, and when he didn't resist, stroked his lower thigh. "Since you're so vital . . ."

She pushed the enchantment through her fingers into his body, closing her eyes, feeding it power. A glamour. So simple it might just slip by his awareness. She willed him to remember their affair. How he'd been entranced by her.

He laughed and shifted his weight, letting her hand fall away. "I must admit you are still much younger and full of energy, my dear. Not tonight."

Nina pouted just a touch, enough to appeal to him but not suggest any feminine silliness. "As you wish, Val." She rose, and as she did so, pretending to brace herself, she pressed the spell deep into his legs, the heady smell of lilacs in the sun, the sensuous drowsing of bees inside flowers, the musk of the buck in rut.

She leaned close, bending in front of him to display the curve of her breasts. Cupped his face so the damask rose oil on her wrist gave off the scent of a garden in full bloom. She brushed his dry lips with her mouth, leaving a trace of the spell there.

"Perhaps another time," she said. Glancing down, she detected a slight swell in his trousers and smiled to herself. She had done her work for the night, planting desire and self-doubt in this aging, but still powerful man. She'd established an energy line between them that she'd slowly pull taunt to reel him in.

Nina gathered up her shawl and wrapped it around herself. Picking up her glass, she caught him watching, a slight frown on his face. "What is it?"

But he only shook his head. "Just leave it," he said, pointing to the glass. "Benson will take care of everything in the morning."

So he hadn't noticed. Not yet. The spell would seep in slowly. She'd check on its progress tomorrow night.

"As you wish. Good night, Grand Mage." She gave a slight bow as she left the room, gathered her things in the women's dressing room, and slipped out into the night. Cold, brilliant stars lit the sky, watching her progress as she drove toward town.

Gerald went into the kitchen and asked Estelle to make a tray for Elizabeth.

Estelle rubbed her hands against her white apron. "I know just what to give her to tempt her to eat," she said with a smile.

"Keep it light. She's still got a lot of psychic work to do."

"Leave it to me. Now, what about you, sir? When did you eat last?"

"Breakfast?" he asked.

"No, sir. You haven't eaten since yesterday morning. I'll serve you in the family dining room."

"Has Arnold eaten?"

She shook her head.

"Would it be an imposition to prepare a buffet for everyone?"

"Imposition? To do my job, sir? I'm only too glad to do something for my little poppet." She wiped her eyes with a corner of her apron.

Gerald smiled at Estelle's childhood name for Anne. "She's going to be all right. Both Anne and the baby. Don't you worry."

Estelle choked back her tears, then squared her shoulders. "I'll send in a tray for the nurse as well. You'll have a spread in the formal dining room in half an hour. It's big enough for all of you." She put her hands on her ample hips. "But you can tell that Preston that I will not order takeout pizza for him."

"Quite right." Gerald laughed for the first time since they'd found Anne unconscious.

He went up to his rooms for a quick shower and change of clothes, then called the entire group together in the formal living room near the front of the house. After they'd filled their plates from the offerings of cold cuts and cheese, bread, salads, and potato leek soup, he asked Arnold if he'd detected any more problems.

Just as he was about to answer, Preston ran into the room and surveyed the trays. "Where's the pizza?"

"You will eat what we feed you, young man," Abernathy snapped. "We called this meeting fifteen minutes ago. Where were you?"

"Talk, talk, talk. I've been working." He grabbed a plate and slathered two pieces of bread with Dijon mustard and mayonnaise, then piled on roast beef, ham, three types of cheese, lettuce and tomatoes. He carried his Dagwood sandwich to a seat at the table and took a bite.

Gerald timed his question perfectly. "Have you found our money yet?"

Preston's eyes bugged. He chewed frantically. Finally, he spoke around the wad of food in his mouth. "Yeah, man. I already told you where it is. I found a back door into that Knight guy's computer."

"Let's go then," Gerald said.

"Dude, can I eat first?"

Gerald had watched him devour an omelet, a heaping pile of hash browns, three pieces of toast for breakfast and two bowls of Estelle's famous soup mid-morning, but the kid still looked like he was sculpted from a handful of shadows.

"Five minutes," Gerald said. "Abernathy, Arnold, would you join us?"

Once the group had reassembled around the computer monitors in Gerald's study, Preston took them through his discovery. "Here are the transactions. Three disguised as stock trades, two as commodities, another to a real estate firm allegedly buying a manor house in the south of France. They're all dressed up to look legitimate. But," he held up his finger dramatically, "they all go to this bank in the Caymans."

Gerald leaned forward to study the list of withdrawals. If they hadn't taken place at practically the same time and drained his funds, they would have seemed legitimate.

"What ties them to Knight?" Abernathy asked.

Susan asserted herself. "If you look at the next monitor, sir, you'll see the stream of orders that seems to come from three of your offices. But several layers in, they all trace back to the same IP address."

Gerald stared at a long string of letters. "How do you know this is Knight?"

"We did a reverse DNS lookup on Google on that IP Address," Dana explained. "It usually gives the name of the company it's tied to. This is a small IP service provider and its only point of presence is in Northern Maryland just outside D.C."

"Here is Mr. Knight's property from Google Maps," Susan said.

An aerial view of the Maryland countryside swam into view. Susan clicked in closer and a stone mansion complete with turrets, gables and mullioned windows filled the screen.

"That's it, all right," Abernathy said.

"I still can't believe he's the source," Gerald said. "I mean, we're talking about Valentin Knight here."

"I know," Abernathy said. "I wonder what's happened to him."

"Or maybe he was a crook all along," Preston pronounced.

Both of the older men looked at him with distaste.

After a pause, Gerald said, "You suggested that you could get our money back."

"Just say the word." Preston's fingers hovered over the keyboard.

"Please proceed," Gerald said.

Preston's fingers flew and a string of code ran across one of the monitors. Gerald studied the map and the list of withdrawals, but nothing changed there.

Suddenly, all the monitors went blank.

"Son of a—" Preston pounded the enter key several times, but nothing changed.

Then a black screen appeared with huge letters that read,

Hello, Mr. Le Clair:

Your computer has been encrypted.
The hard disks of your computer have been encrypted with a military grade encryption algorithm. It is impossible to recover your data without a special key.
Hand over the child and you'll get your money back, minus a small service charge.

You have:
3 days, 15 hours, 59 minutes

"Fucking hell," Arnold snarled.

"Trace this." Gerald spit out. "Find out where this came from."

"Dude," Preston muttered, his face white, "there's like no way to break this encryption. We're dead in the water."

The clock clicked to 58 minutes.

"What do we do?" Arnold asked.

Preston folded his hands. "We wait for further instructions."

Chapter 14

Nina luxuriated in a hot bath scented with Egyptian rose oil, preparing herself. Steam filled the air, and she settled in deeper, relaxing her shoulders and neck. Tonight, she'd go into her private mediation chamber and activate the next level of her spell, pulling the line between her and Valentin taunt. She heard a faint chime from her computer in her office down the hall. That particular sound alarm meant Zebulon's trap had been activated. A warm rush filled her torso, both sexual and predatory at the same time. Her plans were proceeding as she'd hoped.

She got out of her bath and dried off. Wrapped a silk robe around herself and walked to the office, enjoying the lush carpet she'd recently had installed in anticipation of wealth beyond her childhood dreams.

She nudged the mouse next to the laptop and the screen sprang to life, displaying the warning. The encryption program came from Knight's computer, but Zebulon had arranged for her to sign on to Knight's computer remotely. He'd assured her the spyware would be invisible.

She settled into her chair and smiled. Now she owned the Le Clairs—lock, stock, and barrel, as the saying went. The message Zebulon had sent led them to believe if they handed over the baby, they'd get their money back. They would never comply, of course, but the promise would burrow into their hearts like the worm Zebulon had uploaded to burrow into their computers. It would send them into an emotional tailspin, make it hard for them to focus, undermine their ability to undo the spells, to defeat Mordred.

That part had surprised her. Mordred was real enough. In the middle of her daily meditation regime, he had appeared, brushing through her wards like they were flimsy spider webs, when she knew for a fact they were strong. She'd learned from the best.

He'd announced himself as the Wronged King. It had taken a minute to figure out who he was. "We had almost won, both you and me. You had your wizard all to yourself for eternity, trapped in crystal. I had struck a blow to my father, the Pretender."

"Are you talking about Arthur?"

"Of course."

"But he killed you."

Mordred waved a ghostly hand, dismissing this as inconsequential. "I dealt him a death blow in turn."

"But the Sisters of Avalon took him away on their barge."

"Yes, their Death Barge." He laid emphasis on the words.

"That's not how the story goes," she said with a shrug. "It is said that Arthur will return. Nothing is said about you."

"Now is our chance to set the record straight," he said. "Word has reached me that a great one in this lineage is about to be born to remake history. If he is allowed entry into this," he gestured around to her meditation room, "physical realm, our chance will be lost."

"Who is about to be born?"

Mordred's lip curled, but he didn't answer.

"Then tell me who the parents are."

"Anne Le Clair and Michael Levy—the two who betrayed my father to begin with and set all this in motion."

This answer puzzled Nina, but she pressed on. "Tell me more about this word that reached you."

Mordred drew closer and placed his index finger on her third eye. She allowed the contact, closed her physical eyes, and waited. A light formed beneath Mordred's finger and turned the color of smoky quartz. Inside the murky light, a scene unfolded.

She found herself in a large chamber. Nine Sentinel Stones stood around the perimeter glowing faintly. The ceiling of the cave glinted in response, mica picking up the light and bouncing it back. A rounded ceiling dotted with crystals reflected light, stars within the earth.

This is where I found the Orion crystal, she thought.

Nina watched as people arrived. First Anne, surrounded by a pack of white hounds with spots of red. Two women dressed as priestesses of Avalon, one older in a white gown. Then Michael accompanied by an older sturdy fellow. And finally Cagliostro dragging with him a man, his shoulders roped with muscle, his hair braided with shells and beads that sang as he moved.

They all stopped before the most glorious being she'd ever seen—tall and blond, his skin translucent ivory, eyes the color of crushed violets. She recognized him instinctively—Gwyn ap Nudd, Lord of the Fae. She fought the urge to kneel.

The scene grew misty for a while as people spoke. The older man who'd come in with Michael ran to a beautiful woman who reached her arms out to him. Then Cagliostro seemed to change and a woman even more radiant than Gwyn appeared, her skin alabaster, her lips mulberries, and her hair red curls the color of flame. Cagliostro walked into faery with her.

Then the scene cleared, the voices audible. Michael and Anne held their crystal keys out to the Lord of Faery and he blessed them.

Then he said, "There is one more thing." Gwyn smiled at them, his expression playful. "On Samhain, we hunt the souls of the dead. But on this night, the eve of Beltane, souls wishing to be born come through our realm." He placed his hand over Anne's womb. "A great being is coming to you."

"Oh," Anne murmured.

"You mean?" Michael began.

"Guard this one well," Gwyn said.

The scene faded and Mordred's face swam into focus. "Gwyn ap Nudd himself spoke it. But we still have a chance to alter the outcome. He said to guard the child. That means he is vulnerable."

Nina hesitated. "Are you certain this child is Arthur?"

"I have seen it," Mordred said.

Still, Nina thought, did she dare go up against this great Lord of Fae who wielded such consummate powers?

A memory surfaced.

"He is the greatest mage in many generations, Nimué." The woman who spoke picked up an earthen mug and took a sip. Her sleeve fell down her forearm, revealing an intricate Pictish tattoo. "Count yourself lucky to have studied with him and let that be enough."

"Still . . ." Nimué let the request hang in the smoky air between them.

"You remember the concoction," the woman said. "There is nothing I can do to stop you using it."

"They defeated us, Mother."

"And yet, here we are," the older woman replied.

The two drank their ale in silence for a while.

"Combine this with what he has taught you. Perhaps you can best him." She grabbed Nimué's hand and squeezed.

Nimué winced.

"But if you fail, it will be your death."

Nina smiled. She had succeeded then. For a long time, she had held him locked in crystal until something had awakened him and he'd found a way out of her prison. Now she would best him again. But one thing at a time.

She convinced the spirit of Mordred that once the Le Clairs handed over the child, she would bind the soul just as she had bound Merlin all those centuries ago, leaving the coast clear for the "true king," as he called himself, to enter the newborn infant. She would have the most powerful magician captive and she would use that power to make herself rich beyond her dreams. Then she would explore the hidden realms, forbidden knowledge.

Mordred's blind ambition surprised her. He had been the Sun Child, born of the Beltane ritual. Yes, the son of Arthur one could argue, but not necessarily in the line of inheritance. Even if Guinevere had birthed a son, it didn't mean he would become king. Most of the time, the tribes in those times had chosen the successor not by birth, but deeds. Still, Mordred's obsession had come at an opportune moment. It added a whole layer to her previous plans, making it much more likely she would succeed.

Nina settled into a trance-like state and sent a probe to Mordred. After a few minutes, she felt him stir.

It is done, she sent. *They have received our demand.*

She felt a surge of savage joy in the connection before she broke it. Let the Le Clairs stew. Now it was time to reel in her big fish.

Preparations for Arthur's tour took four days, and Guinevere spent most of her time supervising the stores that would go with them. Not that she knew much of campaigning, but she knew what they'd need to see them through until harvest. Before the warriors left, they must attend the ceremony to prepare the fields for planting, so Arthur stayed the next day for the breaking of the ground. The young men tied their draught horses to their ploughs and competed to see who would make the deepest, straightest furrow. There was much bawdy joking about ploughing fields and bedding maids. Everyone's blood was up with the rise of spring.

That night, many a couple sported in those furrows, blessing the land, bringing fertility to the animals and people as well. Leigh, the old wise woman who tended the sick and delivered babies, mixed up a special herbal concoction for Guinevere to drink in hopes she would catch a child. She held her nose and chugged it down, trying not to make a face, but Leigh laughed. "Aye, girl, it is a nasty mix, but it has done the trick many a time."

Guinevere wiped her mouth. "Thank you."

Later that night Arthur led her to a special bower that had been made for them in the center of the field and laying her down in the soft earth, made love to her as if he were just returning from months on campaign rather than preparing to leave for one. But amidst the thrusts and the heat, Guinevere's thoughts strayed to Lancelot. She wondered who he was with this night.

The next morning, Guinevere had the honor of blessing the corn, and the women, filling their aprons with the golden grain heads, went out and slung the seed across the fields, singing as they went. With the fields prepared for summer, Arthur rode out the next day with a great clanging of swords, braying of hounds, and churning of hooves. But early that morning as the birds began their song to the sun that would soon crest the hill, he'd tumbled her again in their bed, then dressed to leave. "May I return to growing grains and a widening belly, my lady."

She smiled and kissed him goodbye. Below, he spoke to Lancelot with Guinevere listening at the window. "I head for the spring of Sulis, then into Wales to visit our kin and the lords to the west. I should be back before midsummer, so we can ride east."

"Yes, my lord. My men and I will guard your homeland."

Arthur turned to the old soldier who had marched with his father. "Ronan, your honor is beyond reproach and your arm is strong, but you must still recover from the injury you received last season."

Ronan hung his head. "I would march with you, my lord."

"But who would counsel Sir Lancelot in taking care of my lands and guarding the queen? There is none other I trust as much as you."

Ronan nodded, his eyes reddening. The old man had loved a campaign, but age had caught up with him. He was too proud to snore in the sun like his hound did now on the side of the wall, although he deserved it more.

"Keep her safe," Arthur said in a quiet voice that still reached Guinevere's ears.

"Yes, my lord."

Arthur slapped Lancelot on the back, then mounted his white stallion and rode out, the knights following, making a fine sight with their burnished armor and banners. Arthur's mastiff rushed ahead, his red tongue hanging out, eager for the road.

With the fields planted, the folk handed off the responsibility for the crops to Mother Nature and life slowed. They turned to making repairs, keeping the vegetable gardens weed free, and the young girls made garlands for their hair with the early flowers, hoping to catch the eye of a favored boy.

The furrows greened with the lengthening days, at first reminding Guinevere of the first fuzz on a young man's chin, but soon the stalks took on definition. She had hoped to be growing herself, but two weeks after Arthur rode out, her blood came. Hiding tears, she took to the woods pretending to hunt for herbs, but allowing the growing leaves and trickling stream to soothe her heart.

Why could she not conceive? She had asked the healers for herbal potions, drunk the most vile concoctions, laid with poultices on her abdomen. She'd asked the priestesses for rituals. Even mentioned to Merlin when he visited that she would be grateful for magical help, although he said such was the business of the priestesses and wise women. But nothing availed.

Perhaps it was not the ground, but the seed. But would men ever admit to such a thing? She would speak to Leigh, ask her if she had a remedy. Arthur would probably drink it, revolting as it might be, if they kept it between themselves. He was desperate for a son. He had stopped saying he did not care if the first was a girl or boy. Now, he wanted an heir.

As she climbed a small hill that led up from the creek, she heard a snuffling in the woods. She froze. Looking around, she noticed a myrtle bush rustling. She moved back behind the thin trunk of a young black pine and crouched down, glancing around to find better cover. It seemed to be a large animal, given how much the undergrowth was moving. Perhaps a boar or bear. Either one was dangerous.

Then she heard a whistle. Lancelot stepped into view from the other side of the hill, a bow and quiver hanging from his shoulder. "Here, girl," he called, and a Clumber Spaniel ran out from the bush, legs and stomach wet with muddy water. She stood panting, tail wagging, then shook and threw water everywhere.

Her much larger mate galloped down the hill and slammed into her shoulder, playfully snapping at her mouth, trying to induce a tussle. Two smaller Welsh Spaniels came up around Lancelot's legs, then sniffed the air and took off straight for Guinevere, braying as they ran.

Lancelot notched an arrow.

She stood and stepped from her meager cover, waving her arms. "It's me, Guinevere."

Lancelot lowered his bow. "My lady, we mistook you for dinner."

The dogs surrounded her, rubbing against her legs, tails a blur. The larger dogs headed for her with a yelp, but Lancelot ran down from the top of the hill and headed them off so they wouldn't jump up and smear her clothes. He held his hand out to pull her up a slight incline. When she took it, a warm tingle ran up her arm. She pulled away, but he grasped her firmer, thinking she'd stumbled.

"My lady?" he questioned.

She allowed him to lead her to the deer trail, not needing help, but not wanting to make him question her again. And really, not wanting to break contact. "You are hunting, I see," she said, trying to force her attention away from his wide shoulders, his handsome face flushed from running with the dogs.

"I thought to bring back a few birds. Pheasants or quail. Perhaps duck."

"Are you headed for the lake?"

"Yes, would you do me the honor of walking with me?"

She looked down at the ground, into her basket, hesitating, anything to avoid those luminous brown eyes.

"Or do you need to get back with your harvest?"

"Oh, these will keep. I've wrapped them in a damp cloth." She looked up and found him studying her, his lips curved in a tentative smile. "All right."

"Excellent," he said.

They walked back down the hill and Lancelot offered her his hand when they came to the creek, but this time she declined and jumped from rock to rock, nimble, keeping her balance, then waited for him on the other side, laughing.

"I see you have good woods craft, my lady."

"Please, you may call me Guinevere."

Lancelot bowed with a flourish, a mischievous gleam in his eye. "Guinevere it is. Where did you grow up, Lady—uh, Guinevere?"

"On the Isle of Anglesey, my lord." She said this last with emphasis.

"Please, call me Lancelot. Is Anglesey very different from here?"

"Milder, perhaps, because it is so close to the sea, although the damp in winter can penetrate to the bone. The isle is a rolling, green land with small hills. A few mountains, but not like Yr Wyddfa. I grew up near the sea where we had marshes."

"Lovely," he said, looking at her as if he were not discussing the island at all.

"And you, Lancelot. Tell me of your homeland."

"Llydaw is close to the ocean, so we have many cloudy days. But when the sun comes out, it is glorious," he said.

They walked on, chatting about their favorite childhood games and pastimes, until the dogs gave voice and flushed out a covey of partridge. Guinevere fell silent and watched. The birds took flight and Lancelot pulled an arrow quickly, notched it, and took aim. He felled a large bird, then a second in rapid succession.

He shouldered his bow again. "We'll leave the rest to make more birds," he said, somehow making simple good sense sound suggestive.

Guinevere blushed.

He pretended not to notice and whistled for the dogs to bring the birds to him. He strung them together, threw them over his back, and they walked back as the sun prepared to set, the dogs running ahead, then coming back to nose their hands and urge them to hurry. Dinner awaited, they seemed to be saying, but neither Guinevere nor Lancelot wanted to move any faster.

They drew closer together in the quiet gloaming, their conversation lulled, and they settled into a silent communion. Guinevere found herself walking closer to him, although the path grew wider and easier to traverse as it rose out of the woods and stretched across the open field. Lancelot's presence was like a small fire in the gathering cool of twilight, subtly warming her, making her breath come faster than the walk demanded. A silver sickle moon rode the western sky accompanied by the jewel of one bright star.

Footsteps approached in the dim light and Lancelot put himself in front of her.

"My lady?" came Ronan's voice.

"I'm here," she answered. "I found Lancelot on my forage and went further into the woods with him on his hunt."

"When you didn't return as expected . . ." Ronan trailed off.

"I'm sorry to have worried you," she said, moving away from Lancelot and drawing herself straighter.

"Thank you, Lancelot, for looking after the lady," Ronan said.

"It was my pleasure." His voice, husky in the night, sent a shiver through Guinevere.

"Are you cold, my lady?" Lancelot reverted to more formality with Ronan next to them.

Guinevere shook her head no, not trusting her voice. His presence had awakened something deep within her and she didn't want to surface from the easy familiarity they had found between them. Yet, the settlement stood before them. She must gather herself, go in, greet people normally, see if dinner was ready.

Lancelot seemed to understand and walked forward, putting an arm on Ronan's shoulder. "I've found two fine partridges, but we might be too late for cook to include them in dinner." He hoisted the birds up.

"Never too late for partridges," Ronan said, and the two men walked together, talking of hunting, Lancelot praising the pair of Welsh Spaniels.

Cook took the birds and roasted them, so they had them after the stew. The men drank mead into the night and Guinevere excused herself early, curling up in her bed, remembering the tone of his voice in the dark, the touch of his hand when her footing was not sure, the solid warmth of him beside her.

After that day, Guinevere took to walking with Lancelot in the afternoons when she could be spared from overseeing the household. She mentioned to Hester one morning as they sort through the spinning that she needed to keep their royal guest entertained.

"I'd love to entertain him," Hester swooned.

Guinevere laughed. "He is quite handsome."

She showed him her favorite spots—the meadow overlooking the lake, dotted already with wild flowers. The ancient oak that stood slightly apart from the other trees in the wood as if they revered the ancient one and didn't want to crowd him. She found reasons to walk close to his men as they sparred in the courtyard, listening to the ring of swords, watching for his dark crown of hair, standing almost a head taller than most of his men. His sword fighting was like a dance, graceful, almost elegant, but he struck with deadly skill, swift as an adder lying in the shadow of the woods, but noble as the hart with a full crown of antlers.

In the evening, he sat next to her, easily holding the whole gathering in thrall with a story from his home. They listened to Heilyn, whose sight was fading, but whose fingers still knew his harp, as he sang the old tales of glory or sang songs of woe or of love. She bent her head to him to hear his soft words of praise for the song or her eyes. He was familiar to her, as familiar as the scent of baked bread in the morning or the sound of a lark singing its joy to the rising sun. It was as if they had been in the middle of a conversation that had been interrupted and now they came back to it naturally, as if they were not just meeting, but returning to an old acquaintance.

They rode together, Guinevere on her smoke gray mare, he on his prancing black stallion, often dismounting and walking the horses part way so they could walk close together, making small talk, sometimes just enjoying the closeness of walking arm in arm. One day, before boosting her up on her mare, Lancelot grasped her waist and, turning her, held her body against him, staring into her eyes. "Guinevere, if I had only found you sooner."

She looked away, down to her feet, at the side of her horse, anywhere but in the pool of those deep, dark eyes. "My lord," she said, hoping to recall him to propriety, but he lifted her chin with his finger and kissed her, softly at first.

He drew back. Her eyes filled with tears.

"Guinevere?"

"I never thought to feel this. It was my duty to marry him. I love Arthur, but—"

His lips stopped her tumble of words. She clung to him, the warmth in her belly bursting into fire. Their kiss deepened and he pulled her to him.

They heard hoof beats from down the hill and drew apart, Guinevere gasping, her body demanding to be satisfied. Two destrier stallions came into view. The riders wore Arthur's livery. "Oh, no," she whispered before she could stop herself.

As the riders drew near, Lancelot hoisted Guinevere onto her mare and mounted his stallion, restive to challenge the newcomers. She did not recognize the men.

"My Lady Guinevere," one knight spoke, dipping his head. "Arthur sent us to guard in his stead. He sends his apologies to you and Sir Lancelot." His voice lilted up at the end of the sentence.

Lancelot rode forward. "Lancelot du Lac, nephew to King Hoel."

The man looked from Lancelot to Guinevere's flushed face, then a rather sinister smile curved his lip. "King Arthur will be delayed at least another two months."

Guinevere mastered the spark of pure joy that shot through her at this news.

"He has sent me to guard Camelot until his return."

She studied the man's face. There was something familiar about it. He had the same aquiline nose as Arthur, the same thin mouth.

Could it be? she wondered.

"Have I made your acquaintance, sir?" she asked.

"At the wedding, my lady, but there were so many people there. My name is Mordred, son of King Arthur and a priestess of Avalon."

Chapter 15

Elizabeth dreaded the upcoming ritual, dreaded allowing the grief of Isis to sink deep into her heart, dreaded slogging through the search, through the well-known story. Didn't she have enough worries with two precious lives on the line without having to mourn the loss of Osiris? Usually this ritual was for the initiation of a priestess. Tonight, what would it accomplish?

Elizabeth had tried to contact Michael in Egypt once more. Tahir told her that Michael was not available, that he was going after Anne. When she'd asked what that meant, he said it was a secret of his order, something he could not discuss, even with a high initiate such as herself. She'd have to trust him, just as she had to trust Dr. Abernathy leading the rite, and Winston as Anne's doctor, all the members of the lodge she'd worked with all this time. As she had to trust Anubis. And Isis.

She thought of handing her part over to Winston's wife, Cordelia, who was as well trained as she was, but she felt the disapproval of Anubis even as the thought crossed her mind. So she showered, then dressed in the tattered robes of a wanderer and spread ash on her face, appropriate for the grief of Isis.

Downstairs in the ballroom, the rest of the lodge were gathered, sitting in meditation, assuming the roles assigned them for the ceremony. Elizabeth released her ordinary consciousness easily, knowing the lodge was in the capable hands of Dr. Abernathy as high priest. He led them into the temple, handing each a scepter or head piece appropriate to the Neter they would play. Anne lay in the corner, quiet, lost in her own dream of Camelot and her forbidden love.

Abernathy nodded to the nurse, who silenced the monitors, but sat close enough to keep an eye on them. The quarters were called, then he began reciting the litany. Each person stepped forward to recite their assigned piece, with Elizabeth repeating what she'd already seen in vision—her marriage with Osiris, his mating with Nephthys, the birth of Anubis, and Set's murder of his brother.

"Each person at the banquet tried the box to see if they would fit. One was too tall, another too short. One was too fat, another too thin."

Good Lord, it's like Goldilocks, Elizabeth thought, her irritability getting the best of her. She pushed down a hysterical laugh.

Get a grip on yourself. There has to be some good reason for us to perform this ritual tonight. Otherwise, Anubis would not have insisted.

Abernathy continued, not seeming to notice. He spoke of how Isis searched while Elizabeth moved through the temple, asking participants for a great box made of cedar and inlaid with ebony, gold, and silver. Only the children had seen it, they said, floating down the Nile. At last, Elizabeth sank into the story, and the next person she approached seemed not to be a lodge member at all, but a blue-skinned being with pendulous breasts and a large belly, but sporting a beard. Lotus flowers grew from the Neter's head.

Isis greeted the androgen. "Hapi, Lord of the River, Lord of Fish and Birds of the Marshes, have you seen my lord? Set has murdered my love and nailed him in a coffin of cedar. Have you seen the Lord Osiris?"

"I carried the body of the Great Osiris, encased in his coffin of black and red, gently in my waters. One day we reached the great green sea." Elizabeth had a dim sense that Bill Hardy was speaking to her as Hapi, but then Isis surged forward, more strongly than she ever had before. Elizabeth pushed back a bit. It was never safe to allow a spiritual being to have full reign, even her own spiritual guardian.

"Hapi, son of Horus, we thank you for your kind service to my lord. Do you have knowledge of where the coffin went after that?"

"I heard two ibis birds talking as they searched my waters for supper one evening. They had flown over the shores of Phoenicia where a great tamarisk tree grows. One said there is something hidden within the tree, something that sings a song of Egypt."

"I must sail to Phoenicia."

The lodge sang of the ocean, then fell into a crooning chant that sounded much like waves in the sea.

David and Alycia stepped forward and acted out the discovery of the great tamarisk tree by King Malcander and his wife, Queen Astarte. The tree had grown around the casket of Osiris, hiding it from all eyes. The only hint of his presence was the scent of juniper berries and pine nuts.

"How beautiful this tree is. See the green shine of the leaves. Listen to the birds singing in its many branches," said King Malcander.

"It is a tree worthy of our royal hall," the queen said.

Abernathy's voice rang out, the deep resonance filling the temple. "And so the tree was cut and placed in the palace of Byblos as a great central pillar, and it became famous throughout the land. All who heard about it desired to see it, and many made the pilgrimage.

"One day, an old woman, haggard and bent, dressed in rags, appeared at the gate."

Isis raised her voice. "I have come to see the tamarisk pillar and desire entry."

The lodge mimed the soldiers guarding the gates. "Only the great ones can come in. You are a beggar, a low woman."

"We cannot allow one of such bad character to enter."

Isis raised her hand, and a light came forth, striking the soldiers in the eyes, so that they cried out and saw the truth of who stood before them.

"Great Goddess, please enter."

But before she did, Isis forbid them to speak of her true identity.

Abernathy took up the tale again, his voice resonating through the hall. "When Isis approached the tree, she knew it contained the body of her lost love, but she had to find a way to remove it.

"Isis went to the town baths to refresh herself from her long journey, and there washed and plaited her hair. The maids who served in the palace marveled at this and asked if Isis would do the same for their hair, never knowing they asked a Goddess for help. When the maids returned to their work, the beauty of this new style and the scent of lotus and myrrh that rose from the maids struck Queen Astarte. When questioned, they told the queen about the lady at the baths, and Astarte sent for her."

Elizabeth stood before Cordelia, who said, "I have it in my mind to ask you to come as nursemaid to my children, little Prince Maneros and my little baby Dictys, whose health is failing."

As Elizabeth felt the power rise in the ritual the Lodge of the House of Isis was enacting, Nina began her own solitary ceremony, calling in the directions and sealing her own temple in the attic of her brownstone in Washington, D.C. Riding the high of the success of her theft, she channeled that energy to call all the seductresses from legends around the world. She bent over a flat, silver dish filled with water that she'd gathered from White Spring, calling each by name.

She listened for the sound of waves washing ashore on the Isle of Anthemusa, the famed island of the Sirens. They heard the wind gust and a sail snap full. They knew sailors were trying to pass them by, so they rushed as one down to the waters and sang, intertwining their voices together in a complex weave that burrowed down to find the hidden desires of each sailor, weary from work and the company of only men. Their song promised rest for toil, ease for tired muscles, lying back in warm water to be massaged and stroked into complete relaxation. To dine on the richest of food, the headiest of wines, until those hungers sated, the deeper desires would be fulfilled, one after another in an entwining of bodies in as many combinations as the sailor could imagine.

Nina pulled in the incredible beauty of Helen of Troy, the daughter of Zeus and Leda, who had been abducted twice and sparked a war because she was the most exquisite of women. Then the seductive brilliance of Cleopatra, who she knew was not as beautiful as Helen or even Elizabeth Taylor, but who had still seduced the leaders of Rome and almost saved Egypt.

Nina took the Orion crystal in her hand and blew her spell into the stone, calling out to Valentin to awaken and come to her. Then she looked down through the water and saw the irresistible and devious Delilah, who ensnared the indestructible Samson, calling out to her. Mata Hari, the erotic dancer and spy, adding her deadly eroticism to her brew. Then the innocence of Marilyn Monroe as a cover.

She felt something feeding back to her through the crystal, like a nibble on a fishing line. She'd established this connection a few nights ago at the regular meeting of the lodge when she'd stayed behind and given Valentin a drink, kneeled before him and pressed against his thighs.

She visualized the Visha Kanyas, the Poison Maidens of India, chosen as infants, made immune to poisons through childhood, trained in seduction even as girls, hired to seduce powerful men and kill them in their own chambers. Sought for their cunning and strength, admired for their beauty and sexual prowess.

Then she showed him her old face, Nimué. She sunk into that life as deeply as she could without losing her connection to the present and breathed the old spell through their link.

But to seduce a man like Valentin Knight, Nina knew she must appeal to more than his sexual appetites. He was older, after all. Not as quick to desire a sexual connection. What drove him? What desire dwelled in his innermost heart?

The desire to know. It had always been that with him, both in the past and now. So she called upon Athena, who came forward, her owl on her shoulder, seeming to offer access to divine knowledge. She asked for Hypatia, who held the keys to the Library of Alexandria, that great repository of ancient knowledge. She whispered she could take him back to before the fire, before its destruction. She could show him all its secrets.

Were these high, light-filled goddesses really cooperating with her or were they demonic spirits only wearing their faces? She didn't know nor did she care. As long as Valentin took the bait.

Deepest of all was his desire to penetrate the very secrets of life, so she called upon the Great Goddess herself, the Black Madonna, Isis Veiled, and She came through the thick, honeyed atmosphere of the ritual, thick with the scent of rose and musk, the feel of warm skin, carrying the Key of Life. Nina knew this was the real Goddess and was momentarily stunned that She had responded. Why would she cooperate, but before she could think of any answer, Isis held out the Great Ankh to Valentin—and he reached out and grasped it.

Nina had him.

She allowed herself a moment to luxuriate in her victory. She felt him coming, the fishing line being drawn in. She called Gregor to tell him Knight was on his way.

Then she changed from her ritual robe to a black velvet dress, dramatically cut to reveal the swell of her breast and a necklace of sparkling diamonds. The Orion crystal key hung just above them.

Soon she heard car tires outside, then the engine turn off. The car door slam shut and finally the knock on her door. She waited to catch her breath, then opened her front door. There he stood, glassy-eyed, confused, wearing his pajamas. He was alone. He'd driven himself. His forehead wrinkled in his confusion, "Nimué?"

"Welcome, my Lord Merlin. Welcome back."

Chapter 16

"To hell with waiting for further instructions," Arnold said. "You traced the source of this code to Valentin Knight's home computer, right?"

"Yeah, sure, but they've got us locked down," Preston repeated.

"Isn't there any way to unlock it?"

"We'll run an interdict, man." Preston whirled around in his office chair and started ticking off points.

"And what is that?"

Preston heaved another dramatic sigh. "We'll need to burrow through at least a four-layer firewall, but there's no chance of that happening quickly so we need to get direct access to his computer."

"What else?"

Preston ticked off all the problems on his fingers. "His computer is in D.C. This guy's rich, so he's probably got security tighter than a nun's cooch."

"No need to be vulgar," Gerald objected.

Preston ignored him. "Plus, I need some heavy duty software and a Rubber Ducky to implant the latest version of EternalBlue directly. Then I'll decode his passwords. Once we find the money and move it back, I'll want to plug in a PoisonTap to keep watch in case he tries this little trick again."

"Leo?" Arnold asked.

"No problem," he said.

"Yeah, right." Preston rolled his eyes.

Arnold ignored him and asked Leo, "How fast can you get it?"

"Here in New York? Tomorrow morning. But we're flying to D.C., so once we're there, I could have it in an hour."

"Sure, man, like you're some kind of super spy," Preston said.

"How long would it take for you to do all that once we've secured the site?" Arnold asked him.

"No way." Preston's face changed from sarcasm to disbelief. "Are you guys serious? Who the fuck are you?"

"If we told you that . . ." Arnold left the rest of the sentence unstated and tried not to laugh.

Preston's gaze darted from Arnold to Leo and back. "You're shitting me."

"How long?"

"Depends on the passwords, but maybe fifteen minutes, give or take."

"Get ready. We're wheels up in an hour."

Once on board, Arnold and Leo sat on two couches that faced each other, a table in between bolted to the floor. Preston sat by himself absorbed in computer games. "I need a break," he'd said. Arnold spread out the print-outs Preston had given them, and he and Leo reviewed the blueprints of Valentin Knight's home. Then they checked out the Google Maps of his property and the surrounding area. They agreed on the best approach, then found a list of his security personnel.

"You know any of these people?" Arnold asked.

Leo scanned the list. "I knew Kate back in the Secret Service."

"She good?"

"Naturally," he said with a touch of smugness. "I don't know his head of security though."

"What's his name?"

"Tyrone Williams."

Arnold typed the name into the FBI search engine that Leo had given him access to. "Too many results. Do we have a middle name? Any distinguishing characteristics?"

"Cut the search age to under forty. The middle initial is J."

Arnold refined his search parameters and hit enter.

"There." Leo pointed to a name halfway down the list. "The address is the same as Knight's. He must stay on site."

Arnold clicked on the name and some information popped up. "Born in Montgomery. Finished high school. Football scholarship at the University of Alabama. Majored in P.E. Ex-Navy Seal eight years ago. After that, his record has been redacted."

"Must be black ops, then private security for Knight."

"Your government connections always come in handy," Arnold said.

"The Le Clairs could have gotten it on their own."

Arnold poked Leo in the shoulder. "I'm glad you're with the family now." He meant more than the Le Clair family. Although Arnold considered himself a peripheral member of the Le Clairs by now, he thought of Leo as a brother.

He sat back and rubbed his eyes. "Let's get some rest."

Leo yawned. "Good idea." He nodded and flicked off his overhead light, then stretched out on his couch.

Arnold did the same. He and Leo shared a long history. They trained together in the Marines, then been recruited to the same CIA black ops team after distinguished service in the Gulf War. After a few missions in the Middle East, Eastern Europe, and Central America, they'd gone their separate ways. Leo joined the Secret Service and Arnold was recruited for corporate security by the Le Clairs. He switched over to head of family security soon after.

Leo served two White House administrations before President George Le Clair was assassinated during his term in office. Leo had not been on duty that night, but he always told Arnold that he felt some measure of responsibility for it. Maybe if they'd trained harder. Maybe if they'd sent an extra man or two. Maybe if they had better intelligence. So, he'd come to work for the Le Clair family when they'd been assigned a permanent detail from the Secret Service. Maybe it was misguided guilt, but Arnold was glad to have him since they'd always worked well together. They'd become fast friends and even if Leo was reassigned, Arnold was sure he'd keep up with Leo the rest of his life, which was sure to be longer because of his fighting and logistical skills.

Flashing the Le Clair name gave Arnold's team access to land at Andrews Air Force Base where they were met by the rest of their team. Frank had bulging arms and shoulders and a trim waist. He held top rank as a sharp-shooter in case they needed long-range capability, but he was handy in any fight.

Ken always had the latest haircut, this time a quaff—cropped short on the sides and topped with a mass of curls. He wore rimless glasses and the all-black tee, pants and parka standard for the job, but somehow he made it look like Armani. He reminded Arnold of a young lawyer trying to make partner, but in fact he was a multi-talented freelance agent, skilled in breaking and entering as well as surveillance. He always worked Arnold's last nerve, but somehow, he ended up hiring Ken a lot.

Frank greeted him. "What's the plan, man?"

"Frank, Ken, you know Leo."

Nods all around.

"This punk—"

"Hey!" Preston objected.

"—is Night Wing." Arnold injected as much sarcasm into his voice as he could manage.

Frank laughed, making Preston flush red, but Ken pointed at him. "Didn't you hack the stock exchange the day Congress gutted the Dodd-Frank Act?"

Preston gave a little flourish with his hands and bowed. "I'm glad to find my work is appreciated in some quarters." He glared at Arnold, who ignored him.

Leave it to Ken to know, he thought.

"You all know the situation. Looks like Valentin Knight has gone over to the dark side of the force and stolen the Le Clair's money. We're here to get in," he pointed to Ken, "hack their computer and return the funds." He nodded to Preston. "Dana is backing us up online in Massachusetts."

Ken handed Arnold a packet. "I've given you EternalBlue and PoisonTap, a Rubber Ducky. I threw in a couple extras."

"Sweet." Preston held out his hand, but Ken slapped the package into Arnold's large palm. Then he winked at Preston.

Arnold interrupted this budding bromance with a sharp command. "Let's load up."

The group piled into a black SUV with heavily tinted windows and Joan, their pilot from Maris, took the wheel. As she negotiated the numerous freeways leading out to the countryside surrounding Potomac, Maryland, Arnold reviewed the operation. Preston connected the iPad to the onboard screens in back and a map of Knight's property and the surrounding area popped up.

"Knight's acreage runs along this wooded area on the west side." Arnold ran his large finger down the property line. "The house is just over two klicks from this trail."

Ken studied the map for a minute, then nodded.

Arnold continued. "Dana will gain access to their security system, bring down the cameras and motion detectors. We'll go in through this basement door here."

Ken clicked his phone and brought up his own set of blueprints. "What about the kitchen service area? They take deliveries. Might be easier to breach and we can skip this stairway." He pointed to the screen on the back of the SUV seat.

Arnold and Leo scooted closer to the blueprint and Frank held his hand out for Ken's phone.

"There's a security satellite office right down the hall," Arnold said.

"Best to get to them as fast as possible. Disable any response. Is this Knight's private office?" He pointed to a large room toward the front of the house.

"That's it."

Leo spoke up. "We were thinking of going through the French doors of the office. Avoiding detection all together rather than disabling their response."

"Too risky," Ken said. "Can your girl jam the cell towers?"

"We'll use Titan," Preston interjected.

Arnold looked around at his team and each man nodded.

"Sounds like a plan, then," Arnold said. He leaned forward and asked Joan, "What's our ETA?"

"Fifteen minutes unless we run into traffic. Not likely at this hour."

Everyone took the time to double check their equipment. Preston had already hooked up the hard drive to his laptop and was running through the programs stored on it, emitting gasps of delight each time he clicked a link.

Ken got his attention. "We don't talk on approach. We use basic military hand signals. Do you know them?"

"I don't need—"

"Yes, you do. Now, pay attention. Your life depends on it." Ken showed Preston basic field gestures and made him repeat them until he had them down. The others checked their guns, extra ammo, knives, and flashlights. Arnold's team carried Beretta APX Compacts for this job, but Leo was used to the SIG Sauer from his Secret Service work. They all carried silencers. No sense alerting the neighbors.

Joan switched off the headlights half a mile before the turnoff in the woods. Once they arrived, she turned off the engine, and the group stole out of the vehicle, quiet as hunting owls. Arnold handed out night vision goggles, and everyone checked the infrared and thermal imaging, Ken showing Preston how to use them.

Arnold scouted out a faint deer trail a few feet in from the road and the others followed, Preston sounding like a bear in the undergrowth. Arnold signaled a stop, but Preston didn't notice and ran smack into Leo.

"Son, you're too loud. You'll get us shot," Arnold said. "Try not to make a sound. Watch where you step, avoid sticks, even twigs, and pay attention to signals."

Preston drew a breath to protest, but Frank's hand wrapped around his throat before he could say a word. He leaned in and said in a whisper, "I will not get killed because you're a fucking moron. Straighten up."

Preston still tried to answer, but Frank tightened his grip and the kid nodded frantically.

Frank let go and Arnold signaled for the group to move forward. This time Preston sounded more like a small mammal rooting through the underbrush. Better. Arnold guessed it was the best he'd get from him.

They descended a short hill. At the bottom, the path ran along a small creek, water trickling beneath rocks and pooling around a deep part of the bank a few feet away. They crossed it and wound around a tall stand of ash trees. The terrain rose slightly and the sharp scent of pines filled the air. A few yards more and Arnold saw lights on an outbuilding. He signaled a halt.

Leo and Frank stepped to either side of him. Leo dimmed his night goggles and switched to high resolution. He checked for movement. Frank switched to thermal imaging.

"Nobody," Leo mouthed.

Frank signaled his agreement.

They climbed an old split-rail fence and moved across the field like the shadows of passing clouds. Preston seemed to be improving. Arnold reached the barn first and waited against the faded red wall. Inside he could hear horses shifting their weight, the nicker of one to another. They seemed restless. The other men arrived within thirty seconds. Arnold pointed right to Frank and left to Ken. The two moved off soundlessly.

Within a minute, Ken returned, his night goggles hanging around his neck. "Something's up," he murmured to Arnold. "All the lights are on in the big house. Team of two checking the outer buildings."

Arnold waited for Frank, who appeared within a minute. "Place is like a hornet's nest that's been kicked over. Searching the house for something."

"Same plan?" Arnold asked.

"Let's get closer. See if there's anyone in the security office."

The team moved around the barn, hugging the walls, then ran behind a horse trailer. Security lights blazed, lighting up every inch of the sloping green lawn that led to the back entrance.

"I'll check the front," Ken whispered to Arnold.

Arnold nodded and signaled for the rest of the group to wait. Ken snuck to the front, then took off in a sprint to a sprawling oak closer to the house. Then he just disappeared. Arnold shook his head. The guy was good. He'd give him that.

They waited two minutes, listening to the shouting from the house and side yard. What the hell was going on?

Leo stepped up beside Arnold. "I'll go around the other side."

Arnold nodded. Leo slipped off almost as skillfully as Ken, except Arnold tracked him until he disappeared around the side of the kitchen entry.

They waited. Two more minutes went by. Then another two. Just as Arnold was about to go after them, Leo came walking around the side of the house, his arm around Kate, the woman he knew from Secret Service who now served on Knight's security team.

"What the fuck?" Arnold burst out.

Chapter 17

With Mordred's arrival in Camelot, life became more formal. Guinevere sat next to him for the evening meal and answered his questions as best she could. Lancelot sat farther down the table. She was grateful he was out of her direct sight. It made her duties easier to bear. The new harpist did as well.

Mordred's retinue rolled in on their slower wagons a few days after his precipitous advent, and along with more supplies, troops, and the usual cook had come the harper, this one a Druid by all appearances. Thin and willowy, like the music he played, Carataos was young and soft-spoken, but with a face scarred by an illness. He, too, had been born in Avalon, then gone to train with the Druids.

After he played the first evening, Guinevere lingered at the table until Mordred and his men had gone out to drink and play dice in the yard under the summer stars. The servants cleared the meal. She picked up her mead and walked to the corner where Carataos sat.

"I am grateful you are here."

He ducked his head slightly. "It is my honor to play for you, my lady, one from the old lands."

She smiled at the acknowledgment of her home island. "Have you seen Merlin about?"

Carataos smiled, his long angular face softening. "Aye, the mage travels with Arthur."

"Oh, it seems he is still his favorite student," Guinevere said.

The harper chuckled. "So it would seem."

She watched as he loosened his harp strings and with a soft cloth, stroked the honey-colored wood. His movements were careful, tender, reminding her of Lancelot's touch. Warm desire filled her. If only Arthur had not asked Mordred to come. Was it a chastisement for her inability to give him an heir? Surely his presence proved the blame did not rest with Arthur. Was he preparing him to rule next? It would be unprecedented for a Sun Child to rule the mundane world. She did not trust him. There was something devious in his nature. He nurtured some dark secret. She would not like to see Camelot pass to such a one.

A plan hatched in her mind. Perhaps it was not too late. Births were not like clockwork.

"If you are willing, perhaps you could lead the mid-summer ceremonies."

His too large lips formed a smile, then he nodded. "If m'lady so desires, it would be an honor."

A few days later, Guinevere saw Lancelot trot out to the north woods alone, his black stallion pulling at the reins, tossing his head, eager for a run. The preparations for mid-summer in two days were well in hand. Mordred and his men had ridden out to the southern meadow to joust. Guinevere told Hester her mare needed exercise and slipped away to the stable.

Once out of sight of the settlement, she let her mare stretch out along a path that ran through an open meadow. Ducking close to her horse's neck, she let her run like a cloud scudding before a swift wind. The mare reached the top of the meadow and continued into the woods, the path broad here beneath the hawthorn and oak branches stretching above, forming a wide tunnel. Her mare slowed and she settled into an easy canter, then a trot. The horse's sides heaved, so Guinevere slowed her into a walk and let out the reins to allow her stretch her neck and cool off. They walked out from the woods to a higher meadow and there at the end, against an ancient stone wall, she saw the black stallion freed of his bridle, grazing.

Lancelot leaned against the wall, hand hovering near his sword. He must have heard her horse's hoofbeats. When he saw her, he leaned back, arms at his sides, a wide smile on his face, and let her come to him.

And go to him she did. She slid off her mare and took off her bridle, letting her out to graze. The black stallion turned his head and snuffled a welcome, and she joined him standing close enough to take advantage of his long tail chasing away the flies from her face. She paid him the same favor.

Suddenly shy, Guinevere laid the bridle next to Lancelot's tack, smoothed her skirts, and only then did she look up at him.

"My love," he said, his voice urgent and husky. He took two long strides and grabbed her up in his arms. He pressed his face into her neck, kissing the hollow at the bottom of her neck, then let her slide down his body until her face hovered near his. "I think we have waited long enough."

A small whimper escaped Guinevere in answer, and he claimed her mouth, letting her slide further down and find her feet again, but she leaned into him. His arms encompassed her, strong, safe, right. She surrendered to his probing tongue, letting him hold her up.

Lancelot grunted, a hart relieved the season has finally arrived, and picked her up, carrying her to a blanket he must have spread earlier. Had he known she'd come, she wondered? He laid her down, gentle now, pushing her hair away from her face, kissing her forehead, her temples, stroking her cheek. "You are the most beautiful woman—"

Guinevere stilled his words with her own mouth, amazed at her brazenness. Their kiss deepened and his hands strayed to her breasts. She thanked the goddess that Hester had been too busy to dress her this morning. Her bodice opened easily and Lancelot bent to pay them homage.

Lost in his touch, in the tug of his mouth, the playfulness of his tongue, Guinevere laid back and gave herself up to Lancelot's explorations. He reached down and pulled her skirts free from their entangled limbs, then raised them. But he did not do as Arthur would have. He bent between her legs and paid tribute there, surprising her enough that she raised up on her elbows, but his skill made her gasp and she laid back, enjoying the arts of the French.

She melted, her heart opening as her body did. The tension mounted, and she spasmed beneath him. He waited for her to settle again, then with maddening slow deliberation, took himself in hand and pressed against her small mound, until the heat built again and she thrust her hips up, trying to capture him. But he chuckled and eluded her. She groaned her frustration, but at last he moved into her, only slowly at first, enjoying his teasing, until at last it seemed he could hold back no longer, and he thrust all the way. She climaxed once again, but this time he did not pause, but continued to move, slowly at first, then building to a gallop and they burst into ecstasy together.

They laid back gasping. Guinevere felt as if she had been a virgin until this moment, even though she'd been a married woman for several years. They curled up together, watching the sky, listening to the birds and the horses munching nearby. Neither spoke. What was there to say? She was married to the High King of England, he an ambassador from another king wishing to confirm their alliance. But they had today. And perhaps a few more if Mordred's report was true.

After a while, Lancelot turned to her and began all over again. He had amazing stamina. They dallied there, enjoying their love play uninterrupted. But then Guinevere realized the shadows had lengthened, and the sun had moved into the western sky.

She sat up, groping for her clothes. "Lancelot, we must get back. I'll be missed."

Looking down at him, his face changed suddenly—his eyes warm and dark, his nose curving down to a full mouth and square jaw. He pointed to a pendant laid out on a counter with other jewelry. He seemed to be asking her to pick one.

She seemed to be in an odd jewelry shop.

She blinked and Lancelot's face swam back into focus.

". . . I'll take that path and it will bring me back from a different direction. Does that sound like a plan?"

"What?"

Lancelot gave her a questioning look. "Ride back the way you came. I'll take the long way round. That way we won't arrive at the same time or from the same direction."

"That's a good plan, Michael."

Lancelot took hold of her forearms and looked into her face carefully. "And who is this Michael? I thought I only had a marriage of duty as a rival."

Guinevere blinked, then shook her head. "I don't know anyone by that name."

He smiled. "Then I have made you take leave of your senses with my attentions?"

She kissed him lightly. "Yes, my love, you most certainly have."

He laughed and helped her capture the mare, slip on the bridle, then lifted her into the saddle. "You have made my heart sing, my lady Guinevere."

"Gwen," she said. "Arthur calls me Gwen."

"Then I shall call you Guinevere. Now, ride."

As the story of Isis unfolded, Elizabeth grew restless again. Something seemed off. She had hoped by reenacting this ritual, retelling this myth, that she would gain insight into their present situation, or perhaps the knowledge to loosen Mordred's grip on Anne and the baby. She knew Egypt had succeeded in bringing the enlightened one to birth through this very story. Isis had conceived Horus and given birth to him, then Horus triumphed over Set. She knew Camelot had failed to do the same for England in their time. While Nephthys' mating with Osiris had produced the great Anubis, Guinevere had failed to produce a child, either with Arthur or Lancelot. That story still hung in the balance, waiting for an ending.

Arthur was the once and future king. The legend that he would return and bring his golden age of Camelot to fruition still haunted the Western imagination. Would reenacting this successful story help to break Mordred's hold? How? Would it somehow move this story forward? But nothing new was coming to her, and she felt as if she was just going through the motions by rote.

Abernathy took up the tale again. "Isis bowed before the queen, took the baby, and at night gave him her finger to suckle. He soon flourished, but as he did, a desire grew in her heart. Isis yearned for her own off-spring, an immortal child fathered by the Great Osiris, whose body stood enclosed by the tamarisk pillar in this very palace. So, she decided to turn little Dictys into a God. Every night, Isis would place the child in the fire."

As Abernathy narrated, Elizabeth mimed the actions. She approached the central crystal, pretending it was the fire, and held her hands above it.

"Isis assumed her form as a swallow and the fire burned away the mortal parts of Dictys as she flew around."

Yes, put me in the fire. Make me immortal. Mordred's voice rose from the crystal.

Alycia had already stepped out to play the part of the terrified queen, but stumbled to a stop when she heard the voice.

It startled Abernathy into silence.

"You seem quite immortal to me," Elizabeth snapped.

Shaken by Mordred's interruption, Elizabeth took a moment to center herself, then nodded for Alycia to continue the ritual.

"You are trying to kill my child. Guards." Alycia cried out.

Abernathy stepped forward. "Startled by Queen Astarte's interruption, Isis assumed her goddess form and stood, a beacon of light crowned with the throne. As this happened, the guards rushed in, surrounding King Malcander. Amazed by the presence of this goddess, they all bowed."

Elizabeth said, "I am Isis, Queen of Heaven, Mistress of the House of Wisdom, the Neter of Magic and Science."

The whole lodge bowed to Isis, and Elizabeth felt herself being subsumed by Her presence.

"Queen Isis, you have honored us with your presence. You have healed our son. What gift may we give you?" David in King Malcander's role asked.

Abernathy answered, and the lodge enacted the story that he told. "Isis asked for only one thing—the tamarisk pillar that only she knew held the body of her beloved Osiris. King Malcander granted her a ship to carry it back to Egypt, and she set off, calming the waters, until she reached the delta of the Nile. Hapi welcomed them both. Isis hid the boat near a floating island and laid the chest out. She opened it to gaze at her beloved, then closed it and finally rested.

"But Seth went out to hunt that night and from a distance spied the chest of cedar inlaid with ebony and ivory, gold and silver. He knew Isis had found the body of Osiris, and since a Neter can never truly die, knew she would soon call upon her magic to resurrect him. He flew into a fury and, lifting the body of Osiris from the coffin, tore it into pieces. Some say fourteen, some forty-two. He scattered these pieces up and down the length of the sacred Nile for the crocodiles to eat."

For a moment, Elizabeth was one with Isis as she learned of Set's treachery. Isis felt weightless for a moment, suspended in air. Her mouth gaped, a fish stranded in the sand desperate to breathe. She shook her head, her arms stretched out in front of her as if to push the knowledge away.

"No, it can't be," Elizabeth choked out, and she and the Goddess Isis fell to the lodge floor and wept. They wept for the loss of Osiris, the beloved. For the loss of so many in her family, her brother George, her fae-touched sister Cynthia, and grandson Thomas. They wept for the state of the world, yearning for the return of the light.

Abernathy moved forward and put his hand on Elizabeth's shoulder. When he felt her sobs lessen, he spoke. "Now Nephthys, the sister of Isis, could no longer bear the cruelty of Set, so she took Anubis and joined her sister on the banks of the Nile. 'We shall search for him,' Isis declared, and took a boat of papyrus to travel the Nile and find the pieces of Osiris. She would put them back together and blow the Breath of Life through his lips.

"Anubis assumed his jackal form and hunted the banks for his father, to bring him back a second time."

A chill ran through Elizabeth, shaking her body physically, as she recognized the link between the two stories, but before she could say anything, Abernathy's recitation went on smoothly like a gentle breeze over her head.

"Piece by piece, Isis reassembled the body of Osiris, and in each place that she found a part, she had the priests build a shrine and conduct his funeral rites to fool Set into believing the body of Osiris was buried in that place. But in secret, Isis laid out the pieces of her beloved in a sacred sanctuary until she had rejoined them all. All but one piece. The member she would need to mate with him and engender within her womb the Golden Child, the Sun Child, the Falcon God."

Tears of joy gathered in Elizabeth's eyes as she felt the energies of the two stories coming together to heal what had been rent in the past. Oblivious of her realization, the lodge continued the ritual, and she rode the wave.

"So Isis shaped a phallus from pure energy, some say of gold, and in the shape of a swallow, she hovered over the body and became pregnant with the Divine Son. After Isis had accomplished all this, she had her priests perform the funeral rites and the spirit of Osiris passed into the Halls of Amenti where he rules to this day. But when the Nile floods, he returns to spread his green over the fields, and when the harvest is ready, he is cut down once more and he returns to rule the Land of the Dead."

Chapter 18

Elizabeth rose from the center of the temple, her heart singing, and returned to a seat beside Anne. Anubis smiled at her, but Mordred still glowered, restless, not understanding the shift in tides that was loosening his grip on Anne and the child. Anne murmured something, but Elizabeth didn't catch what she said.

Abernathy continued the story. "When Horus grew into a young man, he gathered an army and went in search of Set in the southern deserts of Egypt. Ra brought his chariot of solar light down to help Horus, but Set took the form of a boar, black as a thunder-cloud, fierce to look at, with tusks to strike terror into the bravest heart. Not knowing the boar was Set, Horus gazed on it in wonder, and Set sent a blast of fire into the face of Horus, harming the clear vision of the Falcon King."

Elizabeth suddenly saw Michael on the inner planes. "Arthur has slain the black boar already," he said to her, and he showed her his vision of being in the forest and the young Arthur riding by.

"Ra shielded Horus from the light in a dark cave until he regained his vision," Abernathy said.

She has captured him, Mordred shouted in their minds, and he gave a trill of victory echoed by many voices of an army they could not see.

Dr. Abernathy stumbled in his oration.

Chilled by the cacophony, Elizabeth looked into the crystal ball and was suddenly blinded by crystal walls. Then Mordred swam into view, a triumphant leer on his face.

Behind him, she saw something move, a figure caught up in what looked like mirrors. As she focused, the scene cleared. Merlin stood surrounded by a cave of crystal. He beat his fists against the sides of the huge faceted stones.

Then the scene morphed. The crystal gave way to a room in a modern building, Merlin's magical robes to a suit coat and vest. And finally, the face. His long, gray beard disappeared, revealing beneath pajamas of all things. The gray mane hanging over his shoulders shortened into well maintained silver haircut. The man crept around the room, poking and prodding the walls, trying the windows, looking for anything to use to escape. Then, he stiffened as if suddenly knowing he was being watched. He turned and stared straight into Elizabeth's eyes. The eyes were the same—piercing, timeless, full of sad wisdom.

With a start, she recognized Valentin Knight.

Where are you? she sent.

Lady of Avalon, is that you? I need your help.

He is still caught up in the legend, Elizabeth realized.

Anubis moved into view and addressed Knight. *Grand Mage Merlin, mentor of the Once and Future King. Help your lady complete the ritual and you will be free of this witch forever.*

Guinevere made it home from her morning with Lancelot and fobbed off inquires by claiming she'd fallen asleep in a meadow. "The summer days are so beautiful. I dozed in the sun."

Hester accepted her story, but Leigh studied her more carefully. Guinevere ran into the kitchen to escape her, then up to her room, where she stretched out on the bed, remembering her morning with Lancelot, retracing every touch, every kiss, as if it had been her first time. And indeed, it had felt like it. With Lancelot, her body and heart sang as one. She knew this was true love. Perhaps this was why her womb had not quickened. Because her heart had remained lukewarm. She loved Arthur, but more as a companion, a friend. With Lancelot, she felt as if she were on fire.

That evening went smoothly, she thought. She kept her mind and eyes off

Lancelot until he called for the harper to play a love ballad. The first song praised the beauty of a man's intended, and the company sang along at the chorus. The second told the tale of star-crossed lovers, the lady betrothed to a lord to seal alliances but whose heart belonged to a gallant knight. Carataos' face might be marred, but his voice was as beautiful as a lark welcoming in the sun on the first spring morning free from frost. Light and sweet as the lilac bush when singing of beauty, but in a sad song, haunting as the moon just glimpsed behind heavy clouds or a shadow barely seen, flitting between trees, ghostly and ominous.

Guinevere wiped tears from her cheeks once he finished, then looked to find Mordred studying her. Flustered, she tried to cover her reaction. "His voice is very moving, don't you find, Sir Mordred?"

"He is well trained, but perhaps the matter of the song affected you more?"

Guinevere tossed her blond curls. "What of you, sir? Do you pine for some lovely lady tucked away in her father's house, but promised to another?"

Mordred snorted at her remark and called for more of the wine Lancelot had brought from King Hoel.

As if he sensed the tension, Carataos began a lively jig and many people got up to dance while others pounded their mugs in time with the music, sloshing mead on the table. Guinevere slipped out once Mordred joined in the revelry.

Summer grew into fullness, and Guinevere had never been so happy. Still Arthur did not return, and she settled into life in Camelot without him but with her love, the knight from France. She had grown used to Arthur's absence during the campaigns against the Saxons. Now as he sealed the peace, she became wily in ways to slip off and spend time with Lancelot. One night quite late, a slight noise in her chamber woke her. She sat up, her bed covering falling from her, but before she could cry out, Lancelot unshuttered his lantern and revealed himself.

"Lance, what are you doing? Mordred is more than suspicious," she whispered.

"Nobody saw me, love. I couldn't sleep thinking of you lying so nearby."

And so he took to sneaking into her chambers more often and it seemed no one was the wiser. He left while the owl still hunted the field mice, well before the morning lark stirred, and they thought themselves safe.

One night after he left her, she could not sleep, remembering his lips, his touch. Restless, she went to the window to watch the deep purple sky dotted with stars lighten to lavender and wait for sunrise. She heard the stable door open and one of Mordred's men led out a dun gelding. At the end of the yard, Mordred met him. They stood a while, talking low, but they were too far away for her to hear. Then the man mounted and rode off, walking the horse to keep quiet until he reached the road leading across the meadow.

Guinevere went back to bed, trying to imagine how she'd learn the purpose of this secret mission. Next morning as soon as she could, she told Lancelot what she'd seen. He spoke to Mordred that night.

"Sir Mordred, do you have need for a group to ride out to see to the peace? Have you heard of any Saxons about?"

Mordred's thin lips formed into a dour smile. "No, my lord. We have well and truly defeated those yellow-haired beasts." He speared his venison and ate.

Lancelot waited until he swallowed the mouthful. "Have you news from our king?"

"Nothing, my lord." Mordred sat back with his ale and called for a battle song from Carataos. It was loud and long, stopping Lancelot's questions.

But a few days later, toward evening, a commotion sounded in the meadow and soon destriers appeared, the mount of knights. A white stallion led the group, followed by a standard bearer with Arthur's coat of arms flying in the breeze. Sir Kay and Sir Lamorak accompanied him, but no others of the Round Table. The horses charged into the practice yard and clattered to a halt near the door. Arthur jumped from his stallion and entered the hall.

"Where is Gwen?" he shouted.

Chapter 19

When Kate saw Arnold's group, she reached for her sidearm, but Leo grabbed her arm. "Trust me," he said.

"I want some answers," she snapped and pointed the gun at Arnold. He saw it was a Glock, probably a G33 subcompact, but it was hard to see in this light.

He raised his hands in the air even though Leo could probably disarm her. Frank and Preston did the same. They each sported little red dots above their hearts.

"What's going on?" Arnold asked.

"You're the ones sneaking in here intent on—" she shook her head. "What are you doing? Was it you?" She pointed her chin at the others.

"Was it us what?" Arnold asked

"Did you kidnap him?"

"Who?"

"Don't play Abbott and Costello with me. Mr. Knight."

"Wait, you're all out here looking for Mr. Knight?"

"Yes."

"Knight is missing?"

She took two more steps toward Arnold and studied his face. Then she holstered her Glock. "You really didn't know."

"Of course not."

"Then what the fuck are you doing here?"

Just then Ken came marching around the other side of the house, hands in the air, a look of chagrin on his face. Tyrone was behind him, gun trained on his back.

"Stop," Tyrone commanded. His gaze darted from Kate and Leo to Arnold and his group. "What the fuck is going on?"

Frank slapped his knee, guffawing. "You got caught."

"Oh, shut up," Ken said.

Tyrone pointed his gun at Frank. "I said, what the fuck is going on?"

Arnold noted Knight's team favored Glocks. Tyrone's looked like a standard G31. It would be his second choice.

Kate stepped forward. "That's what I'm trying to ascertain, sir. They didn't take Mr. Knight."

"How do you know?" Tyrone asked.

"This is Leo Strickland. He's in the Secret Service. Assigned to the Le Clair family."

"Le Clairs? As in President George Le Clair?"

"That's right," Leo said. "We're here investigating a financial hack that originated from Mr. Knight's personal computer."

Tyrone stared for a few seconds. "That's impossible."

"We felt the same way, but the trail is solid," Arnold said.

"And who are you?"

"Name's Arnold. Head of Le Clair security," Arnold never gave anyone his last name.

"Man, I traced it back here and I don't make those kinds of mistakes," Preston shouted.

Tyrone pointed the Glock at him and Preston started to cry, much to Arnold's delight. He bit his lip to stop from smiling.

"Night Wing here is one of the best," Leo said.

"Did you say Night Wing?" Tyrone lowered his gun. "You the guy who hacked Wall Street the day Congress gutted the Dodd-Frank Act?"

"That's me." Preston said, recovering from his scare.

Damn it, how come everyone knew this except me? Arnold thought.

"Mr. Knight is missing?" Arnold asked.

Tyrone studied Kate, who nodded, then holstered his Glock. "We found him gone at 2:00 am. No notice."

"Is a vehicle missing?"

"Yes, in fact."

Preston snickered. "Maybe he went to see his girlfriend."

Tyrone actually bared his teeth at Preston, who blanched and moved behind Arnold.

Arnold gestured to the rest of Tyrone's security team who had gathered behind him. "Obviously you think there's foul play."

"We do. Mr. Knight stopped driving a few years back. He never goes out without at least one bodyguard."

"The Le Clair computer has been locked by a military grade encryption algorithm that originated from Mr. Knight's computer. Our plan was to infiltrate the house and override the encryption."

"Well—" Preston began.

"Shut up," Arnold snapped.

"A financial hack, you say?" Tyrone asked.

Arnold dug his toe into the ground, then looked up. "It looks like Mr. Knight stole the Le Clair's fortune and has absconded with it."

"Why would he do that? The man is a billionaire," Tyrone asked.

"Did Knight leave his computer?" Arnold asked.

Kate looked to Tyrone for permission to speak and he nodded. "Yes," she said. "We can prove what we're saying. All this is on his system."

Tyrone gestured for Arnold's group to enter the house. They walked in the back door, through a gleaming kitchen complete with an expansive Typhoon Bordeaux granite island in the middle and an eight burner gas range with a side grill. Arnold kept his eyes peeled as they moved into the hallway.

Preston pushed past the security teams. "Where is his office?"

"This way," Kate said and escorted them to Knight's study. An expansive oak desk took up most of the room, which Preston took possession of. Books filled one wall. The desk was lit by a green banker's lamp.

One of Tyrone's security team escorted a young woman into the room, brunette with striking gold-flecked brown eyes.

"This is Sylvia. She does our cyber security work. She'll be watching you." Tyrone pointed to Preston.

Preston pulled out a black box and hooked Knight's computer and his laptop up to it. Sylvia bent to help. They ran a few more cables to what looked to Arnold like an external hard drive, then Preston settled back in the black leather chair. Arnold felt apprehensive as Preston turned on Knight's computer.

The group crowded behind the two computer experts to watch.

A log-on screen appeared.

Preston typed furiously and Kate grew uneasy.

"Sylvia, please tell us each step Preston is taking," Tyrone said.

"Certainly, sir. Preston is running a program to find Mr. Knight's log-on ID and his system password. Once we're in—"

"We're in," Preston announced.

"Now, he's looking for the key to unlock the ransomware. Mr. Knight has probably left it—"

"Got it," Preston announced.

Kate raised an eyebrow in surprise.

"Now he's looking for the encrypted system file," Sylvia explained.

A list of files filled the screen. Preston scrolled down and highlighted one. Kate leaned in. "Let me see this."

Preston opened the program. Only one name listed—Gerald Le Clair. He clicked on the name and showed Kate the code that had captured the Le Clair computer.

Kate frowned. "I'll have to trust you on that."

"Now, he will decrypt the encrypted file. Just to be sure, we'll decrypt the Le Clair drive," Sylvia explained as Preston went to work.

After a series of confirmations, he sat back. "That part's done."

Arnold called Gerald. "We've decrypted the computer. Check your system now. Preston says to reboot it."

"Reboot?"

"That means restart it."

"Are you sure this is safe?"

"Yes."

"Why are you talking in a normal tone? I thought you were going in dark."

"When we got here, we found Knight's security team searching the premises. Seems like Mr. Knight is missing."

"Missing?"

"That's right."

"But, what does this mean? Was he kidnapped? Maybe he isn't behind this after all."

"It could be, but let's take this one step at a time. Next, we're looking for your money." Arnold nodded for Preston to continue.

Preston worked with both Kate and Arnold watching him closely. Dana continued her play-by-play. "Now we're looking for the transactions that moved the Le Clair money."

"Strange," Preston suddenly said.

"What?" Kate and Arnold asked in unison.

"The transfer originated from this computer, but there's no trace of any deposits into Knight's accounts."

"He's into Mr. Knight's accounts?" Tyrone asked in alarm.

"Dude, what did you think I would do?"

"But, how did you get in?" Tyrone asked, walking closer to the desk.

"Please," Preston said with disdain.

Tyrone started to say something else, but Preston put his palm out, interrupting him. "He hasn't opened any new accounts or made any transactions in the amounts he stole or in amounts that add up to them. Knight doesn't have the money."

Arnold groaned and put his face in his hands. "But you said you'd found it."

"Hold on, dude," Preston said. "All is not lost. Maybe somebody used Knight's computer to do the hack. I'll keep looking, but it may take a little while."

"How long?" Arnold said.

Preston sighed dramatically and looked up at the ceiling as if appealing to a higher power. "Like, how do I know?"

"An hour? A day? How long?"

"A day? Please!" Preston was the picture of offended pride.

Arnold waved his arm. "Just keep looking."

One of Tyrone's team ran into the room. "Sir, we may have found something on the traffic cams."

"What?"

"Knight's car."

Tyrone looked at Arnold. "I realize your priority is your employer's money, but mine is finding Knight, so if you'll excuse me."

"May I come?" Arnold asked. "Maybe I can help."

Arnold's cell rang. He checked the name and answered immediately. "Preston says it might not have been—"

Gerald interrupted him, his voice urgent. "We have information about Valentin."

"Wait," Arnold said to Tyrone, who was heading out of the room.

Gerald continued. "I just asked the guardian of the temple about the ritual and he said Knight has contacted Elizabeth on the inner planes."

"Where is he?"

"He doesn't know. He's not only been kidnapped. He is under some heavy spell. He seems to think he's Merlin and that Nimué has taken him to the crystal cave."

"What the fuck?" Arnold shook his head. He tried not to use that kind of language, but this situation kept pulling it out of him.

"What?" Tyrone asked.

Arnold held up a finger, listening to Gerald.

"It makes a kind of sense. Both Anne and Michael are now reenacting the Arthurian story on the astral."

Arnold ran a hand over the top of his head. How was he going to explain this to Tyrone?

Gerald went on. "I think whoever has glamoured Knight also took the money. Trace him. In the meantime, Katherine and I will look for him in other ways."

"Katherine?" Arnold shouted. "That doesn't sound good."

"She felt something was wrong and showed up. She's a gifted psychic and is ready to help her daughter and grandson."

Arnold knew he'd said this last for Katherine's benefit.

"We'll let you know as soon as we have anything concrete."

"Roger that," Arnold said, although how Gerald could call what he and Katherine were doing concrete escaped him. He would trust their results though.

He explained what had happened to Tyrone, who just shook his head.

Kate put her hand on his shoulder and said, "It's hard getting used to these mystical types."

Leo laughed. "And yet, they get results."

"Let's go look at those traffic cams," Tyrone said. "We can rescue him before the woo-woo does." He waved for Sylvia to follow them.

Guinevere came down the steps slowly, her heart beating as fast as a captured bird's, but when she reached the main hall, Arthur spread his arms in welcome. "My love," he said, and hugged her close.

She returned the squeeze, then kissed his mouth. "I am glad to see you, my lord. You didn't send word. We would have prepared a special celebration."

"I finished up in Caerleon, so rode swiftly. The rest of the men will arrive in a few day's time. Then we can celebrate."

"That is excellent news," she said. "Mordred said you would be another month."

He frowned. "Yes, Mordred."

She studied his face. He seemed a bit withdrawn, maybe too careful, but it could just be the fatigue from a long, hard ride.

Lancelot appeared in the doorway.

Arthur's smile lit the room like the sun coming out from behind a bank of dark clouds. "Lance!" The two hugged as men do, pounding each other's backs. "It is good to see you, brother."

Guinevere relaxed. He didn't know.

Mordred's face darkened like an impending thunderstorm, but he said nothing.

The household was in a flurry to unpack the small group's gear, then feed them. Several went off to their wives and children and squeals of delight sounded from afar. The grooms appeared to take the horses down to the stable to tend them and give them their grain. Likewise, boys appeared to lead the dogs to the kennels to feed them, tend their paws, and treat any injuries. A great baying set up as the rest of the dogs greeted them.

Arthur washed up and changed, then met Lancelot and Mordred in the hall to eat. Ronan limped into the room and Arthur rose to greet his old retainer. "Please, sit with us. I'm telling the news."

Guinevere's stomach threatened her if she ate, so she took up her spinning and sat in a corner, close enough to overhear, but she only listened to the tenor of their voices. Lancelot's clear baritone voice played havoc with her concentration and she tangled the thread twice before disciplining herself to concentrate. She watched the two men in her life, Arthur with a fair face, cheeks reddened by the sun. Lancelot with his clear brow and dark, mysterious eyes. They bent their heads together, one golden as a sunflower's face, one black as a raven's wing, Lancelot offering his counsel and friendship, Arthur accepting with no hesitation. What would she do?

Lancelot was the love of her life, the love spoken of in ballads and poems, the man who set her ablaze with his touch, who settled her heart with his companionship. She was easy with him, never felt self-conscious, always in harmony. Now that she'd found him, now that they'd loved, how could she live without him?

Yet her duty lay with Arthur. He was a kind man, careful, thoughtful, a strong leader. She liked him, loved him in her way. But he did not light the passion in her that Lancelot did. She did not kindle under his attentions. Her hope that true love would yield a child had not proven true. She had not conceived. She'd hoped for it, but last week had brought another disappointment.

Her eyes strayed to Mordred, and it startled her to find him watching her. She nodded, then lowered her eyes to her spindle. She must give Arthur a son. Otherwise, would the clans choose Mordred? She dreaded this. Something dark and devious lay in secret at the center of that one's heart, a worm suddenly discovered at the center of a red rose.

That night, after welcoming Arthur into her arms and trying to push thoughts of Lancelot away, she lay quiet for a time, then broached the subject. "My Lord, I am disappointed that I am not carrying your heir yet."

Arthur turned toward her and kissed her forehead. "There is time yet."

"It is kind of you to say, but perhaps I cannot conceive." Tears filled her eyes. "I fear I am barren and you need an heir."

"Oh, Gwen, my love." He wiped her cheeks with a corner of the bedclothes.

She took a deep breath and plunged forward. "I fear Mordred will not be a good leader."

His hand stilled. "Has he done anything?"

"Not really. There's just something about him I don't trust. As if he's hiding something or he is holding some deep grudge."

Arthur lay silent for so long she thought he'd drifted off to sleep. Then he said, "We still have time, my love."

She propped up on her elbow. "Arthur, I want you to listen. If I do not conceive, perhaps you send me away and take another."

He grabbed her and pulled her against him. "Never! I would never send you away for such a thing."

"But, my Lord, you must have an acceptable heir. It is your duty."

He put his finger to her chin and turned her face to him. "It is not so long ago that the clans chose the king."

"But you are the High King—"

He interrupted her. "It matters not."

"The clans have another custom. It is acceptable to break our handfasting and take another for any reason." She watched him in the dim candlelight.

He just shook his head.

"You have united England," she whispered. "Would you have all you've fought for overturned by a barren womb?" Then she laid a finger on his lips before he could answer and blew out the candle.

Chapter 20

Arnold restrained himself from asking how Tyrone's team had gotten access to the traffic cams. Instead, he watched Sylvia track Knight's car as soon as it hit Highway 190. Once it reached Interstate 495, the silver Jaguar XJ was easy to trace. They followed it into Georgetown, but lost it under tree limbs until it reemerged in a street lined with brownstones. The car parked and a figure emerged. The image was too fuzzy to be sure, but the height and weight looked like Knight. Except he seemed to be wearing his pajamas. He walked under the trees and it was impossible to say exactly which house he went into.

"Run these addresses. See what names pop up," Tyrone said.

"Yes, sir," Sylvia bent close to the screen, her big black glasses sliding down her nose a bit.

Arnold wondered about this mania for clunky glasses. What these kids saw in fifties' fashion, he'd never know. He shook his head and refocused.

The owners of all the buildings in a four-block radius popped up.

"Any rentals?" Arnold asked.

"That will take some digging," she replied.

"Check the owners first. Start with these four houses, then expand. See if the police or FBI have anything on them. Find their employers."

She typed for a few minutes, then sat back. "These houses here," she opened a tab that displayed the traffic cam shot, "are owned by these people." She opened another tab that listed the real estate in the area.

Tyrone and Arnold leaned over her shoulder and they read the list.

Mr. Stephen Wood

Ms. Margaret Schuster

Mr. Robert Jones

Ms. Viviane Lake

"Run a quick check on these names," Arnold said.

"Yes, sir."

Arnold gestured for Tyrone to step aside. "He was in his pajamas. Any sign of dementia?"

Tyrone shook his head. "Sharp as a tack."

"When did he last have a physical exam?"

"I don't really keep up with that," he said. "Let's look at these owners before we dig into his medical history."

Arnold always kept up with the medical history of the Le Clairs. He believed in being thorough. "But, why would he suddenly drive off in the middle of the night not even dressed?"

Tyrone shook his head and moved back behind Sylvia. She pulled up four files and displayed them side by side. They all read through them, searching for any connections to Knight.

"This Wood guy works for an oil and gas lobbying firm."

"A possibility. Maybe they want to stop Knight's new project."

"But they've rented the property," Sylvia pointed out.

"To whom?"

She squinted at the screen. "Mr. and Mrs. Thomas Redman. Police officer and teacher."

"Do we have pictures of these people?"

Sylvia worked for a few seconds and pictures popped up. She pointed them out by name.

"Wait," Kate said from behind them. "Doesn't she look familiar?"

Tyrone nodded. "She does. Think she has any aliases?"

Sylvia grabbed the picture and opened a face recognition program. "The same woman appeared with four names, Viviane Lake, Alice Bailey—"

"Alice Bailey, my ass," Arnold spit out.

"What?"

"She's a famous psychic. And she's dead."

Sylvia kept reading, the light from the computer screen reflecting off her glasses. "Simone Weil, and Nina Lockhart."

"Nina," Kate shouted.

Sylvia jumped, almost knocking over her coffee mug.

Who'd had time to make coffee, Arnold wondered.

"Nina Lockhart. That name rings a bell," Tyrone tapped his chin, thinking. "I believe she's on the list of people admitted to the house for Mr. Knight's magical activities." He said this last with just a shade of distaste.

Arnold smiled, remembering his initial distrust of the Le Clair's mystical goings-on. It took a while for a practical man of action to see that magic produced results and even longer to admit it to fellow operatives.

"Let's run a full background check on this Nina," Arnold suggested.

"We should have a dossier. We research everyone who has regular access to Knight," Tyrone said. He ordered one of his team to go fetch it.

"Wait," Sylvia said. She waved them over to the computer screen running the traffic cam images. They watched a group emerge from under the canopy of trees. Knight shuffled between a man and a woman, his arms over their shoulders. The man and woman wore black clothes and baseball hats.

Arnold pointed at the screen. "Do they ever look up?"

"No, sir," Sylvia said.

The group rolled Knight into the back of a white van. The woman climbed in after him, and the man got in the front and drove off. The next camera picked them up as they merged onto 35th Street NW and followed them down to the river where they went through the Canal Street Tunnel. When they emerged onto the George Washington Memorial Parkway, two more identical vans were spread over two lanes. Two vans stayed on the Parkway and the third merged onto Lee Highway. Sylvia split the screen. On the Parkway, another van merged from the next exit.

"It's a service van. There are thousands in the D.C. area."

"But at this time of night?"

Arnold nodded. "True, but food delivery, cleaning services—they're all out in the wee hours."

"Could you get a license plate?" Tyrone asked

"Looks like it's been deliberately smudged," Sylvia said.

"Blow it up. Look for any identifying marks," Tyrone instructed.

"That will take a few minutes," Sylvia said.

"Let us know when you have something."

Tyrone's man arrived with Nina's dossier. "Want to check out Ms. Lockhart?" Tyrone asked.

Arnold and Leo accompanied Tyrone into the dining room where he unfastened the documents and spread them on the dark table. He switched on the chandelier above. "Be my guest. I'm going to go see if the rest of my team has found anything."

Arnold and Leo went to work.

Guinevere went down to breakfast the next morning late and found that Mordred and his men had left before dawn.

"Did they say why?" she asked.

"It's nothing to worry about," Arthur said, but she could tell something troubled him. There was something he wasn't telling her.

Lancelot sat at the table pushing porridge around in his bowl with a wooden spoon. The silver cutlery only came out on diplomatic occasions. "Did he speak with you before he rode?" he asked. Apparently Arthur hadn't shared his concerns with Lancelot either.

The rest of Arthur's men rose from their table at the far end of the room and went out to the yard, leaving the three of them alone for the first time since Arthur had returned home.

"I was still abed," Arthur said. "Perhaps he was called back to Lothian on urgent business."

"But to leave without speaking to you?" Lancelot asked.

Arthur shrugged. An uncomfortable silence settled over the room. Lancelot avoided Arthur's eyes and studied the table in front of him as if the answer to Mordred's departure lay there. Guinevere watched steam rise from her bowl. If they were not careful, Arthur would know something was wrong. If he didn't know already.

Guinevere shook off her fear. She mixed honey into her bowl and took a bite. "Yum," she said, "I love it when cook has berries for the porridge."

Arthur seemed to gather himself up and with an effort smiled. "Yes, it's good to be home."

"What are your plans, my lord? Will you ride east soon?" Lancelot asked.

"I want to get caught up with Ronan on how things are here. Walk through town. Check with the heads of the guilds. Look at the fields. Perhaps we can talk tomorrow."

"As you wish, my lord."

Arthur reached over and put his hand over Lancelot's. "Arthur, my friend. Call me Arthur."

Lancelot nodded and his shoulders seem to relax. "It's good to have you home, Arthur."

The High King looked back and forth between them, something in his face making Guinevere uneasy. Then he said, "You two are my best friends."

Guilt twisted her stomach and she pushed her porridge away. Lancelot stood and touched Arthur's shoulder. "I will always be true to you," he said.

And yet we have already betrayed him, she thought.

Guinevere did not see much of either man in the next few days. Arthur visited with the guild masters and inquired about the state of the crops and the livestock, then met with his closet counselors to discuss his plans for the rest of the summer. At least that's what she presumed he was doing. He came to bed late and did not disturb her sleep, although she feigned it. She lay listening to his breath soften and become regular as he fell into sleep.

She yearned for Lancelot's touch, but did not dare seek him out. Nor did he look for her. At meals, they were a bit stiff in their interactions, both deferring to Arthur. If he felt anything was off, he did not show it.

A few days after Arthur's return, the rest of his knights and fighting men arrived, and Guinevere was driven off her feet taking care of the household, helping Leigh by foraging for healing herbs for those injuries that occur even in peace time, seeing that the food stores would not be overdrawn. The harvest looked promising. She sat at table, listening to the stories of their adventures, the news from the clans, entertaining the knights. Heilyn, the old harper, enjoyed the addition of Carataos, and the two conspired to play many ballads that were rarely heard. One night they had a harping contest that had the hall stomping and cheering.

But a week later, Mordred arrived bringing with him Iddawe, Melehan, Agravain, and a group of soldiers. Mordred strode into the great hall with the kings of the west surrounding him. He called out for Arthur as if he were a servant.

Arthur arrived after Mordred had bellowed his name a few more times. "What is this racket?" he asked, as if he were addressing naughty children. "Iddawe, Melehan, welcome to Camelot. Agravain, it is good to see you again. Had I known you were coming, we would have chambers ready. But come, sit." He looked to Guinevere, who hovered in the passageway behind him. "Please order ale and food for our friends. They look thirsty from their dusty ride."

"That won't be necessary," Mordred said. "We will not take ale from the hand of a dishonorable woman."

An ominous silence fell on the company. Arthur glared at Mordred, then finally said, "I offer you the hospitality of my hall and you come here to insult my lady?"

"We come here, the rulers of all the lands you have brought together under your banner, to speak with you about a weighty matter. Let us adjourn to the meeting hall."

Arthur turned to Ronan. "Let all the knights know we will assemble with Sir Mordred's guests in the High Hall in one hour."

Guinevere fled up the stairs to their chambers, then looked wildly around. It had come, the moment she dreaded had come. They would tell her secret. These men would tear apart her heart like a rabbit among hounds, her true love that had finally ignited her spirit and made her life full of joy and hope. Their vile words would degrade the union of their bodies. Her shoulders shook with her weeping and she sank down on the floor next to the bed, arms around her legs, her head on her knees.

How could she explain to Arthur that she loved him as a friend, honored him as a wise sovereign, had never wanted to harm him, but that Lancelot—

he was like a bright comet that had swooped in and lit up the night sky of her heart, setting her ablaze? She could no more have resisted him than she could have resisted taking her next breath.

The door opened and she heard footsteps. Hands reached down and came to rest on her shoulders. "Oh, my darling Gwen. I am so sorry."

Surprise choked her tears. "You? Sorry? It is me who is sorry, my lord."

"I knew it was a marriage of duty, but I hoped you would come to love me."

"Oh, Arthur," Guinevere leaned into his warmth. "I do love you, but not like . . ." Sobs overwhelmed her again. How could he still be so good?

"Mordred sent a messenger to me in the west telling me about you and Lance. I rode here not to stop you, but to stop him from harming either of you."

She looked up into his face, astonished by what he'd said.

"I can't explain it, Gwen, but I love you both. You as my wife and Lance as my heart's brother. What can I do?"

He was lost. His eyes begged her for an answer.

Resolve straightened her spine. She sat beside him on the bed. "You must do as I said when you first came home. You must send me away."

"No, I could never—"

"You must, Arthur. Say I have not given you an heir. Send Lancelot back to France. Then you can marry again and produce a son to contest with that Mordred." She spit out the name.

"I must go speak to the knights who've supported me."

"Should I come down?"

"I think you must."

Arthur left and Guinevere looked around the room at the familiar dressing table, the bed, her chest of clothes. Where would she go? Perhaps she could return to Anglesey, live in that small cottage that nestled at the top of a cliff overlooking the sea. It was lonely, yes, but people would shun her anyway. Perhaps she could escape to France with Lancelot, live out their days herding sheep or cultivating grapes. But he was King Hoel's nephew and could no more escape court politics than she could. He would not be shunned. Damn the Christians and their ridiculous ideas. Her marriage contract with Arthur under clan law was the longest—five years. She had stayed with him seven already. According to the old ways, she would be free to go with no repercussions.

She walked over to the wooden chest that held her cloths, ran her fingers over the mirror that had been a gift from her father on her wedding, opened her jewel box and looked at the amber necklace she had worn the first day Lancelot had arrived. She called for Hester and instructed her to pack enough clothes for her, but to leave her finery behind.

"What is happening, m'lady?"

"I don't know, Hester, but I must be prepared to leave. Please don't ask me any more questions. I don't know how to answer them."

Hester came and wrapped her arms around her mistress. The tears she'd been holding back fell.

"Now, now, mistress. All will be well. You'll see."

But Guinevere was certain this was far from the truth. She dried her eyes and dressed in a plain, black dress, then made her way downstairs.

When she arrived in the hall, the knights sat around the table, with those she knew to be loyal to Arthur clustered around him. Galahad, Tristan, Kay, even Gawain and Gareth sat on his side of the table, ignoring where their banners decorated the walls.

Mordred sat on the other side of at the Round Table with several of his men, although they didn't belong there. Agravain stood behind him. Gaheris sat close to him. The rest of the knights seemed confused and sat, tense, hands hovering near their belts, although no one carried weapons into this chamber.

All Mordred's men muttered when she walked further into the room and took her place standing behind Arthur. Then she noticed another empty seat. Lancelot was not here.

"Sir Mordred from Lothian has called us together to consider what he calls a weighty matter," Arthur began. "He has seen fit to insult the queen. Let him explain."

Mordred pointed to Lancelot's empty seat, but before he could speak, Arthur spoke up.

"Where is Sir Lancelot?" Arthur asked. "Sir Tristan, would you go with Ronan to look for him?"

"My Lord, I would be loath to leave your side." Tristan eyed Mordred.

"Please," Arthur said in a soft voice.

"As you say, my king."

The men spoke in low whispers among themselves as they waited, the room filling with the kind of tension that forebode an enormous thunderstorm. But this storm would not bring refreshing rain and wind. It would bring blood.

Tristan rushed into the High Hall, Ronan struggling behind, his face red. "He is gone, Arthur. Sir Lancelot asked the stable boy to ready his horse, and Lancelot rode out over an hour ago."

Mordred rose, a look of savage victory on his face. "One traitor has fled. The other stands here bold faced in her shame."

Arthur just shook his head.

Mordred pointed his finger at Guinevere. "I accuse you of adultery. You have lain with the king's best knight while he was away. You and Lancelot are traitors."

"Do you have proof of this?" Arthur asked.

Agravain stood. "I myself saw them in wonton display in a meadow, thinking themselves undetected. Lancelot snuck into my lord's own bed in his absence, such was his villainy."

"I confess I have been disloyal, my lord," came Guinevere's quiet voice. "I am ready to be set aside."

Arthur stood and motioned her to stand beside him. He controlled his face, but his eyes spoke his grief. "You have broken your vows of marriage and lain with another man. I reject you and send you to the nunnery in Caredegion where you will live out your life."

Not there, Guinevere thought. She tried to speak, but could only nod her head. Tears flooded her eyes. Lancelot had deserted her. Arthur was sending her to Caredegion, a prison to her. A deep pain tore through her abdomen and she groaned, grabbing at the air. Leigh's hand grasped hers.

"I'm here," she said. "Your horse is ready. I will ride with you."

"I will send a few soldiers to accompany you, Gwen." Arthur stood staring at her with yearning in his eyes. Then he moved to her and whispered in her ear. "Please forgive me."

Suddenly, Anne's body jerked and her hands reached for her rounded belly. A moan came from her lips. Then she raised one hand and groped in the air for support.

Elizabeth rushed over and grabbed her hand. "I'm here."

The nurse probed Anne's abdomen. Anne cried out and tried to push the nurse's hands away.

Emma looked up at Elizabeth. "We've got a contraction."

Elizabeth stroked Anne's cheek, calling her name. "Time to come back now," she crooned.

Anne's eyes fluttered open, but remained unfocused. Then she closed them again and remained quiet.

Emma noted the time of the first contraction and checked Anne's vitals. Anne seemed to have settled back into her trance.

Elizabeth gathered herself and returned to finish the ritual. They were making headway, but they still had to stop Mordred from trying to enter the baby.

Chapter 21

Elizabeth nodded to Abernathy for him to continue. He took a deep breath and resumed his part of the Isis ritual.

"In the dark cave, Horus gradually regained his sight and when he did, he set out to avenge himself on Set. The Neter was so overjoyed at his clear vision again that both sides of the Nile burst into spring as he made his way down it.

"He gathered those loyal to him until his army stretched across the sands and they fought many battles with Set, but the final one took place at Edfu. In their boats, the forces of Horus and Set drew near to each other among the rapids of the First Cataract of the Nile. Seeing the greatness of Horus' army, Set took the form of a giant red hippopotamus and appeared over the hill of Elephantine Island.

"Cursing Horus and his mother, he called up a raging tempest. The thunder rolled across the heavens and fell in sheets over the boats of Horus and his army. The wind whipped their sails and beat the water into huge waves that rose over their boats and threatened to swamp them. But Horus held against the tempest, the prow of his craft gleaming like a ray of sun.

"Enraged, Set straddled the Nile and opened his great jaws to devour Horus and his host in one gulp, but Horus, calling upon the magic that was his birthright, expanded into a twelve-foot warrior, holding a harpoon twice his height with a blade as wide as a man. Taking a strong stance, he hurled the harpoon at the hippopotamus just as he opened his jaws the widest, and the blade flew through his mouth and imbedded itself deep into Set's brain.

So did Set, Son of Nut, mate to Nephthys, pass into spirit.

"But even death did not stop him. Once Set stepped over the threshold of this world, he took his grievance to Thoth, who prophesied Horus would defeat Set once and for all, and on that day, his father Osiris would rise from the dead and return to earth, bringing with him his illumined followers and returning the Earth to paradise."

That day has come, came a voice from the center of the temple.

Caught in a swirling vortex, Michael was buffeted by what felt like strong winds. He spiraled around in tighter circles as if he were going down through a funnel. At last, he fell heavily to the ground, the breath knocked out of him. He lay there, gasping, grateful the earth stayed put.

After a minute, he pushed up on his elbows. A tall sycamore tree rose above him, sheltering him from the sun. Where was he?

He'd been riding a horse, desperate to escape Mordred and his supporters. He'd planned on reaching the coast, finding a hiding place. Then he'd search out Guinevere. Arthur would not sentence her to die, surely. He'd send her away somewhere. Perhaps to Avalon. That would be best. He, Lancelot, would find her. They would run away and hide somewhere. Live out a life together.

But where was his horse? He looked around and found himself alone on a high hill. Reaching for his sword, he found nothing. His hands brushed unfamiliar garments. Thick blue leggings that hung loose and a tunic that seemed to button up the front. He'd never seen such clothes before.

A realization rose in his mind like a jousting knight stampeding toward him. He threw his hands in front of his face to stop it, but the thought overtook him.

Michael. My name is Michael.

Lancelot, a second voice replied. *My name is Lancelot.*

Then Anne's face swam up into his memory. Anne laughing. Anne listening. Anne covered in dust sitting under the paw of the Sphinx.

He shook his head against such an improbability.

Anne, my love.

Guinevere, will I ever see you again?

This second voice seemed to think Anne was that famous queen.

What of Guinevere? Where was she? He still yearned for her. Yet Anne had the same honeyed hair, the same fire in her heart. But Anne was his wife, not centuries dead like the famous queen. She laid at home unconscious.

Because of Mordred.

Rage filled him. He had lost these two women because of that bastard. He would find him and kill him. Tear him limb from limb.

Then another memory came. He reached under the collar of his shirt—yes, now he remembered what it was called—and searched wildly for a silver chain. The chain should hold a crystal key, much more powerful than its size suggested. But it was gone.

Stolen by Mordred.

He'd come here to get the crystal key back to save Guinevere.

He shook his head. No, Anne. He'd come to save Anne.

He remembered a huge granite box. A tall Druid telling him to get in. Tahir nodding, telling him everything would be fine. He'd been in Egypt. But he wasn't back there. That must mean his mission wasn't finished. He remembered jumping around in time before getting in the box at the Serapeum—yes, that was where he'd gone. Before that he'd seen through the eyes of Uther, then the Lady of Avalon. His time as Lancelot, however, had been different. More immediate. He'd not been separate from Lancelot. They had been one person.

Michael pushed up from the grass and walked out from under the sycamore tree. He gazed down into the valley. Two armies faced each other. They wore medieval armor and rode courser horses. He crept closer to the edge of the hill.

Two knights rode forward. Michael's vision telescoped, as if he were still partially in the swirling magic of the vortex that moved him through time. He could see them clearly. One sat astride a magnificent white destrier stallion and held a green shield with two golden gryphons back to back on it. Another rode a bay destrier and carried a shield with a purple background and a golden two-headed eagle.

Arthur and Mordred.

The final battle.

Michael had to get down there and recapture the crystal key. Mordred was channeling its power to win this battle and control Anne. Mordred planned on replacing the soul of their child and be reborn instead. He had to stop him. If he was going to change history, this was his chance.

Michael ran along a faint deer path, hugging the hill closely, running low. He came level with the rear of Mordred's group of men and hid behind a cluster of purple willow. Arthur and Mordred had dismounted and moved together in the center of the field. Behind them, far enough to give their lieges privacy, stood two knights on each side, one holding the horses, the other with his hand hovering over his sword ready to defend his leader.

A line of privet bushes jutted into the field farther down. Michael moved toward them, then worked his way out as close to the two leaders as he dared. He crouched in the shadow of the last bush.

"—will not step down," Arthur was saying.

"You have failed the land." Mordred pitched his voice for all to hear. "You have not produced an heir. Your wife and best knight have betrayed you."

Arthur ignored this last part. "I have produced offspring, as you have pointed out."

"In the Beltane ritual. I am the son of the Sun and the Lady." Mordred puffed his chest out.

"And yet you claim to be my son," Arthur answered, his voice calm, but somehow carrying through the whole valley. "You cannot have it both ways."

Mordred glared at him, his eyes so full of a feral rage that Michael's courage wavered. "If you want me to follow the old ways—"

"Old? Are our traditions old already?"

Mordred smiled like a man who hears the trap he's laid snap shut. "I'm glad to hear you say this. If you honor our traditions, you agree to submit to them?"

Arthur hesitated. "What are you asking?"

"Give your life to the scythes. When the grain is cut, let it cut you down as well. Give your life's blood to the fields. Bring fertility and abundance back to Camelot."

"This requires a young and virile man. You are more suited to it than I."

"So you admit to being old? To being impotent?"

Jeers and laughter erupted from Mordred's followers.

Arthur pitched his voice so only Mordred could hear, but Michael was close enough. "Stop this now, Mordred. Tell me what you want."

"I want my birthright."

"Be reasonable. The clans will decide that."

Mordred's face flushed a deep red, the cords of his neck stretching as he screamed, "I want to be High King."

"You are destroying all the good work we have done uniting England. It will come undone—"

"Snake," one of Mordred's men yelled out. "It's an adder." He drew his sword and swung it at the snake.

But the armies had not heard what the knight had said. They only saw the flash of the sword lit by the sun. Shouts rose all around. The knights drew their swords and galloped in, screaming as they rode. Foot soldiers followed, war cries rising everywhere.

Soon mayhem ruled. The battle had begun.

Elizabeth stared at the large crystal ball, shocked by what she'd just heard.

That day has come, the voice had said. And it hadn't been Mordred.

All those assembled gaped at what was forming inside the ancient crystal ball. The faceted depths cleared and Set appeared with the face of an ant-eater carrying a *was* scepter. Mordred stood beside him, his sword drawn.

We have come to finish this war, they shouted in unison.

Abernathy turned to Elizabeth, his face confused, yet he did not voice his question. They both knew this would break the spell of the ritual. This should have been the end of the rite. Traditionally, the story concluded with Thoth's prophecy that one day Horus would defeat Set once and for all. But tonight, something new was happening.

The armies of Set and Mordred formed behind them, growing louder and more menacing, then all at once, they poured through the crystal onto a battlefield.

Before anyone could react, Elizabeth and Abernathy were pulled through with them. The other Lodge members were caught in the whirlwind and followed.

"No," Elizabeth screamed, and looking over her shoulder before the veil closed, saw Anne convulse in another contraction. The baby was coming too quickly.

Then she heard a sound that woke up a distant memory of being a warrior. The singing of a sword slicing through the air. She dodged just in time.

Michael moved toward the place he'd last seen Mordred, intent on recapturing the crystal, dodging men locked in combat. A courser reared above his head, mouth open in a scream, and lashed out with his hoof. Michael dropped and rolled beneath the horse, coming to his feet on the other side. He silently thanked Arnold for his martial arts lessons, but wished the skilled fighter and strategist was here with him now. Arnold, Leo, the whole security team.

He looked for the distinctive shield, saw a flash of purple further on, and moved toward it. A foot soldier lashed at him with the business end of a pike. Michael sidestepped, then reached for his sword. He cursed when he found only his belt. Encumbered by the long weapon, the soldier tried to run, but Michael gave him a hard shove and moved on.

The purple shield seemed to stand out in the sea of men, horses, and banners. He moved toward it again. Another foot soldier stepped in front of him, swinging a halberd. Michael let Lancelot's muscle memory take over, and the man was soon dispatched. Michael pushed down guilt. He picked up the halberd and kept moving forward, dodging horses and grappling men.

A sword swept in front of him, and Lancelot twisted the halberd, hooked the sword, and pulled it from the man's hand.

Nice move, Lance.

Thank you.

Michael shook his head, surprised by the answer, and kept moving. He cut down a foot soldier who ran at him, but then found himself staring at a blue chariot drawn by two Arabian horses with blue plumed headdresses. The chariot sported a green scarab on the front and blue and gold trim.

"What the hell?" Michael stared.

Two men stood in it, one driving the horses, the second with a bow and arrow pointed straight at him. The man loosed the arrow and Michael dove behind two men locked in combat. The arrow pierced the throat of Arthur's man. The chariot bowled past.

Michael backed away from the fray and surveyed the battlefield. Medieval warriors grabbled with each other. A knight rode past and swung his sword at the neck of one of Mordred's men. Then a group of warriors marched by wearing blue and white striped headdresses, gold breastplates, and sandals that laced to the knee. They carried long spears and shields with an emblem that Michael fought to recognize. But it was Egyptian. There was no question.

Then, far in the distance, he saw a tall, golden being, at least seven feet tall if not more, with the body of the man and the head of an ant-eater.

Michael sank to his knees. This was not possible. The Egyptian Neter Set strode across the battle field laying waste with his scepter.

He shook his head. Closed his eyes, then opened them again. But Set remained.

Forget Arnold. They needed Merlin. He looked around wildly for any sign of the wizard.

Chapter 22

Nina watched Valentin Knight rise from in front of a three-foot tall quartz crystal he'd been whispering to and resume pacing. The room she had locked him in was a room ringed with mirrors and lined with large crystals into which she'd whispered spells, spells to confuse the mind, to weaken the will, to ignite in him the overwhelming, irresistible sexual compulsion he'd felt for her so long ago thanks to the spell she'd discovered in her past, a spell coming all the way from the cult of the Goddess Diana. A subliminal tape played into the space, low chanting, whispers and moans, the sounds of lovemaking, all interspersed with Nina's voice speaking the spell over and over too low to be heard clearly.

She wore a long, diaphanous gown, shimmering with iridescent colors, pulling in the eye, confusing the mind. Revealing flesh at certain moments, concealing it at others. She vaguely remembered stealing Merlin's book of spells long ago. Reading it page after illustrated page. Demanding that the trapped wizard explain them all to her. Practicing the spells there until she had perfected them. But somehow it had not been enough. Something had been missing. Because here she was.

Now she was trying again. But this time, she knew that words on a page were not enough. She must have the power of his mind. She would break that beautiful mind, master his will, take his power. This time, with the Le Clair's money and Knight's magical power, she would have it all. Wealth, power, invincibility. She would learn to live long like the old prophets in the Bible. Hundreds of years. She would master magic. She would be rich beyond measure.

She opened the door to the room.

Knight turned to her and spoke in a language she did not recognize. She listened and after a moment, something about it tugged at her deep memory. He walked up to her shaking his head, eyes confused, pleading. He repeated what he'd said. Reached his hands out, begging.

The sound of his words reminded her of the first time she drove south on the M5 and suddenly hearing a different language coming from what she thought was the BBC. After a while, the station identified itself as BBC-Wales. Yes, that was it. She almost laughed, but stopped herself. He was speaking Old Welsh. It was plausible Merlin had spoken that language.

Knight was in too deep. She'd have to back off on the spell. Bring him back a bit, but not too far. She made her way to the sophisticated sound system she'd asked Gregor to install. She turned off the track of herself repeating the spell.

She waited.

"This Nina Lockhart is a piece of work," Arnold said, pushing the bio he'd been reading across the table to Leo. "She's got another alias—Evelyn Apple. There are warrants out on this name in France, England, and the US. I'd have to show these to Elizabeth or Michael, but I think all these names have something to do with Arthurian legend."

"Didn't they say it was Mordred—" Leo scrunched his shoulders in discomfort "—talking through the crystal."

Arnold smiled. "Something like that."

Leo pointed to the laptop screen he was perusing, returning to the world of verifiable facts. "She recently traveled to England. Rented a car in Salisbury. Had to show a driver's license, so she used the Viviane Lake identity. That's how we found this record."

"Did she leave a trail?"

"Nothing I can find. Must have used cash. Think it's worth it to ask one of the hackers to look on security cams?"

Just then Tyrone rushed into the room. "We've got a location for the van."

Arnold and Leo jumped up and followed Tyrone back to the security office.

Sylvia turned the monitor so they could all see. "This was the best image we could find of the license plate of the van."

A close-up of the plate showed it covered with mud.

"We kept changing the colors until we came up with this." AP-016- popped out in the image.

"We couldn't make out the last number, so we ran all ten possibilities. Five of these numbers belong to a laundry service. Those trucks were all at hotels in the greater DC area picking up loads." Sylvia flashed through pictures so fast he lost track.

"Two belong to a food delivery service. They delivered to an Indian restaurant called Indigo and Bistro Bohem, serving Czech food. They were parked behind the business all night."

Tyrone shifted his weight back and forth on the balls of his feet, apparently eager to get on with finding Knight.

"The other three belong to Hertz. Only one has been rented in the last week, by—"

"Viviane Lake," Arnold and Leo said in unison.

"Right," Sylvia said. "How did you guess?"

"Never mind. Where's the van now?"

Sylvia hit a key and an image of the van parked beside a ramshackle warehouse. "On the outskirts of the city on the way to Baltimore."

"Any cams we can hack into?"

"Nothing close enough, sir."

"Who owns the building?"

"A company called Clas Myrddin. It's Gaelic for Merlin's Enclosure," Sylvia said. "We haven't done a background check on it yet."

"More Arthurian references," Leo said. "We can guess what you'll find."

Tyrone nodded. "We're headed out. Keep us alert to any change at the warehouse."

"Yes, sir."

"Let's go."

They headed for the door, but Preston flagged them down. "The money. It's not in Knight's accounts anywhere. It was transferred to accounts in Switzerland and Antiqua."

"Any names?" Arnold asked.

"No, but I did run across a strange company name. Or maybe it's an on-line fantasy game?"

"Let me guess. Clas Myrddin?"

Preston looked annoyed that Leo had stolen his thunder. "How'd you guess?"

"They own a warehouse near Baltimore. They're holding Knight there."

"You found him?"

"We're headed out. Keep trying to get that money back."

"No problem," Preston said.

Arnold imagined there would be all kinds of problems ahead, but patted Preston's shoulder. "Good man."

Preston watched him leave, his mouth open in surprise.

Nina waited a good half hour, watching Knight carefully. He continued to test the walls of the room, moving around randomly at first. Then his movements became more systematic. He went back to one corner and walked the entire perimeter of the room, pushing the mirrors, inspecting the seams between them. Finally, he sat cross-legged in front of a large faceted rainbow quartz about three feet high, placed his hands on either side, and began to tone. He was coming around. She didn't want him fully awake.

Nina took the sacrificial knife from the altar, her fingers running over the gems on the handle. It had been the first item she'd bought on the black market. Another famous artifact, supposedly used to end the life of Pythagoras by one of his disciples. Since then, several dark lodges had used it in ritual sacrifices.

She slipped into the room she'd built to simulate the crystal cave of old and locked the door behind her. Gregor stood guard outside. She walked to Knight's side and crouched beside him, matching his soft chant, harmonizing her breath to his, coming into sync with him. He looked into her face. She sat cross-legged across from him, maintaining eye contact, laying the knife across her lap. The chant softened, then fell away completely.

She reached out and pulled Knight's hands onto his knees, right palm up, left palm down, then matched her palms to his. Pushing forward, knees touching, she stared into his eyes, probing psychically. She found no defenses, only confusion and a soft love for her. Surprised, her heart softened for a moment, but she shrugged it off. This man had refused to teach her what she wanted in the past all because he did not approve of her ambition. She continued penetrating his psyche, diving deeper, searching for the key to unlock his knowledge, to let it spill out like a child come to term, bursting out of the birth canal with a rush of water and blood.

First she found childhood memories, both Merlin's and Valentin's, playing with his brother in the local creek, the Druids riding in, choosing him, taking him away. Valentin being taught by his own parents the basics of magic, the ethical rules. For Merlin, at first lonely nights, his secret crying in his bed, sobbing into his cover. But the growing fascination of lessons. She watched him learn the rudiments of magic, then quickly grow proficient.

Valentin was initiated into a lodge. Nights spent studying, meditating on the Qabalistic Tree. Venturing into eastern methods. She watched the two learn spells for healing, communicating with animals, for invisibility. Divination through water and crystal, sigils and their meaning, the uses of sound. She watched his visions pour out—as Merlin, the need for Arthur's parentage, listened to the chant he used to change the appearance of Uther, saw the once and future king be born, the patient tutoring, coming and going to check on the child. Watching as he grew into a young man.

Valentin's love for all things Arthurian. His lifelong feeling that somehow the once and future king would come again. Merlin's vision of Arthur's marriage to—wait, it was not Guinevere, but some dark-haired beauty she did not recognize. So, was this where the mistake had been made? Then Guinevere and Lancelot locked in passionate throes of lovemaking and Arthur's heart broken at losing them both. The knowledge that Nimué would betray him.

Wait. He'd known?

"Yes, my love, I knew."

Nina jumped, but didn't break contact with Valentin. She opened her eyes.

He was watching her, his gray eyes soft, a sad look on his face. "For this. So that Mordred would come to you. So you would try again."

"No, I did this for myself. I did this to gain your power."

Nina took the knife into her hand and held the point over Knight's heart, pressing hard enough to bring up a ruby red drop of blood. Knight looked down, impassive, then back up at her, pity written on his face. Nina flinched, then redoubled her chant, pouring her desire into it, louder this time. Fueling the spell with her fury at learning that Merlin had submitted to her willingly. A willing sacrifice. This could undo it all. If he died, the benefit would rebound to his spiritual progress and the world at large. But perhaps she could still win his power. She would wound him, leave him alive, her prisoner, until his will broke. He was old. How long could he hold out?

She heard a rustle behind her. "Not now, Gregor," she said between clinched teeth.

She felt the prick of something sharp at her throat.

"Let him go," someone whispered.

Her eyes flew wide. This wasn't Gregor. What was happening?

"Now."

"Never!" Nina turned the sacrificial blade around and slashed at the unseen figure behind her. But the knife found only thin air.

The stiletto at her throat slipped in and severed her carotid artery.

Nina dropped the dagger and grabbed her neck, hot blood spurting over her hand. She looked up.

In the mirror she saw a woman, dressed all in black, a balaclava covering her face. Hazel eyes watched her with detached envy.

Nina panted as more blood ran down the arm onto the floor. Dizzy, she put an arm out to hold herself up, but it slipped and she fell to her side.

Her killer caught her before her head hit the floor and laid her down gently.

"Enjoy your homecoming" the woman whispered.

Nina's breath stopped. Her body shuddered, then went still.

A light opened above her and with a huge surge of joy, she flew toward it.

Chapter 23

Michael crouched down behind a dead horse and tried to get control of his breathing. The animal's mouth was open in a scream, and he unconsciously reached out to stroke its neck. It was one thing to travel back in time and meld with Sir Lancelot du Lac, then find himself in the middle of the final battle that ended Camelot. But Egyptian warriors? The Neter Set? This was some Alice in Wonderland stuff. He had to focus. His job was to retrieve his crystal from Mordred. He had to ignore everything else.

Standing, he searched the battlefield for any sign of the renegade. The Egyptian battalion of foot soldiers fought right in front of him and they seemed to be on the wrong side. This group was making mincemeat out of a cluster of Arthur's soldiers.

Focus. Anne and the baby are depending on you.

But just as he narrowed his vision, none other than Grandmother Elizabeth stood before him, a dagger in one hand, shield in the other, looking quite comfortable with them.

He just stared.

"Michael, is that you?"

She must be here on the astral plane, he thought, her body safe back in the temple.

Then she poked him with the flat of her blade. He felt the cold steel on his arm.

"You're really here?"

"Yes, Mordred and Set pulled us through."

"How— What— This is impossible."

She chuckled, and with a nod said, "Nevertheless, it is happening."

One of Mordred's men loomed up behind Elizabeth, but before Michael could react, an arrow pierced his throat and he fell.

"I must tell you." Elizabeth grabbed his attention again. "Anne is in labor. We have to end this battle correctly."

Guinevere pregnant? With my child? Lancelot's thoughts pushed forward.

Michael shook his head against the tumult of emotion from the knight. "In labor?" he asked.

"Yes. I can't say how long it will be, but labor is progressing rapidly." She looked deep into Michael's eyes, then emphasized each word. "We must stop Mordred from trying to inhabit the child."

"I'll kill him," Lancelot yelled.

"Yes, but that won't be enough," Elizabeth said.

"I'll get the crystal," Michael said.

"I'll be right behind you," she answered.

Michael scanned the sea of men and horses, schooling himself to stop reacting to the bizarre mix of cultures battling before him. His eyes lighted on the purple shield again behind a group of Arthur's men. Gathering his courage, he strode toward it, dodging an arrow on the way. A man came at him with a long knife and he grabbed his forearm and twisted at an extreme angle. The man fell to his knees. Arnold's martial arts training was becoming automatic now. He whirled around.

Mordred was right in front of him, locked in combat with Arthur. Rage filled him, the rage of a husband fighting for the life of his wife and baby. The rage of a lover, fighting the man who'd forced him to leave his beloved. But he was not here to kill him. He was here to steal his power, to take back the powerful crystal key that had already opened too many doors. He reached out to grasp a gleam of silver he saw at the back of Mordred's neck, but he missed his chance as Mordred surged forward, his sword reaching under Arthur's armor and piercing his side.

Arthur screamed, his face etched with agony, and fell to his knees.

Mordred let out a shout of victory. "He is down. Arthur is down."

He closed in to finish the job, but Arthur struggled and raised Excalibur at the last minute, impaling Mordred on the blade. His eyes went wide with pain and shock. His mouth gaped, but no sound came.

Set strode toward them, his long legs eating up the distance.

Mordred pushed at the sword, but his movements were weak and ineffectual. He tried to speak once more, then he slipped into unconsciousness.

Michael rushed up behind Mordred, reached beneath his helmet, and grabbing the silver chain, yanked it off.

Set's eyes went wide and he evaporated like mist under the Egyptian sun.

Arthur looked up at him and smiled. "Thank you, Lance," but before Michael could answer, he was caught up in a whirlwind that blotted out the scene. He felt himself flying up, then he landed with a heavy thud. He lay there, trying to catch his breath. Stretching out his hand, he felt sand.

He squinted into the gloom, but couldn't make out anything. Then he saw a figure approaching him, taller than any human. The figure extended something long toward him and Michael flinched away, trying to evade what he took to be a sword. But the end was rounded and shone a dull gold in the darkness. In the gleam, Michael saw it more clearly. It was a large ankh.

He looked up at the figure and in the gloom made out pointed ears and a snout. Grasping the offered staff, Anubis pulled Michael to his feet.

Anubis leaned down and said, "You did it."

"I did?" Michael asked, but the Great Opener did not answer. He turned and led Michael to the chapel below the sands of the Sphinx where they'd begun this journey.

"But I was in the Serapeum," Michael said.

Anubis walked up the three steps of his pedestal and turned back into stone.

Michael touched the feet of the statue, thanking the Neter, then made his way through the temple, noting that the gold solar disk above Sekhmet's head was missing now. The thieves had been busy while he was away.

He walked up the ramp out into the night. The stars stretched above him, a gibbous moon dimming their glory only a little. Michael headed to Tahir's house, wondering how long he'd been gone. Once he reached the street, a low rumbling came from behind him. The earth trembled. The sound of an avalanche, rocks crashing against each other.

He turned and saw a huge plume of dust rising from what had been the newly opened temple, now choked with rock, sand, and rubble.

Elizabeth stepped toward Arthur and Mordred, but three of his knights surrounded him. Percival moved the quilted padding under Arthur's armor aside. The gash oozed blood when he pulled the fabric up. Elizabeth pushed forward to inspect the wound.

"My Lady," Percival said, "what are you doing here?"

She didn't answer him. Just checked Arthur's vitals. His pulse was weak, his breathing shallow.

Beside her, Gawain took hold of the hilt of Excalibur and pushed Mordred's body off it with his foot. The usurper was dead, but it didn't mean his spirit had left the crystal in her temple back at The Oaks.

Arthur gestured for Sir Bedivere to step closer. Arthur grimaced at the effort to sit up, then said, "Take Excalibur to the lake and throw it into the water. Ride back as soon as you can and tell me what you see."

"But, sire, you cannot mean for me to throw this sword away."

Arthur clasped Bedivere's hand. "Do as I ask, my friend. You will see why once you have done it."

Bedivere took the sword from Gawain and went for his horse.

The fighting around them was drawing down. Word had spread of Mordred's death and many of his men had fled. Some few remained, determined to die with him it seemed.

Elizabeth looked out over the meadow to the edge of the lake and there in the distance, she saw a smudge that grew more distinct as she watched. She laid Arthur back down in the grass, telling Percival to apply pressure to the wound.

"Are you sure, My Lady?"

"Yes, this will save him." She looked around for water, but finding only ale, gave Arthur small sips. After some time had passed, Bedivere ran up to Arthur's side, winded from his ride, and knelt beside him. "I am here, my king."

Arthur's eyes fluttered open. He winced as he took a breath. "Is it done?"

"It is, my liege."

"Tell me what you saw." His voice was barely a whisper.

"The sword cleaved the waters and sank, hilt first."

Arthur shook his head. "This tells me you have not done what I asked. Go back and throw Excalibur into the lake." He pushed Bedivere away with surprising strength.

What is taking the priestesses of Avalon so long to arrive? Elizabeth wondered. *And where is Merlin?*

Elizabeth rose and put her hand above her eyes to block out the sun. She searched the lake. The smudge had grown into the shape of a barge. How long would it take them?

Around her the men were treating the wounded while others stripped Mordred's soldiers of their arms and piled the bodies. She wished there was more she could do, but this was the past. These men, the moaning horses, they had all died hundreds of years ago.

She walked back to Arthur's side and was surprised to see Bedivere getting up from Arthur's side once again shaking his head. He could not have ridden to the lake and back. But this was his third time. Legend had it that this time he would throw Excalibur into the lake.

Mordred's body had been laid out with his sword between his dead hands, his eyes closed. The blood had been washed from his armor.

Arthur stared at him, then looked at Elizabeth with haunted eyes. "What could I have done, My Lady?"

They all thought she was the high priestess of Avalon. "You did your best," she said, kneeling beside him. Gawain had taken off Arthur's helmet. She pushed his hair back from his face. Sweat beaded his forehead.

"Camelot has fallen. The dream is dead," he said.

"Not dead, my liege." Elizabeth turned his face so he was looking into her eyes. "It is postponed. Your dream will become the dream of all of England,

Wales, Scotland, and Ireland. The ideals of chivalry will spread over the world. You will return and bring peace."

His eyes held a look of wonder. "Truly, My Lady?"

Before she could answer, Bedivere approached again, this time with awe written on his face.

Arthur stifled a groan as he rose on his elbows. "Is it done?"

"Truly, my lord."

"What did you see?"

"I saw a hand, a lady's hand, rise above the water and catch the sword."

"The sword is safe." He laid back down, a look of peace on his face.

It was then the priestess arrived and instructed the knights to put Arthur on a litter. The knights lifted him and carried him to the barge, the water rising to their knees. The priestesses got on the barge, surrounding Arthur. Elizabeth stood on the shore watching.

The High Priestess turned to her and bowed. "My Lady, the circle closes. We will bring him to you."

Him? Who are they talking about? she wondered.

Then a whirlwind lifted her and Elizabeth found herself back at The Oaks in the temple. The rest of the lodge stood blinking, trying to orient themselves.

The white van was parked neatly between the painted lines to the left of the one story warehouse. The team listened, but heard nothing except the slight buzzing of a transformer somewhere close by. The aluminum framed windows in front were dark. Arnold signaled for Tyrone and Kate to check the back. They peeled off, one going right, the other left, stepping sharply around the corners, guns drawn. Then they disappeared. Leo checked the van, which was empty except for the hood they'd seen over Knight's head.

"Light in the back on the left." Tyrone's voice sounded quietly in his earpiece. "Flimsy door."

"Copy that," Arnold said.

"There's some strange music playing," Kate whispered.

"Enter on my count. One."

He motioned for Leo and they stood on either side of the front entrance.

"Two."

Tyrone pivoted, gun pointed.

"Three."

Arnold kicked the door. It swung open easily.

He pointed his flashlight and gun into the room and moved forward. A few steps in he stumbled over something large and soft.

Leo pointed his light down.

A man lay on his back, crimson blood pooling under him.

Arnold felt for a pulse. "He's dead, but still warm. She's on a killing spree."

They sprinted through the front room and pushed through the next door, Leo snapping his gun to the right, then front. Arnold covered the left. A bank of electronic equipment filled one wall. Eerie moaning and whispering came from the speakers. On the other side stood a room, brightly lit, filled with mirrors.

They opened the door. Knight sat on the ground staring at the body of Nina. She lay in the same position as the man in the front room, on her back, blood rapidly forming a puddle on the blue Persian carpet beneath her.

Arnold whirled at a slight noise.

A figure detached itself from the wall and moved closer to the light coming through the windows of the room. She stood with her hands away from her body, palms forward, and took a couple more steps toward Arnold. Everyone trained their guns on her.

"Hello, Arnie."

Leo snorted at the incongruity of the nickname.

She pulled off her balaclava.

"Rainey." Arnold lowered his gun. He motioned for the others to do the same. "What are you doing here?"

"Your message said all hands on deck. Didn't you want me?" Her voice was husky.

Leo shot a glance at Arnold. The question sounded like more than a contract killer asking an employer about a job.

"Of course," Arnold answered.

Kate moved to the side of the room and switched on a light. The woman stepped back toward the shadows. She was medium height, well muscled and lithe, with skin the color of well-creamed coffee. Her hair was pulled back in a tight chignon at the base of her skull, but when she'd pulled off her balaclava, a few strands had escaped and now hung in loose curls.

"You killed them," Arnold said.

"The man shot at me. That woman had a dagger pointed over Knight's heart. He was bleeding. She tried to stab me." A look of mild amusement passed over her face.

"It's good to see you," Arnold said.

"Likewise."

Arnold realized the others were staring at them with various looks of confusion, incredulity, and amusement on their faces.

"I think you know Leo," he said.

"Only by reputation. Pleased to make your acquaintance." Leo held out his hand.

Rainey took another step back until her face was in full shadow again.

Arnold pointed. "These folks are Knight's security team."

Rainey might have nodded to acknowledge them. It was hard to tell. Then she waved to Arnold, turned and melted into the shadows of the next room.

Arnold gave himself a little shake, then went to look for Knight.

Knight sat on the rug next to Nina's body, stroking her face. "Goodbye, my love." Then he rose and stepped around Nina, approaching the group, his arms out as if he were welcoming them.

Arnold looked carefully into the face of the man who the Le Clairs considered the most gifted wizard in the Americas, perhaps the western world. An air of grandeur surrounded him, even as he stood there in his pajamas, the buttons mismatched, his hair disheveled.

"Are you hurt, Mr. Knight?" he asked

"I am not a knight," the man said. "You are. Do you not remember yourself, Sir Galahad?"

A shiver ran the length of Arnold's spine. "That's your name, sir. Valentin

Knight," he said, enunciating clearly.

Knight cocked his head at such an extreme angle that Arnold was reminded of an owl. His eyes widened in disbelief. "Do you not recognize me, Galahad? I am Merlin, High Mage of Camelot."

Oh, shit. Arnold thought.

But before he could think what to do next, Valentin Knight put his hands on Arnold's shoulders. "My good man, take me to the Lady of Avalon. I must help her free Guinevere from Mordred's curse."

Given the circumstances, that made a strange kind of sense. Maybe he wasn't entirely crazy.

Arnold stepped to the side and made a flourishing bow he hoped approximated a medieval royal gesture. "Come with me, my Lord Merlin. Your chariot awaits."

Knight followed him out of the warehouse, somehow exuding gravitas in his pajamas and slippers.

Tyrone came up to them. "I'll go to Nina's apartment and collect her computer and anything relevant."

"Thank you, Sir Kay."

Tyrone snorted like a spooked horse. Kate looked hopeful that he'd give her a name from that storied time, but Arnold interrupted Knight. "I'll call my team. Meet us at the airport."

Elizabeth stumbled when she stepped back through the crystal. Abernathy emerged right behind her and reached out to steady her. She studied him for a moment, trying to remember who he'd been in Camelot.

Anne cried out in pain.

Forgetting all extraneous matters, Elizabeth ran to her and took her hands. "Breathe," she said.

After the contraction passed, Anne looked around her, frowning. "How did I get down here? What's all this equipment?"

"You don't remember?"

Anne frowned in concentration. "I had dreams. I was in Egypt, then some castle where I met—" She grabbed the metal sides of the hospital bed and took a breath to yell again.

"Breathe through it," Elizabeth said.

She turned to the nurse. "When did she wake up?"

"Just now," Emma said.

"How long were we gone?"

"About four hours."

"Time between contractions?"

"It was every fifteen minutes, but that was five."

Elizabeth squeezed Anne's hand. "I'll be right over there," she said and walked toward the crystal.

Mordred's face swam to the surface. *I will have that baby,* he said.

She thought back to Knight, how he'd appeared in the crystal asking for her help, only he'd thought he was Merlin and she the Lady of Avalon. Was this the next piece of the puzzle?

Anne cried out again. It had only been about two minutes. They didn't have much time.

Gerald watched with Katherine from the ballroom door. They had joined in with the ritual in meditation, watching what they could. Katherine channeled her energy to Anne. The lodge members had returned. Anne was awake, but it seemed the usurper still lurked in the crystal, determined to be the soul born to Anne and Michael.

He heard a clamor at the front door, several voices shouting. He ran to the front of the house.

"Have you found it yet?" Arnold was talking to Preston.

"The code is complicated. Just be quiet for two seconds."

"Dana, take him into Gerald's study. Let me know when you've got it."

"Yes, sir." The two computer experts walked away. They'd left Sylvia with Knight's system back in Maryland.

Gerald approached Arnold and got his attention. "He hasn't broken the encryption yet?"

"He broke Knight's code, but turns out it was a cover. Nina Lockhart was the real thief. We've got her computer now."

"Nina." Gerald remembered her. A rather unpleasant, but beautiful woman. Young. Ambitious. He'd never figure out why Knight had let her into his elite lodge.

"Wait, was?" he asked.

Arnold nodded. "I'm afraid Nina is dead."

"How—" Gerald stopped dead when he saw Leo escorting Valentin Knight into the house. The man was wearing pajamas buttoned up the wrong way.

"Ah, Sir Tristan," Knight said to Gerald. "What a pleasure to find you here. Can you direct me to the Lady of Avalon?"

Arnold pointed to Knight from behind him and mouthed, "He thinks he's Merlin."

Gerald tried not to shake his head. He was still under the spell to some extent. Could this night get any crazier? It was dark by now. He'd looked out the window and watched the sunset after most of the lodge members had disappeared.

"Right this way, Mage Merlin." Gerald escorted Knight to the temple.

David Wilt, the guardian of the ritual, opened the circle to admit them all. They walked toward the line of lodge members. Katherine ran to Anne.

Winston Stuart stood at the bottom of Anne's bed and was just taking off latex gloves. "She's only dilated eight centimeters," Gerald heard him say.

"No, you can't push yet," Elizabeth was talking to Anne. "Katherine, where did you come from?"

"Please, mother. You think I wouldn't feel this?" She took Anne's hand.

"Ah, my Lady. There you are." Knight walked over to Elizabeth and surveyed Anne and her attendants. "I see we are prepared here."

"That's Valentin Knight," Alycia whispered, her face lit with awe.

"The Merlin of America," Mary replied.

"Yes, I am Mage Merlin." Knight nodded his head to them in acknowledgment and wandered over to the large crystal ball. "And here we have Sir Mordred."

He stared into its depths, mumbling to himself in a language Gerald didn't recognize. Anne stifled a groan and something swirled in the crystal.

"Now, now," Knight said, shaking his finger at the stone as if he were admonishing a child. "We'll have none of that."

He turned back to Elizabeth. "There is one ingredient missing."

Chapter 24

The Le Clair plane landed in Boston's Logan International Airport. Grandmother Elizabeth's secretary, Susan, had arranged for a helicopter to fly Michael straight to The Oaks just south of Marshfield. Once on board the helicopter that reminded Michael of a dragonfly, he put on the headphones and settled back, closing his eyes when the craft took off. The bubble top and small seat made him feel as if he'd drop straight down to the ground. Once they leveled out, he opened his eyes and watched the lights of ships headed toward Boston's harbor.

His right hand crept up to feel the hard edges of his crystal key beneath his shirt. After he'd found himself on the floor of the newly discovered temple in Egypt that he'd flown there to explore, he'd walked toward Tahir's house. With a huge rumble, the ground had fallen in on the new temple just after he'd crossed the street and reached the Pizza Hut. He forced himself to keep going rather than stare at the spectacle. He found Tahir and his family rushing out of the house.

Tahir spotted him. "What happened?"

"The temple ceiling collapsed."

Tahir shook his head. "I can see that. Did you get it?"

Michael fished for the silver chain under his shirt and held up the slender quartz tabby.

"Good. Gerald called. You must get back. Anne is—"

"—in labor," Michael finished for him. "Grandmother Elizabeth told me."

"Elizabeth?" Tahir's eyes widened in surprise.

"Yes. It's a long story, but it will have to wait. They need the crystal. Can you send me back through—"

Tahir raised his palms to forestall Michael's next word. "I have no control over the destination. You'll have to fly."

"But that will take too long."

"Sorry. It's the only option."

The new pilot had shaved two and a half hours off the eleven-hour flight from Cairo. Michael swore he'd started braking halfway across the Atlantic.

The helicopter landed with a thud, and Michael jumped out and tore across the yard. Arnold opened the door. Michael tore through the front rooms, threw open the door to the ballroom and ran across. He halted, arms waving to keep his balance, when he found himself facing David's sword. Then he realized the guardian was unsealing the temple so he could enter.

David waved him in seconds later and Michael ran in, looking around wildly.

"Ah, Sir Lancelot. Always late." Knight held his arms out in welcome.

Lord Merlin. He heard Lancelot's voice in his mind.

Michael didn't recognize the man in front of the crystal ball, but given what he'd seen in the last two days, he was unsurprised by his attire.

"Michael." Anne sat up and reached out for him.

He ran to her and took her gently in his arms. "My love," he said.

Guinevere, Lancelot whispered.

"Yes, yes," Grandmother Elizabeth tsked. "Now, let's get down to business. Do you have the key?"

Michael brought the crystal out from beneath his shirt.

"Good. You know the situation?"

"Mordred wants to stop the birth."

"Not exactly. He wants to inhabit the baby."

A burning fury rose up in Michael. "What do we do?"

"Sir Lancelot," It surprised Michael to find Valentin Knight standing next to him. "Now comes the time to rectify your mistake. Lady Guinevere's betrayal—" he bowed his head to Anne "—and my own failure. If only Arthur had listened and married you, my Lady Claire." He was looking at Cordelia Stuart, Winston's wife and one of the more advanced mystics in the lodge.

Cordelia pointed to herself, her eyes saucers.

"Yes, m'lady. So, it was Arthur's mistake as well."

Knight closed his eyes a moment, seeming to settle into himself. Then he opened them again and looked at each one in turn. "Now, do we have the keys?"

Michael held his up. Anne fished hers out from beneath the hospital gown she'd been put in.

"Since you are indisposed, m'lady, would you allow Lady Viviane the use of your stone this evening?"

Anne pulled the necklace over her head and handed it to her grandmother.

Michael took another necklace out of his pocket, this one topped with an ankh. "Tahir said you might need to borrow this one."

"Most excellent. If I might?" Michael handed the crystal over to Knight who arranged it in his palm, point out resting on his index finger, the bottom resting in his palm. The others did the same. "If you please." He gestured toward the crystal ball in the center.

As they walked forward, others from higher frequencies joined them. Anubis walked forward from the West in his human form, smiling at Elizabeth who took up the High Priestess position in the east. She felt the brush of a wing and saw that Isis stood beside her. Osiris accompanied Michael, and Nephthys took up a position in the South. Merlin stood in the North with Thoth, Master of Magic, beside him.

He held up his stone and chanted in an ancient language, older than the Old Welsh he'd spoken to Nina, a language that vibrated the surrounding room, a language that seemed to have formed the very structure of Earth Herself.

In the crystal ball, Mordred turned and screamed, "No!"

Behind him, a barge came from the mists. A tall woman dressed in white flowing robes poled it. Behind her, a figure lay prone in the belly of the boat, his head resting on the lap of the Lady of Avalon. Seven other priestesses surrounded the other two, holding lamps. From their lips rose a most enchanting song that grew louder as they approached.

Water lapped around the feet of those in the lodge. They could smell the wet reeds, the scent of water lilies. A hunting kingfisher called from the distance. The barge thudded into the sand and the woman poling the boat jumped out.

The Lady of Avalon looked down tenderly at the man who lay in the barge, his armor red with blood from a wound to his side, his eyes closed, face pale. She leaned down close to his ear and whispered, "King Arthur, it is time to come back now."

The man stirred. His cheeks seemed to take on more color. His hair was still the tawny gold they all remembered from their journeys. He opened his eyes. Still the same lake blue. He scrambled to his feet, looking around. His gaze rested on Michael. "Lance! My friend. It is good to see you."

The Lady of Avalon stopped him from taking his hand. She turned him toward Anne and his body seemed to thin out from solid to gauze, then into light. He streamed toward Anne and hovered over the round belly, then melted down into her.

"No!" Mordred cried out, his voice breaking. He sobbed.

"Sir Mordred," the Lady of Avalon said, her voice musical, soothing. She held out her hand. "It is your turn now. Come with me to Avalon. I have many wondrous things to show you."

They all held their breath. Would he obey her? Would he need to be coerced?

The Opener of the Ways moved forward, ready to take the soul to judgment if he refused the Lady's offer.

But Mordred's face softened, seemed to grow younger. He stepped out from the crystal ball and walked into the water. He took her hand.

"Thank you for your service, Mordred. The same as Set, as Judas. Even the Star of the Morning. A hard part to play. You have done well."

Something seemed to lift from Mordred's shoulders. His face shone.

The Lady ushered him into the boat. He laid down in the bottom. She sat and took his head in her lap.

Merlin separated himself from Valentin Knight and got into the boat with the priestesses, leaning down to kiss the Lady of Avalon full on the mouth. A little murmur of surprise rose from the watching group.

Knight looked around at his surroundings, blinking in confusion. Mary Shak went to him and took his arm, whispering in his ear. Gradually, his face cleared.

The priestess poling the boat turned the boat around. Her robe, soaked to her thighs, clung to her. Putting both hands onto the side, she lifted herself into the barge, took up her pole, and the nine priestesses of Avalon pulled away over the lake, taking Mordred to the Isle of Apples.

They all stood watching, astonished at the simplicity of how their struggle had come full circle.

Anne's urgent cry broke them from their reverie.

Katherine helped Anne to slide up the bed and prop open her legs.

Emma lifted her gown. "I can see the head."

Winston and Elizabeth sprang into action.

Michael rushed to Anne's other side and took her hand. She gripped, crushing his fingers. A guttural groan came from her throat. "I have to push," she said, looking to Elizabeth for permission.

"Push," Emma and Elizabeth said at the same time.

She strained, her eyes squeezed tight, her face screwed up in the intensity of the pain.

Winston crouched to receive the baby. The head crowned, then the face appeared. Michael was lost in wonder.

With the next contraction, the baby slithered out into the world. Winston cleared his nose and eyes, and the new baby announced his arrival with a lusty cry.

Elizabeth took up the golden cup sitting on the western altar, filled with water from White Spring for the ritual, and took it back to the now swaddled baby. She dipped the first two fingers of her right hand into the water and drew an equal-armed cross on the child's forehead. "I anoint you in the name of the One. Be welcome."

She handed the grail cup to Anne, who drank and handed it on to Michael. He drank in turn.

"May you be blessed," Elizabeth intoned.

The baby stared up at them, lake blue eyes set in a rose-bud face. A crown of tawny hair topped his head.

"The little master has arrived," Elizabeth heard from the doorway.

Estelle stood there holding a large stainless steel pot, a much more earthly grail. "I thought you'd need hot water."

Elizabeth nodded for the lodge to end the ceremony, and as soon as they settled the directions, David let Estelle come in. She handed off the pot to Emma, then stood beside Anne, cooing at the baby. "What an angel. I told you it was a boy."

Anne sat up straighter, then frowned a bit at a wave of pain.

"What's the little tike's name?" Estelle asked.

Michael and Anne glanced at each other, then Michael nodded.

"Arthur," Anne said. "I think we'd better name him Arthur."

"After the legendary king," Estelle said.

"Yes, after High King Arthur," Michael answered. "The Grail King."

"So, I have soup and sandwiches in the dining room," Estelle announced. She turned to Anne. "Broth for you until the doctor says you can have more." She bustled away.

They all laughed. Estelle's down-to-earth entrance had grounded the energy of this amazing ritual quite effectively.

David ushered the lodge out in the order they had entered, then walked the perimeter, checking for any excess energies or imbalances. When he finished, he looked to the High Priestess. Elizabeth nodded, giving him permission to leave.

Winston checked Anne over while Emma gave Arthur his first bath. "She's fine. I don't think she needs to go to the hospital right away. The baby should go through the ordinary tests though."

Michael picked up the newly washed precious bundle, smiling down into his face.

"Can I eat some of that golden lentil soup Estelle was making?" Anne asked.

"I'll have Susan send you in a tray." She looked at Michael, who was lost in the wonder of first fatherhood. "We'll send in something for Michael, too. Shall we?" She motioned for the remaining group to follow her and leave the new family alone.

Much to Elizabeth's surprise, Katherine kissed them all and followed her out.

Michael got into the bed next to Anne, careful not to jostle her. She took Arthur and let him nurse, following the quick instructions Emma had told her, but the child had no trouble. They relaxed and told each other their stories.

"So, you and I were Guinevere and Lancelot," Anne said. "I guess we're partly to blame for the fall of Camelot."

"Yes," Michael said, "but it seemed that Merlin knew all along that it would happen. Perhaps we need to build Camelot in this world on a larger scale."

Anne snuggled against him. "That sounds like a plan."

Elizabeth watched all her friends and family as they filled their plates and rejoiced in the success of such a long ritual. She overheard the stories they told each other of their glimpses of Egypt and ancient Avalon.

Knight had realized he was not dressed for the occasion and gone upstairs to shower and try on some of Gerald's clothes. She sat, drinking a hot cup of tea, thinking through the last few days, amazed by it all. Then she snapped her fingers. "Darn, we forgot to note the time of birth."

"I wrote it down," Emma said. "Figured you'd want to do the chart for such an illustrious birth."

"Wasn't it amazing?" she said.

Emma nodded. "Exhausting, though."

"Yes." Maybe she should eat something. Just as she thought that, Estelle put a big bowl of golden lentil soup and a large piece of crusty country bread in front of her. "Perfect."

A boy dressed in dark jeans and a black hoodie whom she didn't recognize dashed into the room and announced in a loud voice, "I found it!"

Gerald jumped up from the table, spilling a glass of wine. Cordelia grabbed a handful of napkins and sopped it up. "Did you transfer the money? Is it all there?" he asked.

"Yes, I got it all back. Took a while. It was in Cyprus, the Caymans—" he waved his hands "—all over the place."

Gerald spread his arms wide and hugged the kid, much to the teen's discomfort. "Preston, you're a genius."

Preston, Elizabeth thought. Somehow he reminded her of Bedivere.

"Well, yes," he said, as if this were self-evident, "but there's more."

"More what?"

"Money. Nina had quite a tidy sum herself, into the millions, and now that the witch is dead, it's ours."

The room fell silent. Everyone turned to stare at him.

"What?" Preston asked.

Gerald shook his head. "No, that would be stealing."

"Well, technically—"

"Technically, it would be stealing," Gerald admonished. "Leave Nina's money where it is. She may have family. Besides, we can't upset this auspicious event with such an action."

Preston shook his head and opened his mouth to protest.

Gerald pointed a finger at him. "Leave it. I'll have Dana check. Now, come celebrate. The baby is born. We have our money back. Eat, drink, and be merry."

"Is there pizza?" he asked.

Gerald rolled his eyes heavenward. "This child!"

Just then the doorbell rang and Estelle's face lit with a secretive smile. Arnold and Leo took up position on opposite sides of the door, still in fight mode.

"Oh, for heaven sakes." Estelle hustled over to the door, her large backside swaying with her steps, and opened it.

A delivery man stood there holding five boxes of pizza. "I couldn't find any anchovies, ma'am."

"This will do just fine," she said. "Please put them on the sideboard."

"Sweet," Preston stood aside as the man put the boxes down. Then he opened them one at a time, picking a slice from each.

Gerald fell into his chair and stretched his back. Then he realized. He was a great grandfather. He looked at Elizabeth and whispered. "Hey, Great Grannie," then kissed her full on the mouth.

"Oh, go on," she said, blushing but happy.

She raised her chalice of wine. "Thank you all."

Everyone grabbed a glass and held it up. "To Arthur," Gerald said.

"To the return of the Grail King," everyone said together.

Elizabeth found herself wondering why Arthur had chosen her family and this moment to return. What challenges would he bring to them if he'd come to restore the vision of Camelot?

She tore off a piece of Estelle's warm bread, dipped it into the wine in her chalice, and closed her eyes. She addressed herself to Universal Mind and all those who had embodied the One Mind throughout the ages.

We'll need your help.

Get A Free Power Places Novel
& Free Short Story

Building a relationship with my readers is the very best thing about writing. I occasionally send newsletters with details on new releases, special offers and other bits of news relating to the Power Place series and my other books. And if you sign up to the mailing list I'll send you this free Milton content:

1. A free copy of the first Power Places novel, *Under the Stone Paw.*

2. A free copy of "The Judgment of Osiris," a short story set in Egypt.

You can get your book & story **for free** by signing up at https://dl.bookfunnel.com/a8u8t9wm9w.

Enjoy this book?
You can make a big difference

Reviews are the most powerful tools in my arsenal when it comes getting attention for my books. Much as I'd like to, I don't have the financial muscle of a New York publisher. I can't take out full page ads in the newspaper or put posters on the subway.

(Not yet, anyway.)

But I do have something much more powerful and effective than that, and it's something that those publishers would kill to get their hands on.

A committed and loyal bunch of readers.

Honest reviews of my books help bring them to the attention of other readers.

If you've enjoyed this book I would be very grateful if you could spend just five minutes leaving a review (it can be as short as you like) on the book's Amazon page.

Thank you very much.

About the Author

Theresa Crater brings ancient temples, lost civilizations, and secret societies back to life in her visionary fiction. She is the author of the Power Places series as well as stand-alone novels. Her short stories explore ancient myth brought into the present day.

For more information:

www.theresalcrater.com

theresa@theresalcrater.com

Also by Theresa Crater
Have you read them all?

In the Power Places Series

Under the Stone Paw

Anne Le Clair, a successful, young attorney, has always managed to remain free from her family's gothic past—until now. When she inherits her eccentric aunt's antique necklace though, she finds no escape from its secrets. Anne is immersed in a crash course of forbidden wisdom, secret societies, and her family's own legacy. She soon discovers that her aunt's necklace is one of just six powerful "keys" that, when combined with the other five at the appointed time, unlocks the legendary Hall of Records. However, another group, the shadowy Illuminati, is working behind the scenes to uncover the same powerful secrets—and make them their own.

Buy *Under the Stone Paw*

Beneath the Hallowed Hill

Anne Le Clair travels to Glastonbury with her fiancée, Egyptologist and mystic Michael Levy, to investigate a house she inherited from a mysterious aunt...only to find trouble waiting. One of Avalon's sacred twin springs is failing. Together, Anne and Michael try to restore the water flow, but discover there is much more at stake: the Illuminati master Alexander Cagliostro has activated an ancient crystal tower, tearing a hole in time which threatens much more than one sacred spring. Meanwhile, in ancient Atlantis, Megan, priestess of the Crystal Matrix Chamber, flees the destruction of her world carrying with herself a vital artifact.

Buy *Beneath the Hallowed Hill*

Return of the Grail King

The long-awaited King Arthur returns to be reborn in the 21st century, but an old enemy from the past rises to stop him.

Buy *Return of the Grail King*

Stand-Alones

The Star Family

Jane Frey inherits a Gothic mansion filled with unexpected treasures. A prophecy claims it hides an important artifact – the key to an energy grid laid down by the Founding Fathers themselves. Whoever controls this grid controls the very centers of world power. Except Jane has no idea what they're looking for.

Buy *The Star Family*

Historicals

School of Hard Knocks

When Maggie Winters is asked to perform an exorcism on a young child, she finds the problem traces all the way back to the tragedy that ended her own childhood. Will appeal to readers of The Secret Life of Bees and The Help. "Crater's prose is accomplished and her story engaging." Kirkus Review

Buy *School of Hard Knocks*

God in a Box

It's the guru invasion of the 1980s. After spending her life savings to fly to Europe and become a meditation teacher, Stacey is told to go home. Lesbians are not welcome. She's lost the love of her life already. Will she lose the other half of her dreams now?

Buy *God in a Box*

Acknowledgments

As always, special thanks go to Stephen Mehler for sharing all his knowledge about Egypt, for the four trips we've taken to there together, and for patience while I write. Thanks for Mike Nelson, Rick Mehler, Brandon Clark, and Terry Goble for their expert assistance on hacking language. Thank you to Caitlín Matthews for her help with my title and to her and John Matthews for their books on the Arthurian material. All the mistakes are mine. Thanks to Mark Posey for his excellent help with editing. Special shout out to Team Anne & Michael for their eagle eyes and helpful suggestions.

www.ingramcontent.com/pod-product-compliance
Lightning Source LLC
Chambersburg PA
CBHW072354020726
47506CB00004B/1107